Advance praise for Selina Rosen's second Drewcila Qwah novel, *Recycled*

"RECYCLED is one hot S.O.B. It rocks with writerly rhythm and a beautiful and funny vulgarity. Over the top in the best an most magnificent sense of the word."—Joe R. Lansdale

Praise for Selina Rosen's first Drewcila Qwah novel, *Queen of Denial*

"A rarity of rarities: a book that makes you laugh out loud. Selina Rosen's debut is very much worth noting...sf's answer to Terry Pratchett."—C. J. Cherryh

"A rip-snorting space adventure the likes of which we don't see often enough these days!"—Lawrence Watt-Evans

"*Queen* is funny and pointed. Ms. Rosen takes a Star-Trek-like plot, introducing the social ills of a world that could be our own, and attacks them with ruthless humor. Drewcila Qwah isn't your everyday heroine, with a foul mouth and almost every other bad habit known to civilization, but she's likeable and honest. The language may not be to everyone's taste, but it's no more than a working spacer's dialect. As Drewcila might say, get the %&#^* out of here if you don't like it. It's not applied gratuitously, and you'll get used to it. The style is as rough and ready as the heroine, but *Queen* is a fast read with a satisfying conclusion."—Jody Lynn Nye

"*Queen* is a fun novel, an old-fashioned space opera that moves at breakneck speed from the first page to the last."—*The Tulsa World Herald*, June 13, 1999

"Down-home science fiction? Redneck interstellar adventure? A full-throttle journey through the rural spaceways? Hey, it can happen and happen convincingly when the writer is damned authentic and has lived the tone she's writing about. That's Selina Rosen to a T. *Queen of Denial* cooks—not just with high energy and in-your-face attitude, but with the metaphorical flavors of grits, red beans and rice, and sweet potato pie.

"If there's such a thing as blue-collar sf, this is it. No spiffy interstellar SUVs here—Rosen's characters horse the futuristic equivalent of dented vintage Ford S-10s around the stars. With plenty of action, violence, foolin' around, and a generous tongue planted just a touch firmly in cheek, *Queen of Denial* takes some old and honored tropes of science fiction, and turns them into the kind of bawdy full-bodied entertainment western literature's furnished since long before Shakespeare.

"When MIR morphs into a cut-rate orbital truckstop for space jockeys who can't afford the International Space Station, Selina Rosen's debut novel is the sort of book that'll feature prominently in the spinner rack right between the displays of alien fuzzy dice and zero-gee mudflaps."—Ed Bryant

"Selina Rosen turns Space Opera inside-out to give us a brand new genre: Space Vaudeville!"—Mark Simmons

"*Queen of Denial* is a rollicking, high-spirited romp through space that grabs you by the shirt with the very first page and never lets go. The pace is breakneck, the humor bawdy, and the heroine one of the most original I've seen in years. The love triangle alone kept me in stitches. This book is a must for anyone who enjoys top-notch spacefaring adventure!"—K. D. Wentworth

"Should appeal to anyone who loves a riotous, wickedly funny read."—Jane Fancher

"*Queen of Denial* is a freewheeling, fun and frantic space opera. It takes the usual conventions of pulp action Science Fiction and stands them on their head by featuring a female lead character as tough as any man in the book, and twice as smart. The story moves at a take-no-prisoners pace, keeping you turning the pages fast as possible. And, in the end, arrives at a most satisfactory conclusion. It's a wild ride and quite an accomplishment for a first-time novelist."—Robert Weinberg, author of *The Termination Novel*

Recycled

by
Selina Rosen

Meisha Merlin Publishing, Inc.
Atlanta, GA

RECYCLED

Published by Meisha Merlin Publishing, Inc.
PO Box 7
Decatur, GA 30031

Editing & interior layout by Stephen Pagel
Copyediting & proofreading by Teddi Stransky
Cover art by Don Maitz
Cover design by Kevin Murphy

ISBN: Soft Cover   1-892065-93-2

http://www.MeishaMerlin.com

First MM Publishing edition: June 2003

Printed in the United States of America
0 9 8 7 6 5 4 3 2 1

Just who is Selina Rosen anyway...

Mr Stephen Pagel, publisher extraordinaire, whispered in my ear, 'Would you write the foreword to Selina's new book *Recycled?*' 'Only if I can tell her to Piss Off', I retorted. 'Of course, that's why I'm asking!'

There was an oblong of tables, with a gap in the middle, in the Dealer's Room at the lovely MidSouthCon Sci-Fi convention in Memphis. I was sitting on the inside on the right, facing out, Selina should have been sitting with her back to me on the left. But she hardly ever sits; she stands, she crawls about, she kneels and she pleads, 'Buy my books, oh PLEASE buy my books. If you don't buy my books I'll starve'. Then as like as not she'll pretend to cry.

It's all acting of course. This girl is almost a better showman than I am! She's a larger than life character with an enormous personality. But came the morning when I was trying to have a dignified conversation with a dignified couple of convention attendees, and we couldn't hear ourselves speak—the noise from the other side of the oblong was so intense.

Here, in the good old United Kingdom we have a saying, 'You only make fun of people you like'. I like Selina and I made fun. I called out, 'Piss off Selina'! That of course only made things worse. She howled with laughter and went on howling for the rest of the weekend.

She's a great gal and a damn good storyteller. I commend *Recycled* to you whole-heartedly. It's a smashing read. I read it on the train on my way to another Sci-Fi convention. Sorry— who am I? Why have I been invited to pen these words? Well, first and foremost I'm an actor with over 800 TV appearances and 26 movies to my name (including *Star Wars)* and I have written three (so far) volumes of my memoirs—Stephen said I should give them a plug. Oh, and I have been known to tell young ladies to piss off!

And I'm delighted to say that we've all been invited back to Memphis next year. Guess what will be the first two words I'll say to Selina!

Good luck love—you don't have to beg folk to buy your books you know, your books sell themselves.

Michael Sheard—aka Admiral Ozzel.
Isle of Wight. UK.
March 2003

For Carolyn Cherryh
for being a good friend and an inspiration.

For Lynn Abbey
for always being there with good advice,
a sympathetic ear,
and for getting people to actually read my work.

For Jane Fancher
for laughing at my stupid jokes and not getting mad
when I do terrible things to her in public.

And for Stephen Pagel
for keepin' the faith.

This business sucks!
We all know it,
and it's always good to have comrades at arms.

Recycled
by
Selina Rosen

Chapter 1

"But Drew said..." Stasha started.

"We can't always do what Drewcila Qwah says, Stasha. She does not have the best interests of the kingdom at heart," Zarco said. "She is self serving and mercenary."

"It's true, no one knows the queen's shortcomings any better than I. Drewcila worries about nothing quite as much as her own best interests, and having a good time. But sire, let us, not forget that what serves Qwah-Co ultimately serves the kingdom. She would never do anything that might cut into her profit margins. What's good for Qwah-Co is good for the country. I'm afraid I have to agree with the queen in this matter," Facto said.

"Do you hear yourself, Facto? What you are saying? She is suggesting that we open up trade with the Lockhedes. They threaten to make war with us unless we help them set up a salvaging operation of their own and make trade agreements. In five years she has usurped my authority at every turn, she's made me look a fool to my own subjects, and turned our once regal kingdom into a smoldering trash heap. The Lockhedes threaten us, and she wants to give them exactly what they want, to give in to their demands, and you think this is a good and sane notion!"

"Because it's what we want, too. Everything Drewcila has said is true," Stasha said in a small, if convicted, voice. "It's a chance for a real and lasting peace. A chance to finally unite the planet. What would better serve our people than this? Drewcila says that by making them economically stable they will have no reason to start another war. That by doing business with them we can gain control over them."

"Drewcila says! Drewcila says!" Zarco jumped out of his chair slinging his arms around and started pacing the room. "I am sick to death of hearing *Drewcila says!* I can't believe you, any of you! These are the *Lockhedes* we're talking about! They are the ancient enemy of our people! Their brutality in war is known throughout the galaxy. They have killed, tortured, maimed, and mutilated countless thousands of our people, and now you want to make them economically stable. You think that if they are economically comfortable they won't make war, and I tell you that if we help to make them rich they will buy bigger weapons and come after us to wipe us out entirely. They don't want peace. They want to take over the planet and slaughter us." He glared down at Stasha. "Do I have to remind you that one of the people they kidnapped and tortured was your own dear sister? That those butchers surgically removed a part of her brain making her basically dead to us? Turning her from our noble queen into a beer swilling, toilet mouthed, scavenging whore!"

"Oh that's a little harsh. I don't think my sister's a whore, Zarco."

This seemed to make the king even madder. Facto watched him rant on wordlessly. When he got like this, and he did often these days, there was no talking to him.

He muttered curses on and on until finally he ended with, "...they took my wife, and they turned her into Drewcila Qwah!" and slammed his ass into his throne very unmajestically.

And therein lay the real rub. Zarco said Drewcila didn't have the kingdom's best interests at heart. That she failed to understand the implications of making trade agreements with the Lockhedes. But the truth was that Zarco didn't want peace with the Lockhedes because he hated them for kidnapping his wife, operating on her brain, and turning her into Drewcila Qwah, a woman who had broken his heart and taken his country from him without firing a single shot.

Drewcila had won the hearts of the people. To them he was a puppet leader whose strings were pulled by men long dead; it was Drewcila they trusted. Drewcila who had solved the kingdom's woes, brought them into the golden age of profitable filth, and turned them into a very rich nation of salvagers.

Facto knew that Zarco was growing tired of being treated like a visitor in his own kingdom. He wanted to make a decision. *Any* decision, as long as it was different from Drewcila's.

Even if it was wrong.

Van Gar made his way across the spaceport. Wasn't hard to find Drew's ship. It was the biggest one on the dock, and it had a huge Qwah-Co logo painted on the side of it. Besides, it was the one hanging in party lights with enough noise coming from it to shake the entire space station.

She was having a party. She'd sent him off on a run that a monkey with a screwdriver could have done and used his absence as an excuse to have an orgy.

He stepped over a drunk on the open gang plank. The guy stirred, looked up at the huge fur covered Chitzsky and screamed. Then he passed out cold. Van Gar noticed the uniform and the blaster at the man's side and realized he was one of Drewcila's "royal guards." No doubt his only real duty on this night had been to warn *Her Majesty* of Van's return. He had failed, and it was no doubt this, more than Van Gar's size or intimidating stance, that caused him to panic.

Van Gar made his way through the rabble and revelers, a mixture of the Barions that manned Drew's ship and the usual spaceport scum one found down on the docks. One guy pushed a drink at him, and Van Gar flattened him with one punch. He just wasn't in the mood.

When he got to Drew's quarters the door was shut, and he found to his dismay, locked.

He pounded on the door. "Drewcila! Open this fucking door."

"Ah fuck!" he heard her exclaim. Then, "Who is it?" she asked in a voice dripping saccharin.

"You know who the hell it is, Drew! Now open this god damned door!" Van Gar screamed.

After several minutes the door opened and three men, two women, a midget, and a goat walked out in various stages of dress. They each looked at him and smiled weakly before walking on. Except for the goat which squatted down and managed to piss on his boot before he could move.

Van Gar took a deep breath, then let it out and walked slowly into the room, closing the door behind him.

Drewcila stood in the middle of the room in a red and black silk robe that barely covered her butt, lighting a cigar with her laser side arm. She took a couple of puffs then looked up at him.

"Have a bad trip?" she asked.

"Is that all you have to say?" Van Gar asked in disbelief.

"You get a hair cut?"

"This isn't funny, Drewcila. I come back to your ship to find it in shambles with drunks everywhere. Even the guard is passed out cold..."

Drewcila's eyes narrowed to slits and she hissed. "That bastard..."

"...you're in our bedroom with the door locked with...three men, two women, a midget and...a *goat!*"

"Hey! The goat belonged to the midget," Drewcila defended.

"Every time we're apart it's the same thing..."

"Well, not always the same thing," Drewcila said, smiling in spite of her best efforts to look chastised.

"I'm not amused, Drew," Van Gar warned.

"Well, neither am I...now," Drew said, and this time she didn't even try to stop her grin.

"Just stop!" he screamed. "Don't you see? Didn't you know? When Chitzskies fall in love we mate for life."

"Oh really? That must make it awfully awkward to get anything else done." She started contorting her body into weird angles. "You could drive a ship, but I'm not sure about a land vehicle. And tying your boots—well that would just be right out. Eating dinner would be strange, especially if you had guests..."

Van Gar let out a long throaty growl. "God damn it Drew! I've had it with you. I'm tired of your shit. Don't you understand...I'm at the end of my rope. You...you've changed. All this power and money has corrupted you."

"Ah...and I used ta be such a sweet little thing, too." She walked over and poured herself a drink. "Give me a big fucking break, Van. You knew what I was when we got together. I didn't keep any secrets. The only difference is that I used to be a poor asshole, and now I'm a rich one. I can afford more expensive perversions, and why shouldn't I have them?"

"Because I love you," Van Gar screamed. "Because we're supposed to be a team. I'm supposed to be all you need."

"Wow! Would you look at the ego on you." Drew downed her drink and looked at him with a critical eye. "Cut through the shit, Van. We all know what the real problem is. You want to be an equal partner, and I won't cut you in. It really chaps your ass that everything's in my name. You seem to think that just because we're together...that just because we screw, you should be entitled to half of everything I have. Well there never was a dick worth that, so you can hang it up. You're living off me, so I don't think you ought to be the one screaming around making demands about how I live my life."

She knew she'd gone too far then because she could see his breath rising in his chest as he puffed like some antiquated steam engine. His nostrils were flaring, and she could even make out the veins popping up on his temples. Not an easy thing to do through all that hair.

"I may have worded that just a little too strongly. I think maybe you're taking it the wrong way..." Drew started.

Van Gar covered the distance between them in three huge strides and backed her against the wall.

Drew patted his chest and laughed nervously. "Ah, come on, baby. I didn't mean that the way it sounded."

He looked down at her.

"You just don't give a damn do you, Drew?" Van Gar hissed. She started to give him some flip answer, and he shook his finger in her face. "Don't you dare. You say and do whatever the hell you please. It never occurs to you that maybe I want...need...deserve, more from you. You use everything and everyone to build your empire. How much money do you need, Drew? How much money can you spend?" She started to answer him, and he glared at her. She was silent. "I'm tired of being your errand boy. Just another sex toy. What the hell is in this for me? And no, I don't mean your material shit."

Drew was silent.

"Well!" Van Gar yelled.

"Oh...am I allowed to talk now?" Drew hissed back. She was now every bit as mad as he was, maybe even more so. She started poking him hard in the chest till he was the one backing up. "You know what's in it for you. Three square meals a day. All the booze you can drink. Partying till you puke. Sex with me most any time you want it. Those things used to mean something to you. You want to know who's changed? Well it ain't me, ass bite. It's you...you're the one who's changed. All this commitment bullshit. I don't want that shit, and you didn't use to want it, either. You're not the boy I fell in love with." She bit her finger and looked at him in mock pain. "That's what hurts, baby. That's what really hurts."

Van Gar looked silently around the room at the scattered beer bottles and cigar butts, then he looked Drew up and down.

"You're right," he said, nodding his head slowly. "It's time I went back to my people." He turned and started to walk away slowly. Drew followed. "I ran into a Chitzsky at the last port. He told me my people are building a colony on the planet Utarus. I think that's what's been calling me. I want to go there to be part of building a new world for my people..."

"Are you fucking kidding me, Van? Ah, come on...I mean all right, maybe the midget and the goat were a bit much..." He just kept walking, and Drew had to practically run to keep up. She laughed and slapped him on the back. "Come on, man, snap out of it...So there was a goat in our bed room. Is that really any reason to leave? To go off on some cockamamie bullshit religious pilgrimage? Come on, Van...I mean really...farming and praying and watching herd animals graze. That's not for you. You're a salvager. You're my mate. Do you really want to trade all of this..." she motioned around the disheveled ship as she followed him down the hall "...for some motionless piece of dirt? Trapped in one spot, never again to float out amongst the stars?"

He stopped and turned to look at her.

"What's here for me Drew? To be your lackey? Make me a full partner in our relationship and in the business, or I swear I'm out of here."

So, that was it. Nothing in the world but a bluff. A con to try and get part of her business. Well, she was the Queen of Bluff and the best grifter in the galaxy, maybe the universe.

Two could play at his game.

Drewcila seemed to think about it a minute, at one point holding both hands up mumbling to herself and acting like she was a scale. When it tipped all the way to one side she looked at Van Gar, shrugged, put her wrist-com to her mouth and pressed the button.

"Prepare Van Gar's ship for take off." She lowered her hand and looked at Van Gar. "It's been swell. Have a good trip, farm boy. Take Frank with you. He can bring my ship back after he drops you where you're goin'."

Van Gar's jaw dropped as he watched her turn on her heel and walk away puffing on her cigar. A large green-toned alien of undetermined sex or origin stumbled by, and she grabbed it by the arm and started dragging it back to her room. Not that it really seemed to be putting up much of a fight.

Van Gar turned on his heel and stomped off the ship.

"He did what?" Drewcila screamed.

"He left," Jurak, first mate of the ship, said as he cringed, fearing her reaction.

Drewcila slumped into her command chair on the deck resting her chin in her hand as she leaned against the arm looking thoughtful.

"Damn! That didn't go at all as I had planned," she mumbled. Finally she took a deep breath and let it out. "He wasn't supposed to do that. What the hell has happened to that man? I don't understand him at all. I mean he was supposed to come back, kiss my ass, and beg for my forgiveness. He wasn't supposed to leave. Has he gone completely mad?" The crewman started to answer. "Don't answer me, you moron! That was a rhetorical question. Please, don't tell me he has charted for the Harish System."

"He did."

"What did I just say!? Crap, what an idiot!" Drew took a deep breath and started punching buttons on her console mindlessly.

Jurak just stood there, not quite knowing whether to leave or stay and what to do if he did either.

"What the fuck is this?" Drew screamed, slamming her fist into her console. "Our stock is plummeting." She started punching buttons more carefully now. "What the hell happened?"

He looked over her shoulder at the read out.

"Your majesty...it would appear that the Barions have gone to war with the Lockhedes again," he answered shakily.

"Well ain't this just a zippidy-doo-da day."

Chapter 2

"Are you fucking insane?!" she thundered at the image that filled her screen.

"I will not be party to making deals with the Lockhedes," Zarco replied sharply.

"I didn't say anything about a damn party. Gods! You're such a fucking stupid idiot!" Drew continued, "The agreement would have served us as well as them. Would have made us trillions. Now, instead, it's going to cost us, and cost us dearly. I've already lost two million iggys. Don't you understand economics at all? We weren't in an economic depression. War is murder on a booming economy."

"My job is to run the country with dignity and pride. I don't take orders from the Lockhedes or you..."

"Your job is to sit on the throne and look pretty. Remember, that's what we all decided because as I already said you are an idiot. Far too moronic to be allowed to run something as important as a country. Hell, I'm surprised you can wipe yourself without winding up in deep shit," Drew spat back.

"I will not have you talking to me this way, Drewcila. You are my wife. I am King of all Barious..."

"You are king of the half of Barious that the Lockhedes don't hold, you pompous ass, and if you don't play your cards right, you won't even have that," Drew said. "And don't you start ordering me around because I am married to you—I can make your life a living hell."

"Drewcila!" The veins were popping out in his neck, and his face was getting red. She seemed to be having that effect on the men in her life lately. "You had better learn a little respect."

"You're right." Drewcila smiled. "I shouldn't make fun of the idiots. You stop this war, Zarco, and you stop it right this minute. Do you have any idea what the war machine costs?

You kiss the Lockhedes' ass, you make trade agreements with them, and you do it right now, before my stock plummets even one more point."

"I most certainly will not. Perhaps if you hadn't turned our war machines into scrap metal and our munitions plants into recycling centers, it wouldn't be so costly. Believe it or not, this is my country, mine..."

"All right, all right. Damn! What a crappy mood you're in. Let's say I screw you. Will you let me have my way then?"

There was a slight pause before the king's retort. "I swear, Drewcila! You are the foulest, most vile woman..."

"Yeah, yeah I know. Ya wanna fuck for it or not?"

"Most certainly not. I will not sell my country's future to sleep with my own wife."

"Fine, but it's your loss." She racked her brain trying to think of some other tactic. Giving up, she yelled, "Damn it, Zarco! If I have to come to that planet, you're going to be damn sorry!"

Zarco had no doubt that Drewcila could make him sorry; she usually did. He watched as her face faded from the screen. He paced the floor for a few minutes, trying to regain his composure and slow his breathing pattern. Having a sudden brain storm, he turned to look at Stasha. "You will dress up like Drewcila and go on TV...back up my speech. The people love her. They'll do whatever she says. In order to discredit your words she would have to admit to her little ruse—that she is rarely on the planet and uses you to talk to them—which would turn the people against her so that they will quit worshiping her. I will write your speech at once..."

"I won't do it, Zarco," Stasha said with conviction. "Drewcila is right, and I will not help you lead our kingdom into war."

"Stasha...Drewcila only cares about profits."

"And Facto's point is valid. What serves Qwah-Co ultimately serves the people. You aren't thinking clearly."

"I have never been any clearer on anything in my life!" Zarco looked near to the hair-pulling stage. "Can you believe her!" Zarco walked over and flopped into his throne looking up at Facto and Stasha. "She actually thinks that I would make policy which affects the entire nation in exchange for sexual favors. Tawdry and ridiculous!"

Stasha's face seemed to crumble then. "Don't think that I missed the hesitation in your voice, Zarco." She turned on her heel and ran out of the room crying. Zarco sighed and got to his feet. "Stasha, Stasha please." He went after her. At the door he turned to look at Facto. "It is easier to run the country than it is to attend to the problems of my own house."

Facto nodded silently and watched Zarco go. He certainly wouldn't want to be in the king's shoes. He understood that it would be difficult, if not impossible, to separate one's personal feelings from kingdom affairs, but as the leader of their country he should be able to put the kingdom's best interests above his own personal feelings. He was letting his heart rule his head, and a leader could never afford that luxury. Zarco's very righteous anger for the Lockhedes was causing him to tread the path to war. Drewcila had seen the Lockhedes' requests as a way to make more profit, and—though she'd never readily admit it to any of them—a chance for a real and lasting peace. As Drew had tried to explain to Zarco, peace equaled profit, and profit equaled peace.

Once again, Facto found himself in the position of having to side with Drewcila, not exactly a very comfortable position for him to be in.

As soon as he was sure Zarco was well out of hearing range, he slipped to the door of the king's office and looked out, making sure that no one else was about. Then he went back to the king's computer and hailed Drew. If they were suspicious of Facto, they'd certainly check transmissions from his computer, but whoever checked up on the king? He'd done this in the past, and, so far, none were the wiser.

The king was no leader, and Drewcila...well, she was always off planet gallivanting across the universe. Someone had to be concerned about the fate of the kingdom, and more often than not that duty fell to him.

"Ah, Fucktoe," Drewcila cooed. "How are you today? Did you find something particularly dull and of no interest whatsoever to bother me with, or has it been an unusually boring day...?"

"Since I am going behind my king's back at the risk of my very life, do you think you might refrain from butchering my name with vulgar salvager profanities and making fun of basically my entire life?" Facto asked with a sigh.

Drew shrugged. "I suppose I could, but it wouldn't be as much fun. I thought this was a done deal. That you had convinced Zardumb that trade with the Lockhedes would bring about a real and lasting peace, yada, yada, yada."

"I thought I had. Then yesterday morning...Well, he just seemed to wake up determined not to give in. And once the Lockhedes had declared war...you can't expect him to give in to them now," Facto said.

"Actually, yes I can. God! Why are men so stupid?" she started pacing in and out of the monitor's range, which was very irritating to say the least. "First Van Gar and now Zarco. Are all men such idiots, or is it only men that I become involved with? Perhaps all the really great sex I give them starves their brains for oxygen until they become stupid. I don't know of course, because I don't remember, but I have a feeling Zarco has always been a moron..."

Feeling forgotten, Facto cleared his throat. "My Queen, do you think you could speak to the matter at hand? My time is limited. Every minute we speak is a minute I put myself at risk of being found out."

"I thought I *was* speaking to the matter at hand." Drewcila turned her attention back to the monitor, looked thoughtful for a moment, and then threw her hands in the air and exclaimed, "I can't think like this!"

"Like what?"

"Sober!"

His screen went blank, and Facto was left with all the problems of state as his king went off to try to explain himself to his sister-in-law/lover, and his queen went off on a drunken toot.

Van Gar looked around the space station then back at his ship.

"Finally we will have a new world. A place for us, and only for us," a Chitzsky male almost as big as Van Gar was booming. He, like most of the Chitzskies gathered around him, wore simple white robes draped over one shoulder. Van Gar had never seen so many of his own people in one place. "We will create a world of peace far away from the barbaric races. We will leave behind the turmoil and strife of our life in the stars and once again return to being the creatures of the earth that we were intended to be. No more will we be a scattered people with no homeland. We will leave behind all the possessions of this world and fly off to our new life, our new destination, clean and pure. To Utarus!"

Van Gar didn't hear much after that. He kept looking around at his people with a feeling of awe. He was being offered a chance to do something that really mattered. A simple life of peace and tranquility, far away from Drew and her scams. He could live in truth, prospering by the work of his hands instead of always hanging by the seat of his pants. Perhaps he would once again find love, and this time with a worthy and monogamous woman of his own race. Of course if he gave the "Pride leader" one of Drewcila's ships, he'd damn well better go off to some distant and remote world. Because if Drewcila ever caught up with him she'd no doubt kill him. Frank told him this about a hundred times as Van Gar was tying him to a pole in the bay of a loading dock.

Before you could say "convert," Van Gar was wearing the simple white toga, no shoes, no weapon, had signed over the ship and all his belongings, and was in the cargo bay of a freighter with a thousand other Chitzskies heading for the remote, unconquered planet called Utarus.

It was then that he realized two things. First, that when you got many of his people in a cramped space, sweating, they gave off an altogether unpleasant odor. And second, that Drewcila must have driven him completely mad for him to have ever thought that this was a good idea.

"He did what?!" Drewcila boomed.

Frank, who was tired and ragged from having to hitch a ride in an over-loaded salvager cargo bay, braced himself as he said for the second time, "He...gave your ship to the Reverend Pard Jar of the Holy Church of the..."

"I heard you the first time, moron!" Drew jumped out of her chair and started pacing and mumbling. "Well...two can play at this game. He doesn't want me, then I don't want him. What do I need him for anyway? He smelled funny when he got wet." She sat down again and started patting her knee and looking up at the ceiling thoughtfully. "What the hell is he thinking joining some odd-ball fucking Chitzsky cult? He must be completely insane." Suddenly her face became a mask of rage, and she jumped to her feet. "He gave away one of my ships! Can you fucking believe that shit? Leaving me is one thing, but costing me one of my better ships...well, that's quite another. Jurak!" She waved an arm over her head frantically, and a man ran up to her. "Make me a Hurling Monkey with a twist. Hell, make it a double, light on the fizzy, non-alcoholic stuff."

"But my Queen...we were supposed to go back to Barious. We just got you sobered up. Your sister is expecting you. What of the war? What of the economy?"

"Fuck 'em! Fuck 'em all! Make me my damn drink. Send for my naked dancing boys! I'm depressed, how can I possibly think about anyone else's needs when I'm depressed?"

* * *

"I need to talk to my sister, Jurak. We need her here. Zarco...well, he just won't listen to reason. Our troops are losing ground daily on the borders, and it's only a matter of time 'til the conflict escalates to attack from the air. How long can she stay drunk anyway?"

"Apparently that's what she's trying to find out, my lady. So far it's been about a week."

"Where is Van Gar?"

"Gone..." Jurak dropped his voice to a mere whisper. "He came home from business and found your sister...well, indisposed if you will. He became angry, and he left. He joined some Chitzsky cult and gave away one of your sister's ships. In truth, I think she could have handled losing Van Gar, it's the ship and her plummeting stocks which have her so depressed. The loss of so much money, I think it's too much for her."

"I think my sister's good at fooling everyone. She loves Van Gar, and though she'd never admit it, she needs him. Well, she's made her bed, and now she'll have to lie in it alone. Patch me through to her quarters..."

"My lady, I don't think that's such a good idea."

"Just do it, Jurak. I've seen my sister drunk before."

Except she'd never seen Drew do *that* before. In fact, she wouldn't have thought such an act was possible. Of course, neither of these men was Barion, and one of them seemed to have parts...well, where parts shouldn't have been. Drew saw her on her monitor before Stasha had a chance to log off. She pushed one of the men off of her, dislodged the other, and stood up staggering—obviously drunk. She grabbed a shirt, half way threw it on, and grabbed the neck of a bottle, from which she took a long drink before addressing her sister.

"Hey, sis, how's it hangin'? I was a little busy," she slurred out.

"I could see that," Stasha said pulling a face. "Drewcila, we need you to come home. The country is at war, and Zarco isn't thinking clearly. The people need their queen."

"You can do it. You do a perfectly good job of fooling them. They all think you're me." She walked over and started to rub her free hand up and down the oiled naked body of one of the alien men.

"But I'm *not* you, Drew. I'm afraid that without your guidance our country will fall into the hands of the Lockhedes." Stasha shook her head then, not quite believing her own words. That she expected this drunken, over-sexed mercenary to save their homeland would have sounded absurd to anyone who didn't know what Drewcila was capable of when she was sober—or at least approaching it—and motivated.

"I told the stupid bastard to open up trade with the Lockhedes—to sign salvaging contracts with them. He didn't listen to me. Why should I give a fuck what happens on Barious? Qwah-Co is very diversified. We'll survive. I have my own problems to worry about, you know. Van Gar gave away one of my ships!"

"While I'd like to believe you weren't engaging in the kind of conduct I just—unfortunately—witnessed while he was with you, I doubt that's the case. Drewcila, what did you expect him to do?"

"Well, I certainly didn't expect him to steal one of my ships and join some hokey-assed religious cult. Oh, tell me, Clod. Why do all my men turn on me?" she said looking up at the big man as she bit one of her knuckles.

"My name is Clote," he said, betraying the IQ of a turnip.

"What...ever." Drewcila released him and turned to the monitor, at least for the moment giving her sister her undivided attention. "I can not even start to fuck away my resentment."

"Drewcila...I'm not kidding. You need to come home. You have to talk sense into Zarco. He really thinks..."

"See, that's the real problem. If you were screwing him right, there wouldn't be enough blood in his brain for him to do any thinking..."

"Damn it, Drew..."

"My God, Stasha! You said damn it! Do you even know what it means?"

"Not really, but I'll say something worse than that if you don't quit interrupting me, stop drinking, and put the kingdom first for once."

"Screw the kingdom. What has it done for me lately? As a matter of fact, I'm thinking of pulling my salvaging operation from Barious and taking it someplace where they want to make a profit," Drewcila hissed out. Then she took a long swig from her bottle just to accentuate her point—that she wasn't listening to Stasha.

Stasha took a deep breath and tried to calm down. She knew Drew well enough to know that screaming at her wasn't going to do anything but make her more determined than ever to do just exactly what she pleased. "Drewcila...our people are dying. They're in pain. Can you feel nothing for them? What about showing a little compassion, is that beyond you?"

"Ah, that's too bad." Drewcila took her knuckle and pretended to wipe a tear from her eye. "Boo fucking hoo! Now back to what's really important: me, me, me."

"Must you make everything impossible?"

"No, I only make things difficult. Only you can make them impossible."

"What's that supposed to mean?" Stasha asked in confusion.

"How the hell should I know? I got it off some movie I saw. I didn't get it then, and I don't get it now, but it sounds good," Drew said with a shrug. She finished the bottle in her hand. "Boys, look around and see if you can't find another one of these."

The two naked men started crawling around on all fours looking through the rubble that covered the floor.

"Is this how you want to live your life, Drew? Drunk, wallowing in filth, having meaningless sex with dozens of different, well-oiled life forms?"

"Well, duh!" Drew laughed loudly, flopping back on the bed and showing Stasha a side of her that she would just as soon have not seen. She looked away from the monitor.

Her sister was drowning her sorrow in liquor and cheap sex. Of course she also did that when she was happy, which was no doubt why Van Gar had left. She loved her sister and she wanted to make excuses for her bizarre behavior. She had seen Drew occasionally put the people's needs above her own mercenary desires...or had she?

After all, nearly every decision Drew had made on the kingdom's behalf had managed to turn a tidy profit and increase her wealth and/or her salvaging empire.

Maybe it was time that she quit defending Drewcila. Maybe when all was said and done, Drew didn't actually *have* a better side. Stasha didn't want to believe that, mostly because if it were true, how could she ever hope to reason with her?

If my sister is nothing but a greedy, selfish egocentric bitch, Stasha thought, *how can I possibly convince her to put the kingdom first? She's selfish and motivated only by money...*

Stash tried again. "I suppose you could move your entire salvaging operation from Barious, but it would cost you a small fortune, and you wouldn't be operational for what—months? I wonder how much money you'd lose on the down-time alone? I wonder if even you have enough money to do it."

Drew sat up slowly and glared back at her, then she laughed loudly, "I have a shit load of money, Stasha..."

"True, but I'll bet it's not enough to move the operation. And while this war is going on, the country's rather expensive. Spaceports are in danger, recycling centers are even now being converted back into munitions plants, and then there is that other matter..."

"What matter would that be?"

"That most of your real money—all your iggys—are here in your private, not-as-secret-as-you-seem-to-think safe—at Hepron Station. Hepron Station, which will doubtless be a target in the war. I hope it's a really *strong* safe, Drewcila..."

"Stop!" Drew screamed, slamming her hands over her ears. "Stop! Your cruelty overwhelms me."

"If you don't sober up and come home there's a very real chance that you could go broke, Drew."

"*Nooooo!*"

Drewcila woke some hours later, alone, and with the queen mother of all hang-overs. She had managed to stay drunk for over a week—something close to a record for her—and now she was sober and suffering from the mega-hangover of death. Her eyes felt dry and sticky, her tongue was swollen, and her mouth tasted like she'd been sucking on dirty tube socks. Of course, with all the other depraved things she'd done, who knows? She might have done that, too. She sat up slowly and waited for the room to quit spinning.

She tried to remember why she had decided to sober up. Of course she was having trouble even remembering her name. She got up slowly, stumbled through the garbage to the bathroom, and landed on the toilet with a thump. It took awhile for her to actually start pissing since her body had no doubt forgotten how in the who-knew-how-many-hours she'd been passed out. But once she started, she began to wonder if she was ever going to stop. She started to wonder how pissing constantly might affect her life. It wasn't a very pretty picture. Maybe she'd just piss until all her bones had turned to dust.

Fortunately she did eventually stop pissing. She rose, walked over and looked in the mirror and jumped at the sight of her own reflection. Damn! She looked as bad as she felt. She stuck out her tongue and found that it was covered in large blue and yellow spots. First she thought with alarm that she had some terrible disease, but then she vaguely remembered that they had painted her tongue and her privates with some body dye made from some plant she couldn't remember the name of now. The person who had done it had sworn that the dye was harmless, but her tongue was swollen, and her crotch itched, so she started to wonder just how harmless it was. Of course chances were that her tongue was swollen from too much drinking, and her crotch was itching from too much sex, so who knew for sure? She couldn't remember how long the treatment was supposed to last. They promised her it would enhance her sexual pleasure, but she'd been too drunk to know if it actually did anything besides look weird. She'd have to ask one of the people she'd had sex with, if she could remember who they were.

"Where the fuck is my toothbrush?" She found it floating in the toilet and frowned. "See, there's the shit. Cause when you're drunk, ya just fish it out, wash it off, and no one's the wiser." She groaned and leaned against the wall holding her head with one hand as she flushed the toilet with the other. "Good bye ol' friend," she said as the tooth brush spiraled downward. "I should have stayed drunk. What made me decide to sober up? Is it a religious holiday or something? Hey! I know one of you assholes can hear me. Bring me a tooth brush, and it had by God better still be in the wrapper."

In seconds Jurak was there with a toothbrush—still in the wrapper. "Thanks." She took it from him, stacked about two inches of toothpaste on it from the wall dispenser, and then started brushing her teeth, making the foam erupt from her mouth on all sides as she did so. She brushed her tongue, then spit, getting foam all down the front of her body and the shirt she was almost wearing. Unfortunately it didn't seem to be dislodging any of the dye from her tongue. "Fuck...this day just gets better and better. Why the hell did I sober up, Jurak? And perhaps we had better work on remedying this problem..."

"My Queen, your sister..."

Drewcila turned to face him and shoved him so hard that he almost fell down. "Now I remember! I'm losing money! I'm losing a butt load of money. Crap! Where are we?"

"We're still docked..."

"Are you fucking nuts! Kick anyone who isn't crew off the ship, close the hatch, and get this tin piece of shit in the air, man. Chart a course to Barious ASAP. I'm getting in the shower. When I get out I want us to be untethered and on our way to Barious. Do I make myself clear?"

"Yes, my Queen." he started to leave as she began to strip the shirt off.

"And get the crew to clean this pit up. It looks like the war is being held in here."

"Yes, my Queen." He started to leave again as she was stepping into the shower.

"Oh...and Jurak...?"

"Yes, my Queen," he said with an exasperated sigh.

"Send someone in here. No sense in me showering alone."

"Yes, my Queen." He left.

Zarco listened to the incoming information with a sense of dread. Drewcila was on her way, hung over but sober, and as angry as he had ever seen her.

"Tell the queen I have the matter well in hand here. Her presence is completely unnecessary," Zarco had assured the man on the screen. His reward was the sound of his once be-loved wife screaming at the top of her lungs.

"Tell that pencil-dicked pud that I can hear him...Crap! My fucking head! You listen to me, Zarmoron, and you listen good..." The monitor swiveled to capture the vision of her swollen, all-but-green face, as she glared at him with blood shot eyes, and Zarco cringed. "You're like a turd that won't flush down, you just roll around the bowl wasting valuable resources and stinking up the place. Your hard-headed stupid-ity is costing me money. More importantly to you as the con-cerned King you pretend to be, you are putting your people's lives in jeopardy for no better reason than to continue your pissing contest with the Lockhedes. My ambassadors will be there within the hour. You will sit down with them, and by the time I arrive, I expect to see a peace agreement and salvaging contracts written up. If you don't settle this, and settle it quickly, there will be hell to pay."

Zarco had heard her, and his anger boiled inside him, but, there was something so distracting that concentrating on any-thing else was impossible. "What happened to your tongue?"

Drew mumbled something completely inaudible that he was sure were horrible curses meant only for him before she answered. "It's dye. It will wear off in a few days," she explained, slinging her hand around dismissively. Then she added in a hardly audible whisper, "I hope."

His question answered, Zarco's anger reared its ugly head again. "You will not give me orders. I'm not that trained dog of a hair-covered beast you keep in your bed. I am the king, and I will make policy concerning the country and the war. We will not make peace. We will not make trade agreements or sign contracts with the Lockhedes our sworn enemies..."

Drew waved her hand at him dismissively, in that moment looking every bit like the queen she had once been, instead of the salvaging whore she had become. "My people will be there in an hour. You will sit down with them and try to sort this thing out so that all I have to do when I get there is finish cleaning up the mess that you have made. Close transmission."

Zarco leapt from his chair at the console, slamming his hand down upon it. She'd openly defied him! She looked like death warmed up and she had just closed out on him, yet in that one instant he had seen back to what she once was and he couldn't deny that he still had strong feelings for her.

However, all of this had the opposite of Drewcila's desired effect, for Zarco rose from his chair more determined than ever to carry out his war effort against the Lockhedes. And this time there would be genocide. This time he would rid the planet of their blight forever.

Zarco looked up at the clock on the wall. Drewcila's "people" would be on their way by now. Alien scum, every one of them, and why did she assume that he'd cave in to them anymore than he'd cave in to her?

He'd had just about enough of Drewcila, and more than enough of her little salvager friends. He smiled.

"Come on, salvaging swine," he mumbled, "I've got quite a surprise for you, and for your boss. Quite a surprise indeed."

* * *

Dylan Allen looked with distaste at his two friends. "Why?" he whined.

"Because that's what the bitch said," Arcadia hissed. She wasn't angry. Valtarian lizard people always spoke with a hiss, which made them sound mad to everyone who'd never actually *seen* one of them mad. Once you had seen an angry Valtarian, you didn't forget how they looked or sounded. That was if they let you live.

"If she can't talk him into a treaty and trade agreement, what makes her think that we can?" Dylan seemed permanently fixed to his bed, making no indication that he was going to move. "We're just going to be wasting our time. Let's concern ourselves with trying to keep the operation running as smoothly as possible under the circumstances, and let Drewcila handle the pompous ass herself when she gets here."

"Get your worthless, lazy ass up!" Pristin ordered authoritatively.

Pristin, an Ontorian, was only three feet tall and almost as wide and looked for the most part like a deranged, turquoise hand puppet. However his twelve inch mouth held two rows of razor sharp teeth and the little bastard was amazingly fast. So when Pristin talked, his subordinates listened. This, as much as the fact that he was a brilliant businessman, was no doubt why Drewcila Qwah, the queen bitch of the salvaging empire, had put him in charge of running her operation on Barious.

Dylan sighed and got up, straightening his clothes. They were all wearing basically the same thing—the sleeveless blue jump suit with the Qwah-Co logo. Of course, since they were big shots, their suits were better cut and they had really cool black leather jackets with the Qwah-Co logo emblazoned over the pocket to go with them. Dylan had never really been fond of dressing like everybody else, so of course he'd spent most of his life that way. The real difference between himself and his compadres was that he looked really good in this outfit, which seemed to spotlight his package. He was a good looking man for a human, not that the rabble he hung with were likely to notice. Still it was important to him that he didn't go out in public till every hair was in place. He couldn't really remember the last time he'd actually seen an earth woman. Of course Barion women were nothing to sneeze at, and they seemed to find him "exotic."

He looked into the mirror and combed his hair, pretending not to notice his companion's impatience.

Dylan spent his days on Barious surrounded by alien salvaging scum, and most days that suited him just fine.

In fact, the only thing he hated about his job here was that he occasionally had to go with Arcadia and Pristin to talk with the royal idiot. Zarco was a man who epitomized all the things that Dylan hated most about mindlessly ambitious men. A rich idiot who'd never gotten his hands dirty, literally sitting on his throne, giving orders and making decrees that affected everyone but him. Pristin called Dylan lazy, but that was only because Pristin was an obsessive-compulsive little overachiever. Dylan knew hard work; hell, he still did it almost every day. More importantly, Dylan was the veteran of a dozen battles.

As a young man he'd played college ruckus ball, and everyone had said he'd go pro, but Dylan had bigger plans. He wanted to go to distant galaxies, and the military promised to take him all the places he wanted to go and make him into all that he could be.

He didn't get to go to any of the really cool places he wanted to go, and he soon realized that all they really wanted to make him was dead. It didn't take him long to learn more than he'd wanted to know about war. He knew what it really cost, not in money, but in life. Which was why he'd jumped ship one day and how he'd wound up in the salvaging trade. Salvagers didn't ask many questions, and they didn't care how obviously fake your information was. Especially not when you worked for Qwah-Co.

Zarco didn't know anything about battle. He'd sit in his castle, safe and sound, and let people run to their deaths in a war which was fashioned from Zarco's very personal need for revenge. He'd punish the planet and his people because Drewcila didn't love him anymore.

He had no noble reason.

This was the real reason Dylan was dragging his feet. It was going to be very hard to sit there and listen to the red-faced tyrant spit out a long stream of bullshit about why it was so important that they fight this war, and not tell the dundering asshole just exactly what he thought of him.

"Quit farting around with your hair, and let's go," Pristin ordered, finally having reached the end of his tether.

Dylan put his comb in his back pocket with a sigh, grabbed his jacket off the back of a chair, and threw it on.

Arcadia took his hand in her claw and gave it a gentle squeeze as she started leading him after Pristin, who never did anything but run. Even on his tiny little legs, when your one stride was worth ten of his, he was almost impossible to keep up with.

"Time is money, and money is time," Pristin said, his way of telling them to hurry up, which they didn't. They weren't that afraid of him.

"What's wrong?" Arcadia asked Dylan.

He smiled down at her. "I hate talking to Zarco, and you know as well as I do that we're wasting our breath anyway." He shrugged. It was a real shame that Arcadia found him as physically unattractive as he found her. She understood him, and he her. He had never had a really good relationship with any humanoid woman, and he found her voice very sexy, so if he didn't totally repulse her, he would have shut off all the lights and fucked her in a heartbeat. Of course that was what he did to most females, which was possibly why he'd never had a real relationship with any of them.

"Business runs so much smoother when Drewcila is here..."

Pristin was standing in front of them in seconds, interrupting Arcadia and making them stop short or trip over him. "It's supposed to be our job to make sure that the operation runs just as well without Drew as it does with her. We have failed..."

Dylan didn't like to be told that he had failed at anything. "Wait just one damn minute, Pris. We did what we were supposed to do. We tried to talk sense into the royal dildo's head. It didn't work then, and I don't think it's going to work now. We're just wasting our time..."

"If Drew gets here and the planet is still at war, and no trade agreements have been signed, heads are going to roll. I don't want one of them to be mine."

"I don't think Drew's going to blame us," Dylan said. He smiled. "And you know she isn't going to blame Arcadia."

"You don't think at all. That's your big problem..."

"Why you pile-of-crap-shaped toad, I ought to..." Dylan let go of Arcadia's claw, and pulled his arm back, making a fist.

Pristin bared his teeth and started growling. Arcadia jumped between them, swishing her five foot spike-tipped tail. "Gentlemen, how can we hope to convince Zarco to end the war when we can't even stop fighting amongst ourselves?"

Both males mumbled their agreement, and they started back on their way. Dylan smiled as he and Arcadia continued to walk along behind Pristin.

"What?" she asked with a matching smile, once again taking his hand.

"It just occurred to me that the three of us make the perfect team. But don't tell ol' toad face I told you so."

"His head is bloated enough as it is," she smiled, and then suddenly froze.

"What's wrong?"

Her head started pivoting around. She was obviously looking and listening. Something wasn't right. Dylan let go of Arcadia's claw and pulled his blaster. "Pristin, stop! Arcadia hears something..."

"Don't be ridicu..."

The hall in front of them exploded, and they were covered in what remained of their friend as a contingent of palace guards filled the hall before them. It didn't take a genius to figure out that someone had ordered them shot on sight.

Dylan fired on them, then grabbed Arcadia's claw and started pulling her back down the hall the way they had come. It wasn't easy. Arcadia had been very fond of Pristin, and coming from a warrior race, her answer to any combat situation was to stand and fight until you died. She was firing behind them as Dylan pulled her along. A contingent of guards rounded the hallway in front of them. He thought they were screwed, but then Arcadia started hauling him back the way they had just come, and he realized that she had killed everyone who had initially come after them. So apparently there had been a method to her madness. Now Dylan found that he was the one firing behind them as he was pulled along.

"What the fuck's going on?" he screamed.

She didn't answer, just kept pulling him. The hallway led to the palace grounds. No doubt Arcadia, whose people lived in the wilds, planned to use her knowledge of the great outdoors to lose the palace guards. Dylan, who had been born and raised in the city, and who purposely steered clear of the palace grounds because all that open sky and living stuff gave him the creeps, wasn't so thrilled about her apparent plan, but he followed anyway. He was the veteran of many space battles, but they weren't in space now. They weren't even close to the spaceport. So for now he'd trust the Valtarian's instincts.

Stasha heard the blaster fire within the castle. At her command, her escort led her to Zarco's office, only to find him watching the monitor and laughing in a maniacal manner. Facto was already there, and he turned to face her as she walked in and frowned.

"Zarco...what on Barious is going on?" she demanded.

He turned to look at her. "I have ordered Drewcila's 'ambassadors' executed."

"Is it not enough to make war with the Lockhedes? Must you now make war with Drewcila as well? You know she will not take this lying down. She will retaliate, and the gods alone know how," Stasha said in disbelief. "Have you gone quite mad?"

"On the contrary. I have just come to my senses. This is my kingdom, Stasha. Mine! Not Drewcila Qwah's. I'm about to tear her salvaging empire to the ground and return the glory of Barious," Zarco said. "Step one is to eradicate Drewcila's little spies so that she has to fly in here with no knowledge of what's going on. When she arrives I will deal with her as I should have dealt with her long ago. She will either submit her will to me and go back to being a real and proper wife and queen, or I shall have her executed and put you on the throne in her stead."

"You..." Stasha fought her tears. "I love you, Zarco. Does that mean nothing to you? Has our time together...all these years...was it all just a farce? Do you love me not at all? Do you truly believe that I would want to be your queen knowing that I am now, and always shall be, your second choice? Have you gone so completely crazy that you believe I would have anything to do with a man who would kill my only sister simply because she didn't love him?" She did cry then. "Listen to what you just said. Last night, only last night, you assured me that you loved me. Today you have decided to once again leave me to go after my sister, and if she refuses to be the person you love, then you'll kill her and *make do* with me. And you think that after all that I'd marry you! I swear, Zarco, I thought this whole war was just you using your usual bad judgment in running the country, but I now see that in reality you are completely and totally obsessed. You have, in fact, gone quite mad."

Facto walked over to comfort her, and she collapsed in tears on his shoulder.

"Sire, surely..."

Zarco laughed. "Ah, and Facto, my old friend, my loyal advisor..." He hit a button, and the monitor played back the conversation Facto'd had with Drewcila that morning. It was pretty damning. "How long have you been working for the queen?"

"My duty is to serve both the king and the queen…"

"You know what I mean, traitor. How long have you been working against me with Drewcila Qwah?"

Facto stood tall and looked proud as he held the shattered woman. "Ever since I realized that money grubbing salvager cares more about the people and the country than you do. Stasha's right; you are crazy and my duty, my real duty, isn't to serve you or Drewcila. My real duty is to serve the people of the kingdom."

"Guards!" They appeared seemingly out of thin air. "Take my sister-in-law and Chancellor Facto to the dungeon. They are both charged with high treason."

Two guards each grabbed Facto and Stasha harshly.

"Zarco! I beg of you, seek help, reconsider this madness!" Facto yelled as he was hauled out of the room. "What crime has Stasha committed?"

Zarco held up a hand and seemed to reconsider. He looked at Stasha, who now held her head high even if tears were still streaming down her face. "Stasha, will you make a speech to the people as I asked you to do?"

Stasha's tears stopped flowing as anger gripped every fiber of her being, and she tried to pull away from the two guards that held her. She looked at Zarco, her mouth set in a determined snarl, and for the moment she looked so much like her sister that it made Zarco flinch. "I would sooner die and rot in the dungeon," she hissed.

"Take them away!" Zarco ordered hotly.

"Men, I beseech you," Facto started, as they were pulled towards the dungeons, "the king's thinking is skewed. He must not be allowed to do this thing."

The guards laughed.

"Have you failed to notice," the largest of the guards, and the one wearing Captain's insignia said, "that there has been a changing of the guards?" He laughed. "Your precious salvaging whore demoted the nobility. Made us nothing. Turned our country into a land of garbage diggers. No more. With our help our good king will return the pride of our nation, and we will finally lay waste to the Lockhedes. We will use the wealth the Queen of Filth has filled her pockets and the country's coffers with to build an army that no one can stand against, and topple all who would stand in our way."

Facto shook with the implications. "Don't you see, man? You will only destroy the country. There will be great loss of life, and..."

"Shut up, old man! Only the peons will die, and we shall regain our true station."

They were shoved roughly into a cell. The door shut with a clang and locked behind them.

Facto looked defiantly at the guard as he spoke. "If you allow this lunacy to take place, all that you will have for your trouble is a smoking hole where our once great country stood. I beg of you..."

The guards laughed loud enough to drown him out and walked away.

Stasha went to sit on the hard wooden bed, which was the only furniture in the cell, and tried to contain herself.

"My sister is walking into a trap. One that not even she can escape from," Stasha said.

"Margot is still out. My good wife will find a way to warn the queen." As if to mock him, two more guards walked in, dragging Margot between them.

Stasha looked up and sighed. "Well, as my sister might say, we're fucked!"

Chapter 3

Van Gar hadn't really thought much about being unstrapped, without the benefit of seats, in the cargo bay of a ship during reentry and landing on a planet's surface. Several Chitzskies were badly injured, and no one walked onto the surface of the planet without several bad bruises.

To make matters worse, after talking to several of the others at length, he began to get a picture of just how badly they were being scammed. If Drewcila found out what he had done, after she beat him senseless for giving away one of her ships, she was going to laugh herself into a coma at his stupidity.

He should have known better. A lifetime as a salvager and over eight years in the company of the Queen of Grifters should have made him immune to even the best bullshit line. And the "Pride Leader" just didn't have that good a line.

He felt like the universe's biggest idiot.

Utarus' surface was bare and desolate, with a sparse scattering of blue and red geodesic domes—the only structures in sight. There were the beginning of what might eventually be plants, and many Chitzskies doing the work of machines—moving dirt and rocks in buckets or pushing around wheel barrows. The "Planet Coordinator's" speech started with, "This is our home..." and as far as Van Gar was concerned, it went downhill from there. They learned that the "Pride Leader," Reverend Pard Jar, hadn't come to the planet with them, and that no one knew his actual name. He was "sacrificing" himself, staying in space, roaming the galaxy. And he would continue to do so until he had gathered up the remnants of his people and brought them all here to fulfill their destiny.

What the hell have I done? I left the only woman I've ever loved and a lifestyle I enjoyed to do what? Come to this godsforsaken wasteland to work myself to death. All to punish Drewcila. Drewcila, who is probably drinking the very best of alcoholic beverages, screwing whatever she likes, and living in the lap of luxury while I bake here, working my ass off to make some scam artist—who's not good enough to wipe the sweat from Drewcila's feet—rich. What the hell was I thinking?... That I was sick to death of being that whore's trained boy, that's what. That just once I wanted to be treated as if I really mattered, as if not just any warm body could take my place. So now I'm here, in hell, and there's no one, no one at all, to stop Drew from doing just exactly what she wants to do.

Van Gar started yelling, and didn't appear to have any stopping point. His Chitzsky brothers and sisters all around him thought he was in a home planet-type rapture, and they all started to sing a hymn as Van Gar wished for death.

Drewcila sat at her place on the bridge, at least for the time being everything but business forgotten. They were on their way to Barious as fast as the ship and the hyperspace by-way would allow them to go.

She looked at the figures that poured onto her screen on the left, even as she watched news reports from Barious on the right. Neither made her very happy. Her stock was plummeting all over the galaxy, and the reason for it was clear from the newscasts. Zarco had closed down all recycling operations on the planet and put everyone to work, either drafting them to military duty or rebuilding the military equipment he needed for the war he wanted to wage.

She was shifting shipments of salvage that were supposed to be landing on Barious to be reworked for resale to three of her smaller operations on other worlds and satellite installations, but they couldn't keep up. Key shipments were being delayed, production couldn't maintain their quotas at this rate, and salvage was stacking up everywhere. It was an incredible mess.

Suddenly the screen showing the newscast went blank. For the next several minutes she tried without any luck to reach Barious. Either the entire planet had just blown up, or more likely some one had detonated a communications disruptor. Technology had advanced to the point that such weapons didn't do permanent damage, however it could be hours—maybe even days—before they could repair the damage done by such an attack. Her stocks plummeted still more sharply.

"Heads will roll," Drewcila mumbled.

"What's that, my Queen?" Jurak asked.

"Detonating such a device at a time of war hardly gives anyone the upper hand. You wipe out communications on the entire surface of the planet, and that more or less puts everyone in the dark. So you have to ask, 'who would gain anything from this?' Zarco, of course. Zarco is purposely keeping me in the dark. This could mean only one thing, that he is up to something—something he knows I won't like. The question is what? He doesn't have sense enough to pour piss out of a boot without directions on the side, and his only real motivation, ever, seems to be his winky. So someone else must be pulling the strings—but who?"

She got up and started pacing back and forth, tapping her chin with her forefinger. "Who would benefit by the country going to war?"

Jurak thought for a moment. "No one, my Queen."

"Precisely...So the war isn't the main objective. Closing down the salvaging operation is, and who wants the salvaging operation closed down?"

"No one, my Queen. Salvaging has made the country prosperous."

"Which is why they hate it," she laughed out loud, and then walked over and plopped back into her chair. "It's the nobility, the rich fucks, Jurak. They don't want the country to be prosperous, or the people to be happy, because then *they* aren't in control. They would have been against treaties with the Lockhedes from day one. It would have been easy for them to sway King Panty-waist to their side, because he's one of them." She looked back at her monitor. "So, how deeply and completely are they entrenched?"

"I...don't know?"

Drew sighed. "Jurak, don't take this the wrong way. You're a nice guy and all, but *damn* you're lame."

"I'm sorry, my Queen."

"Crap, not even going to argue with me," Drew muttered under her breath. She sighed again. "Forget about it and get me a beer."

"Yes, my Queen." He went over to the cooler, dug a beer out of the ice, opened it and brought it to her. She sighed again as she took it from him, and waved her hand dismissively.

"Go on, get out of here."

He bowed low and left.

Drew screwed up her face and mocked him. "Yes, my Queen, I'm a fucking idiot. No, my Queen, I don't have any brain at all. Who would have ever thought that the day would come when I'd grow tired of all this bowing and scraping?" She took a long drink of her beer and settled back into her chair to watch her stocks plummet and feel her blood pressure rise. She smiled as she made a decision. No doubt it would be an unpopular one, but it was one that she could live with.

Dylan and Arcadia made their way through the palace greenery towards the back gates to the palace grounds. The gates were well guarded, and the guards well armed, so Dylan had no idea how she thought they were going to get out when they got there. Arcadia stopped short and pulled him against her into a bush full of thorns against the palace wall. As Dylan plucked a thorn from his ass, he remembered one of the reasons he hated nature so much. He soon saw the reason for Arcadia's sudden movement as two guards walked past, just inches from them. Dylan started to breathe again only when they were well gone.

"What now?" Dylan asked in a whisper.

"I was hoping you had a plan," Arcadia said with a hopeless sound in her voice.

Dylan sighed. Short of an all-out attack on the rear gate, and some really good luck, he didn't have a clue. "Have you noticed that they have changed the palace guard?"

"No, they all look the same to me."

"Well, they have. I didn't think anything of it, just thought it was part of a rotation, but now I realize that what they've done is to change guards who were loyal to Drewcila for guards who are loyal to the King. Drewcila's people would never have killed Pristin, and they certainly wouldn't be hunting us down now. I mean, you are, after all, one of Drew's favorite toys."

"And she mine," Arcadia said in a voice filled with a smile. She suddenly jerked him around, and all sign of mirth left her face. "He's setting a trap for Drew."

"Damn! And I was counting on her to rescue us."

"We have to get out and warn her."

"And again I ask how?"

Arcadia started looking around in all directions. She'd never admit it, but her feelings for Drewcila Qwah went far beyond friendship. Otherwise, she more than likely wouldn't have agreed to be one of the multitudes of people Drew slept with. Unlike their boss, Dylan got the feeling that Arcadia wasn't into screwing people just for fun and profit.

"A frontal assault on the main gate?" Arcadia finally said, seeming to come to the same conclusion he'd come to—that it was really their only option.

Dylan shook his head. "Suicide. I'm not ready for that yet."

Arcadia tried her wrist-com for the thousandth time, even more frantic now than she had been before, because she realized that Drew was the real target. Their communicators weren't working—some kind of jamming device had no doubt been implemented to make sure that the people on the outside were kept completely in the dark.

"We have to do something. The courtyard isn't big enough for us to elude the guards indefinitely," Arcadia said, adding to the list of things for Dylan to worry about. Till then he had just assumed that Arcadia was so good at this that she could keep them hidden.

Arcadia's eyes suddenly lit up, and she grabbed his hand and started pulling him along again. When he saw which way they were heading, he pulled her to a stop. "Are you crazy?" he whispered. "That's the bunkhouse."

"Exactly," Arcadia said excitedly. "Lots of flammable stuff..."

"We start it on fire, and create a diversion," Dylan finished, looking at the blaster in his hand. He nodded his head in agreement, and they started moving again.

He had a clear shot through the door at a mattress inside, and he took it. They moved quickly to a better hiding spot and waited. In mere minutes the bunkhouse was in flames, and as they had planned, nearly every guard on the premises went to where the excitement was. They left the back gate with only one guard, and Arcadia shot him.

"I don't like it. I don't like it at all," Drewcila mumbled. Stocks were still plummeting, and Barious was still a complete communication wash out. She'd had to re-route still more barges loaded with salvage.

"Jurak?"

"Yes, my Queen?"

"Re-route all scrap to one of our other facilities until further notice, or we have stopped this idiotic war, whichever comes first," Drew said thoughtfully.

"But, my Queen...our...our other facilities can not possibly handle the extra pay loads. Many people on Barious...They'll be without work if we..."

"I know all that," Drew said hotly, pounding her fist on the console and losing all the data on her screen. "Shit!" she punched buttons till she got the data back. "Don't you think I know all that, Jurak? That's exactly why I didn't want this war. But your idiot king has apparently forgotten who wears the pants in the castle. Which would be who, Jurak?"

"Definitely you, my Queen."

"And why is that, Jurak?"

"Because my king is an idiot?" Jurak guessed.

"Precisely!" Drew looked up at him and smiled. "See, I think you're a great guy. I wonder why none of the others like you?" She looked thoughtful for a moment. "I can't be sending expensive ships loaded with expensive salvage into spaceports in a country on a planet where a war has been declared—not while I'm blind. That would just be insane. Who knows but that the entire country hasn't been over run by the Lockhedes?"

"What about us, my Queen?" Jurak asked nervously.

"What about us, Jurak?"

"What about us flying into a spaceport blind? Maybe into hostile territory?"

"Why, it sucks, of course. Still, what choice do we have? After all…I am losing a shit-pot load of money." Drew got up, practically skipped over to the ice chest she kept on the bridge at all times, opened it and extracted a beer. Out of the corner of her eye she could see Jurak giving her a disapproving look. She stood to her full height and popped the cap off the bottle on the corner of one of the consoles. "Don't get your panties in a knot, Jurak, it's only a beer."

"My Queen, with all due respect…"

Drewcila coughed, "And that would be a lot, 'cause ah me being *queen* and all."

Jurak straightened even more than usual, cleared his throat and waded in, "Your Majesty always starts out with beer and good intentions, then after a few beers…Well, Your Majesty seems to forget that there are matters which need Your concern, and You…"

"My Majesty gets shit faced drunk and starts screwing everything that moves." She looked painfully thoughtful for a second, "and some things that don't. Why is it that you can do everything right most of the time, but you screw up, get drunk even once, and everyone has to throw it in your face forever? Answer me that question, Jurak."

"Drewcila," he temporarily slung away all formality and tried to reason with her on her level. "You're *always* drunk," he reminded her gently.

Drewcila laughed and flopped into her chair, spinning around to face him. "Well, that would be once, wouldn't it?"

"I hardly think that now is the time to...well, tie one on as you say."

"Chill out, Jurak. Have a brew. I know when it's time to work, and when it's time to play. I'm not going to get drunk." She looked at the monitor as if she expected at any minute it might tell her the answers to the very meaning of life itself, then said in an almost detached voice. "There are two things that piss me off more than anything else in the universe. You know what those are, Jurak?" Without giving him a chance to answer, she held up one finger. "Losing a butt load of money." She held up two fingers. "Men who openly defy me, start wars, or go off, give away one of my ships, and join fucking religious communes. So, needless to say, I'm royally pissed off and hardly in a party mood. So smile—unless you're afraid your face will crack—kick back, and relax for a minute. How does my tongue look?" She stuck it out.

"Still blue and yellow spotted," Jurak said making a face.

"Damn! I was afraid of that." Drew sighed and took a long drink of her beer. It calmed her stomach and her nerves. She wondered if she could get in touch with Van Gar. Try to talk some sense into his head. Or maybe, and this was extreme and must mean something, she should tell him some bullshit story about how she was wrong, and she'd change, and quit doing all the things that pissed him off so badly. Just as soon as she figured out what they were...

She missed him. Missed him to the point of distraction. It sucked, too, because it meant she must actually harbor some real feelings for him. In which case it was a good thing he was gone. Life was good. Hell, it was great! She did what she wanted, when she wanted, with who she wanted. She sure as hell didn't want anything screwing up her party. And there was always

Arcadia, loyal and trustworthy. While her feelings might be similar to Van Gar's regarding Drew's behavior, she at least had the good sense to keep her mouth shut.

Well, most of the time anyway.

Drew'd worked damn hard, and she'd gotten everything she'd ever wanted. A huge salvaging empire, a fleet of ships rivaled by none in three galaxies, giant recycling centers, and whole satellites bore the Qwah-Co logo. She had the admiration of her people, power, and more money than she could ever possibly spend.

Now the men in her life were flushing her dreams down the toilet. Van Gar was gone, she still wasn't sure just why, and that idiot husband of hers had started a war which threatened her empire.

Some days, being queen just sucked.

Chapter 4

There was dirt and rocks as far as the eye could see. The nights were cold, and the days were hot. Van Gar spent his days picking up the rocks, putting them into buckets, and carrying them to one of two places. The first was the loading bay: apparently some planet was actually paying the Pride Leader for their rock. The second was the "building site," one of the few large flat places on this otherwise knobby planet. There, a crew of Chitzskies was mixing mud and laying up rock walls to build a large meeting hall which would double as a home for the "Pride Leader." When that structure was complete, they would work as a community to build single family living structures for the population. Currently the "population" was living in prefab, plastic coated, cardboard geodesic domes made entirely from recycled material which were, ironically, a product of Qwah-Co.

Each blue or red piece of every dome was stamped with the Qwah name in the alternating color. Her name glared mockingly down on him as he tried to sleep on the cardboard floor of one of the tiny domes which were meant to house six human-sized beings, and in which sixteen Chitzskies were living.

It was hard to believe that this was the most habitable part of the planet. No doubt this was why the planet had remained in such an "unspoiled" state. It rained very rarely—about twice a year—and the few wells that had been drilled recovered very slowly. Because of this, and the fact that they didn't want to overtax the recycling system, they were only allowed to have a real shower once a week. Showers were scheduled so that the same number showered every day. This meant the entire place always smelled like dirty Chitzsky, a smell which he found more repulsive every day.

So he'd lay there at the end of a hard day's work with his poly-fiber blanket on the cold floor with no pillow for his head.

He'd breathe the putrefying stench of himself and his Chitzsky brothers and sisters, that burned the hair from his nostrils. He'd squeeze his eyes shut, trying desperately to go to sleep so that he could at least momentarily be released from the hell he had thrown himself into. And the whole time Drewcila would be mercilessly taunting him. She was so completely and totally egotistical that she'd insisted on anything the company created being stamped with her name. There he would lie, billions of miles from her, and all he could see when he looked up was Qwah, Qwah, *Qwah!* It should be a constant reminder of just why he was well rid of her. Instead, it only served to remind him of all that he had lost.

To make matters worse, he realized only a few days after landing that he found women of his own race to be entirely repulsive, smelly and hairy, and unpleasant to look at. One of the women, Shreta, seemed intent on bedding him. Naturally, she was the ugliest one of the bunch. She had a nice personality, but try as he might, he not only couldn't get aroused at the thought of sex with her, he'd thrown up the green slop they fed them twice a day just thinking about it. He was quite sure that the poor homely thing's underwear riding up into her crack was as close to sex as she had ever gotten.

A week after landing he had insisted they put him on the very next ship off this hole of a planet. They refused, so he decided not to work. They revoked his eating and bathing privileges. He figured he could out last them. Bathing was no big deal, because in truth he could put up with his own stench before he could put up with everyone else's. When you knew you stank, you could always assume it was you that you were smelling, which actually made the stench more bearable. Sort of the difference between smelling your own fart and someone else's. As for food, Shreta secretly sneaked it to him.

He was sitting on his ass one day, watching the others work, when he saw five "foremen" come together. They were talking and looking at him, and Van Gar was sure he'd finally won. That they were going to send him home. But when they started walking towards him...Well, he'd been in enough fights to know when someone was in an ass-kicking mood. Since he was in one himself, he stood up and got ready. He'd taken more than five people on before, and he'd always walked away victorious.

"Will you go to work now?" the one called Remo asked as they approached.

"No. I will not. We are all being used, we have all been duped by a con man. I want to be taken off this planet and brought to the nearest spaceport as soon as possible."

Apparently they weren't in a talking mood.

He put up a good fight, but they still beat him damn near to death. See, Van Gar had never faced even one other Chitzsky male in battle. They didn't crumple under his punches the way humans, Barions, and most other aliens did.

When they had beaten him bloody, they dragged him back into the field and put a bucket in his hand.

So now, all day, every day, he filled his bucket with rocks, dumped them into a wheel barrow, or carried it over to the building site just like a good little slave to the Pride Leader. All the while plotting ways off the planet and out of the mess he'd gotten himself into.

Shreta had once again worked her way over to pick up rock alongside him.

"How are you feeling, Van Gar?" she asked, even though it had been days since the beating. Truth was she asked him five or six times a day just because her conversational skills were that limited, and she wanted to talk to him.

"I'm fine. Healed. Stupid, but well."

She giggled, "You shouldn't have defied the foremen like that."

"That's not why I feel stupid," Van Gar growled back. She jumped a little at seeing his obvious anger, and he didn't feel in the least bit guilty. "All my life I have felt that we were a highly superior race. I looked down at the other races I en-countered, thinking them inferior in every way. But look at us, at all of us, and especially me. We are total morons. We gave up everything of worth to come here. For what? To haul rock and eat green glop 'til we eventually die on this godsforsaken planet of dust and rock."

Shreta looked at him and frowned. She was even uglier when she wasn't smiling. "We came here to make a homeland. To have a better life."

"And does this," he stood up, held his arms out, and turned around, "look like a good homeland to you?" He let his arms fall to his side and looked into her eyes. "Is sleeping on a cold, hard, cardboard floor in a room full of smelly Chitzskies, eating green slimy shit made out of gods only know what...Is this really better than the life you had before?"

She looked really confused now. "We...we are working towards something. We are building a place for us, and our children and their children. It will take a lot of hard work, a long time..."

"How long? Look around you, Shreta. Rocks and dirt. A few struggling, scraggly shrubs. It will take generations to make this unfertile piece of crap yield crops or sustain herds. We surely won't live to see it, and as for children...would you condemn a child to live the life we live here? How horrible was your life before, that this seems better to you?"

A small crowd had now gathered around them, listening intently.

"I...I was a checker in a clothing store," Shreta said, obviously trying to remember the experience. Suddenly anger marked her features, making her yet uglier. "I always had great clothes because I got them at discount. I was never too hot or too cold. I ate whatever I wanted whenever I wanted." She looked at Van Gar. "We were tricked. That's what you were saying, isn't it?"

Mumbling started throughout the group as everyone recalled all that they'd left behind, all that they'd signed over to the "Pride Leader."

"You there, back to work," a foreman ordered approaching them.

Van Gar walked through the crowd and up to the foreman. "Why?"

"Because there is work to do..."

"So?" Van Gar said with a shrug.

"So, the Pride Leader has set tasks for us to complete, and..."

"When did you stop even pretending not to be ordering us around?" Van Gar asked.

"Yeah," the others said as a group.

"If we're here because it's a better place for us, why do we have to answer to you? Why should we have to answer to anyone? Are we your brothers and sisters, or are we your slaves? And if we aren't your prisoners, why can't we leave if we like?"

"You again!" the foreman said, suddenly recognizing Van Gar. "Brothers and sisters, this man is nothing but a lazy trouble maker. Such negativity will accomplish nothing. The Pride Leader has taught us..."

"His words have the ring of truth to them," an angry young Chitzsky said. "Why should we have to listen to you? Why should we have to take orders from anyone? We were promised freedom from the abuse of the aliens we lived encased by, but what about the abuse that is shelled out by you in the name of the Pride Leader?"

"Better then that, if this is paradise, then why doesn't the Pride Leader come live here with us?" Van Gar added.

"He's...he's suffering out there, so that we can all be brought together here." But now even the foreman stammered.

"For what purpose? So that we can all starve together on this floating turd in space?" Van Gar asked. He'd run more than a few scams himself in the time he'd spent with Drewcila and he could now hear in this man's voice the faltering that always comes before the sell.

"The plantings we've made so far are starting to grow..."

"They are stunted and barely existing. Take in a deep breath. You know what that horrid stench is, my people? It's *us*. Why?

Because there isn't enough water to bathe, much less water crops properly. The more of us there are, the more water we're going to need, and you can't squeeze water from a dry sponge. We can recycle the water just so many times, and then it isn't good for anything but plants, and there won't be enough of it to make them thrive. This guy who calls himself the Pride Leader has robbed us all, and he did it by promising us something that we all felt like we were missing. I know this because I also felt like I wanted a home planet. Someplace that belonged to Chitzskies, that we could call our own. But what were we really missing out on before? We had everything but a rock on which to hang claim and be responsible for."

"The Pride Leader used that small wish in each of us—the wish for a home planet—to take everything we had of value, and force us into a life of slavery so that he could get power and money. He is the greatest traitor to our race that has ever lived. And that's saying a lot considering that our ancestors managed to fight a war so brutal that they wound up blowing up our home planet."

A much larger group had formed by the time he ended his speech.

"What should we do?" the former foreman asked.

"We've already started," Van Gar said. "We tell all the others and win them over. Then we get off this rock, go find this great imposter and take back what's ours."

Drew sucked on her cigar and paced the command deck, going through different options in her head. They were now in orbit around Barious, and every attempt made at communication with the surface had met with the same failure as earlier attempts. She had her best geeks working on it, but it was obvious that whatever the problem was, it wasn't one that they could solve—at least not from up here.

Their hard work had in fact done nothing but confirm what she'd already been sure of: someone had detonated a communications disruptor from one of the orbiting satellites.

The question was who? Without the answer to that question, she couldn't be sure just what sort of reception she'd be getting at the palace.

The Lockhedes were the likely suspects. After all, this whole war had been started because of Zarco's unwillingness to allow them to salvage with Barious. Cut off communications, and you basically shut down the biggest salvaging port in the galaxy, crippling the superior economy of the Barions, and bringing all commerce to a standstill until communications systems could be brought back on line. A few hours would cost them millions—a few days, trillions.

It definitely leveled the playing field.

However, her gut was telling her that it was probably Zarco and whatever idiots were pulling his strings at the moment who caused this disruption. The real problem was that Zarco was a moron, and it would be just like him to start a war that Drew didn't want, and then ruin her business by destroying communications. Yes, it would definitely be like him to shut the planet off from the rest of the galaxy, not to mention making planet-wide communication impossible, all just to piss her off.

Well, if all he'd really wanted to do was piss her off, he had succeeded beyond his very wildest dreams.

If she went in now, she'd be flying in by the seat of her pants. No ground support. No way of knowing whether the spaceport, or the palace for that matter, was over-run by the Lockhedes. She'd have to trust her own instruments to tell her that she wasn't running into things—like other ships. If she went down there and the country had been nuked, it was all just a great waste of time, and she'd need all her time to try and save her corporation.

"Orders?" Jurak asked carefully.

"I'm still thinking!" Drewcila stopped in mid stride and turned to face him. "Can't you see I'm still thinking?"

"Sorry, my Queen." Jurak bowed submissively.

"All this sobriety, and thinking, and having to be responsible..." Drew stuck her cigar in her mouth and held it with her teeth as she ran her hands through her hair. "I had hoped for so much more from life." She took a long drag from the cigar, and puffed the smoke slowly into Jurak's face until he gratified her by coughing. At which point she walked over, flopped into her command chair, and put her seatbelt on. She'd made her decision.

"Strap in, gang. We're going planetside," Drewcila ordered, and gave them exactly five seconds to comply before she started the descent towards the planet's surface. She puffed on her cigar, making clouds of smoke as she concentrated on the ac-tual flying of the ship, while trying to watch all the monitors for any signs of enemy craft. There were three other people whose job it was to monitor such things, but she didn't actu-ally trust any of them to do it.

This was a salvaging barge, but it was a *royal* salvaging barge, manned with an all-Barion crew. They were hopelessly loyal to her, but they hadn't traveled the space lanes as long as she had. They'd never had to deal with pirates or smugglers, and they didn't know all the tricks that an enemy could use to get around detection devices.

The ship had a pilot, and ordinarily she let him fly the ship, but right now, going in blind, perhaps into enemy territory...Well, she didn't trust him to do his job as well as she could, either.

This wasn't the Garbage Scow, but it was her ship, and as long as she was sober, she might as well fly it.

Of course, what would have put her most at ease was to have Van Gar at the controls. No one could fly under pressure like he could. She also missed having him around to bounce things off of. Jurak was the closest thing she had to a friend on this ship, and he was mostly an ankle-biting little lackey whose job it was to kiss her ass. He was too afraid of her to give her honest feedback most of the time, and he wasn't a true sal-vager. He, like the rest of the crew, had never been in the trenches with the garbage.

They didn't truly understand the ways of a salvager. They didn't think like one or act like one. Salvaging wasn't just a job, it was a way of life, an attitude, a certain way of seeing the universe and your place in it.

These people had yet to become one with the trash.

They didn't understand the true circle of life. You are born, you live, you make trash which must then be recycled, you die and you are recycled.

All things are eventually recycled. It was a truth that guided every true salvager.

And she, Drewcila Qwah, Queen of all Salvagers, had allowed herself to get too far away from her roots. Not the roots of her forgotten life as Queen of Barious, she couldn't give a shit less about that. No, what in that moment shamed her to the depth of her soul was that she had allowed herself to move too far away from her *real* roots. She was Drewcila Qwah, and before she was Queen, before she was owner of a major corporation, she was a Salvager. She should be captaining a real salvaging barge, not flying around in some imperial mock-up, giving orders over the computer to a bunch of greenies who wouldn't know a good score of trash if it jumped up and bit them on the ass. She should have a crew of salvaging scum from all corners of the galaxy under her command, and be traveling the galaxy in search of really interesting salvage.

As much as she hated to admit it, even to herself, Van Gar was right. She had changed. Not because she was drinking, partying, or screwing around any more than she had. She had always done that. But because she had forgotten to momentarily sober up and get in the trenches with the filth to find the good stuff. She had allowed herself to become soft and complacent.

She admitted something else, something that caused her a wrenching pain in her stomach. Money really wasn't everything! Being filthy rich wasn't worth anything if it kept you from doing the things you truly loved, if it cost you one of your only true friends.

Just then she saw an all too familiar blip on the bottom of one of her screens that immediately died out.

"Ah, fuck!"

"What is it, my Queen?" one of the techs who should have noticed the blip asked.

"We've picked up a tail. One of you morons try to get me a visual."

In front of her the picture of a star class Lockhede battle cruiser filled the screen.

"Try to hail the ship," Drew ordered.

"I'm sorry, my Queen..."

"They're powering up their canons!" Drewcila announced.

"How do you know that, my Queen?" Jurak asked.

"Because I'm not a moron. Our instruments show a change in the power fluctuation coming from their ship. Shields up! Full power!" she ordered as she began an evasive move to starboard.

"Shields at full power, my Quee..."

"Knock the my queen crap off. Call me Captain. I'm the Captain of this ship, damn it!" The first blast hit them, rocking the ship. "Damage report."

"No damage to the hull."

"Drop shields, fire rear heat seeking missiles now!"

"My Q...Captain, I'm afraid we have no rear heat seeking missiles," Jurak reported, his voice taking on a panicked edge. It was hard to figure out whether his panic was due to their basically defenseless condition and the fact that they were under fire, or the fact that he had just told Drew something she didn't want to hear.

"Well, what *do* we have in our butt?" Drew demanded. "And whatever it is, fucking fire it now!"

"We have a laser."

"I said fucking fire it!" A second blast hit them as they fired the laser canon in their tail.

"Damage report."

"Hull breach in sector seven."

"Seal off sector seven. God damn it! If Van Gar ever comes back I'm going to strangle him for leaving me with you idiots!"

Drew could feel the ship pulling as she made yet another evasive maneuver. "Fire the laser cannon again! God! Do I have to tell you morons everything? Use your fucking heads!"

"The laser was damaged in the last hit and will not fire," the weapons chief reported.

"Beautiful! Fucking beautiful!" Drew made yet another evasive move, and found that the ship was handling worse by the minute. "What do we have in our nose?"

"Missiles, photon blasters, laser canons..."

"Good. Everyone hang on and prepare to fire everything on my command." She brought the ship about by turning nose over tail, bringing them into a collision course with the much larger ship. "Fire!"

The security officer fired their entire arsenal, which hit the enemy ship with a very gratifying display of destruction. The enemy ship lost power, and its orbit began almost immediately to degrade, aided no doubt by the blast it had just received. Drew attempted to correct course just enough—she hoped—to skim the space just above the doomed cruiser. For an eternal moment of time, it seemed to the crewmen on the command deck that Drew was somehow forcing the ship to do the impossible through sheer force of will. Unfortunately, neither the application of force nor the exertion of her will could make the ship respond any faster than it was capable of responding.

The two ships were still too close as they closed, and there was an awful grating noise as their hulls met. Drew lost helm control, and her ship started spinning off course. The entire crew seemed to scream as one as Drew wrestled to regain control of the ship. It wasn't easy, and to make matters worse, Drew saw that dozens of bottles of beer and pounds of ice were bouncing around the flight deck, careening off instrument panels and crew.

"Who forgot to secure the ice chest? Shit! What a ship of fools." Helm control was returning slowly, and Drew was able to regain stability. However she wasn't directing the ship towards the surface of the planet, and yet that was where it was going.

"What is it with this fucking planet? Can't I just *land?* Do I always have to crash? Is a nice, reasonable landing at a spaceport too much to fucking ask for?"

She'd only actually crashed on the planet once before, but that would have made for shitty ranting, so she chose to indulge in exaggeration.

"We're all going to die!" Jurak screamed in panic. The rest of the crew quickly followed his example and started screaming and crying.

"Shee...it! What a bunch of fucking losers! Butch it up!" Drew ordered. Then she added in a mostly inaudible mumble, looking at the readouts on the monitor in front of her. "We're all going to die." She was barely able to slow their descent, and steering them towards a spaceport would most likely be catastrophic. She needed someplace big and soft.

"We could...land in the Galdart Desert," Jurak suggested, struggling for control, and seeming to read her mind. No doubt he was remembering that was how she had survived her first crash onto the planet's surface.

"No!!!" Drew turned to glare at him. "I'd sooner impale myself on a mountain top."

The further they got into the planet's atmosphere, the better the ship seemed to be handling. Unlike the doomed Lockhede battle cruiser, Drew's salvaging barge was actually built to land on planets. "All right, we're closer now. Most of us would die, but a few of us would live." She mumbled as she checked her readouts and maps. "Flying in blind with a damaged ship. Landing at a spaceport out of the question—could hit ships landing or taking off, or hit the station itself, as little control as I have over this tub." She was thinking out loud. "Definitely don't want to land in Lockhede territory, and not going to land in the Galdart desert for damn sure. So, I look for a nice, long, stretch of water."

"Lake Witcha—it's close to the Capital. If they're able to monitor our descent at all, the king could then come and save us," Jurak suggested.

Drew postponed laughing at the prospect of having to be saved by Zarco, and made the necessary course corrections. The ship seemed to respond fairly well to everything but radical altitude adjustments. She started firing retro rockets—only three of the sixteen seemed to be functional, but still the ship seemed to slow some—and they were closer now.

Drew checked all the monitors and calculated the data in her head. She mumbled to herself. "All right. We're closer to the planet's surface, and we still have some retro rockets. If I lost complete control now, but we happened to land in the lake, half of us would die, but the other half would live." The ship shook then as they hit some turbulence, and it took all her skill to keep control of the ship and keep it on course. "All right, people, listen up! Code red! Implement Operation Silly Hat."

There was a communal gasp of horror as the entire crew suddenly realized the gravity of the situation. Then they unbuckled and ran around the ship finding their silly hats and donning them. Drewcila felt Jurak push a hat onto her head, and then watched as the crew dressed in their ridiculous hats and solemnly retook their positions, buckling in.

They were still closer to their destination now, and besides, they were all wearing silly hats. It was mathematically improbable that they would all die in a fiery crash while wearing stupid hats.

Drewcila switched all their power to the remaining retros and cringed as the ship shuddered, as it slowed still more. She wondered if the three remaining retros could survive firing at this intensity long enough for them to land. Short bursts wouldn't do much good at this point.

"Still, we're landing on water, and we're only a few hundred feet from the planet's surface, so some of us might die, but most of us would live."

Suddenly the ground and the lake were visible through the view screen. They were still going way too fast, and it didn't look nearly as close as she wished it did.

As she continued to fire the retros at full power, one of them burned out. With the reduced braking action, their speed wasn't falling off nearly fast enough.

The last two remaining retros sputtered, and then died.

Still, we're close, so close now, and we are landing on water, and...

"We are so screwed!"

Zarco watched in awe as the screen in front of him showed the pride of the Lockhede fleet crashing into the sands of the Galdart desert. The Artvail would soon be nothing more than rubbish in the sand, and what crew hadn't been atomized on reentry would soon be nothing more than Hurtella food

"Did we do that?" Zarco asked excitedly.

"Ah...Well, yes, of course we did," his new head advisor, Atario said. "That was our plan all along. Knock out interstellar communications and then sneak up there and destroy their battle cruiser."

"Not to mention that it kept Drewcila off our backs for awhile."

"Ah, yes...the Queen." Atario laughed nervously. "Sire...what are you going to do about the queen if she gets here?"

"Oh...she'll get here," Zarco assured him, "and when she does...she shall finally be a proper queen."

"What of her big friend?" Atario asked.

"My plan and my conviction have never faltered, Atario. When Taralin arrives, she will be brought to me. We shall reprogram her, and she will take her rightful place at my side. Together we shall utterly smite the Lockhedes and return the country to its former glory. The Chitzsky," Zarco's face twisted into an ugly mask of disgust, "is to be killed on sight, as are any who stand between us and obtaining our goal."

"And Sire...if Drewcila will not relent, if she will not be 'reprogrammed?' If she is in fact one of those standing in our way?"

"She will join us, she must. That is the plan," Zarco insisted.

A man ran into the king's office, out of breath. He bowed deeply then straightened. "Sire, reports have come in that a large space ship has crashed into Lake Witcha."

"One of theirs or one of ours?" Atario asked impatiently.

"One of ours," the man answered excitedly.

"No doubt one of our ships damaged in the attack on the battle cruiser," Atario said quickly.

"Sire," the man continued, ignoring Atario, "a man on the ground who saw the ship fall...They are saying the ship is of imperial class. They believe it is the Queen's own ship."

"Dispatch troops immediately to rescue any survivors," Zarco ordered.

"Done, sire." The man ran out as fast as he had run in.

Zarco swung on Atario. "Atario, you promised me that disrupting communications would not cause her to crash..."

"Sire, she is an expert pilot with an experienced crew. Landing blind should have been no trouble for her at all. Perhaps her ship was caught up in the fire fight when our forces locked horns with the Lockhede battle cruiser..."

"If you have endangered my wife to take out the Lockhedes' battle ship, I will see you drawn and quartered. How dare you engage the Lockhedes in a space fight when your queen was so close! It was irresponsible, and I'd better not find out deliberate. Don't think I don't know how the nobles feel about the queen, or how they would like to deal with her. We have made a pact, but I swear to you as your king, that if any harm comes to Taralin, either accidental or intentional, I shall see all involved die a slow and painful death, marked as traitors to the crown. Lest you forget it, she is the people's Queen, and amazingly popular among the military and the common man."

"I assure you, sire. No plot against the Queen is being hatched. We had no idea where she might be. We can't even be sure that it is the Queen's ship, sire," Atario said quickly, wishing now that he hadn't told the lie about them shooting down the Lockhede battle cruiser, and wondering whether it was better to stick to that lie and hope that Drewcila was alive, or tell the truth and suffer the consequences.

"For your sake, you had better pray that it's not."

"My Queen!" Jurak yelled out as he slung a piece of debris from her body. "Are you all right?"

"Do I look all right, moron? I'm four shades of fucked up, but I'll live," Drewcila grumbled as she helped him shove another piece of ship out of her lap. She slapped his hands away and undid her own seat belt. "I hurt in places I didn't know I had."

She checked her console and found all her screens blank. She looked around at her crew, counting heads, and found that they were all shaken but not stirred. She laughed, clapped her hands together, and screamed at the top of her lungs, "Wow! What a dick on a baby!"

"I believe that is the queen's way of showing her joy that we have all lived through our ordeal," Jurak interpreted for the crew.

"I am a fucking genius!" She laughed, took the silly hat—which turned out to be chartreuse with a red propeller on top—off her head, kissed it, and then stuffed it down deep into the pocket of her coveralls. "Yet another Qwah theory tested and proven."

She stood up and almost fell over. The ship was swaying to and fro, which could mean only one thing. They were floating on the surface of the lake. "All right, people, as much as I'm sure you'd all like to stand around and sing my praises, I have no idea how long this sucker can float or how deep this lake is, so I suggest we get our happy little asses out of this crate before we have to find out."

It wasn't as easy as it sounded. It took them a good thirty minutes to locate the escape hatch and figure out how to open it, and then they couldn't find the inflatable life raft. None of the crew had thought it was particularly important to go through the safety manual and run through emergency drills since Drewcila didn't seem worried about it. Apparently they had come to the conclusion that since she didn't seem at all worried about going through the manual and running them through the drills, that there must be little or no chance that this ship would meet with an accident. After all, Drewcila Qwah was their queen, and more important than that in this particular instance, she was a much more experienced space traveler than any of them were. They'd all assumed that if it had been important, she would have done it.

Drewcila, for her part, assumed the idiots knew how to run the ship they'd been crewed on, and it never dawned on her that she might ought to take the time to run through the safety manual or go through the drills. Van Gar had suggested it once, and she'd wound up screaming at him that he was an old lady, and that they had better things to do with their time. Then she'd easily talked him into an incredibly twisted act which included sugar and zero G.

The thought of it made her smile and momentarily forget the chaos all around her. That is until one of her panicked crewmen ran into her. She shoved him roughly, slamming him into a wall as she addressed her crew.

"All right you panty-waisted rejects, listen up..." she hadn't really thought past that, and they were now all silent staring at her expectantly, which was a lot of pressure since she really didn't have anything to follow that up with. She didn't really have anyone to blame but herself. But that didn't stop her trying. "This is all your fault! What sort of a crew considers itself space worthy, and doesn't even take the time to read the emergency manual? I'm very busy being queen and running the corporation and all. I can't be expected to do such a piddly-assed thing as read manuals and mollycoddle you bunch of titty-sucking babies through a bunch of silly-assed drills..." Towards the back of the group Jurak was excitedly waving his hand in the air. "What...what the hell is it, Jurak? Do you know where the raft is?"

He looked more than a little defeated. "No...I was just wondering if we were supposed to address you as Queen or Captain now?"

Drewcila pulled at her hair and jumped up and down. "Gods! I'm completely, astoundingly, surrounded by morons. Our ship has crashed and we're sinking in a fucking lake, and you're such idiots that you don't even know where the life raft is. Call me shithead if you like, I don't give a damn."

She stood perfectly still, then slowly walked over and leaned her head against the hull of the ship. She held her hand up towards them in a silencing gesture, and said in a suddenly calm voice, "Give me a few seconds."

They all nodded silently and waited as their illustrious leader mumbled inaudible whispers to herself. Finally she straightened, turned to look at them and took in a deep breath.

"Jurak?"

"Yes...Captain," he said deciding that of his three options this was the least likely to get him slapped.

"Do you know where the safety manual is?"

"Yes."

Drew glared at him and spat, "Then go get it!"

"Yes, of course," he said as sudden realization came to him. He ran off in the direction of the bridge and came back a few minutes later with the electronic manual, which he handed to Drew. Drew snatched it from his hand and started punching the buttons.

She sighed deeply.

"What is it Captain?" Jurak asked.

"We're standing on top of the damned thing. It's under these floor panels." She sighed as she looked from the escape hatch they had already opened to the floor beneath her feet. It made perfect and logical sense. "Gee, no wonder we couldn't find it," she mumbled to herself.

It took her another ten minutes to get all the crew off of it so that they could actually remove the floor panels and pull the raft out. The raft was bulky and heavy, and that was before some idiot pulled the handle which started the raft inflating.

"Quick, quick push it out, before it inflates!" Drew yelled.

They only managed to get it half way out before it had finished inflating, successfully lodging it in the escape hatch opening. Drew looked around with total disdain at her crew. "Which one of you morons did that?"

A little guy towards the back of the group sheepishly raised his hand.

"Why?"

"I...it was heavy, I thought perhaps it was a gravitational lifting device to make it lighter."

Drew pulled her blaster and leveled it at the crewman who had erred.

Jurak quickly grabbed her arm. "Captain...I'm sure..."

"The planet will be a much better place if this stagnant member of the gene pool is never allowed to breed." She jerked easily out of his grasp, as the crewman fell to his knees and crawled over to her.

"My queen, I beg of you..."

"Ah, get up, you've ruined it for me now." Drewcila holstered her side arm. Then she turned to glare at Jurak. "The moment is gone." She looked at the lodged raft and threw her hands up with a defeated air. "All right, everybody push."

Fifteen minutes later the raft broke free and floated down to the surface of the lake, which turned out to be a good twenty feet below them. Drewcila grabbed the raft inflating guy and threw him out the hatch and down into the water.

"You grab the raft and bring it back over here. If it gets away and we have to swim, I'm going to blast your ass and leave you for fish bait. Understand?"

For answer the man swam after the raft, caught it by a rope on the side, and started pulling it back.

After a quick check in the safety manual she found the switch which activated the emergency ladder, and they climbed down the side of the ship into the waiting raft.

They started rowing towards shore, at which point Drewcila announced, "Let us never talk of this incident again." To which they all nodded their silent agreement.

They were halfway to shore when the king's army showed up to "save" them.

Drew slung her hands in the air and flopped back into the raft. "Oh, now the bastards show up. Isn't that the way it always is with the cops?"

"I believe it's the military, Captain," Jurak said.

"Police, military, it's always the same thing. Where were they when idiot boy opened the raft in the escape hatch? That's my point. We don't need them now."

Jurak moved to sit beside her and whispered in her ear. "You are a good leader."

She smiled, and patted him on the back. "And you're a great lackey. I won't tell if you don't." She took a deep breath as she looked at the army waiting on the shore getting ready to board water crafts to come to their rescue.

"All right, people, listen up." She cleared her throat. "The king didn't actually want me here, so I have no idea what sort of reception we can expect. You are all going on a long overdue shore leave. Jurak and I will be the only ones going to the palace."

"But my queen, our loyalty is to you, not the king," said wet raft inflating boy. "If you are in danger, we will protect you." The others all mumbled their agreement.

"Gee, that's great, guys," Drew said, acting all choked up. Then she glared at them all in turn and hissed, "Listen up you sentimental dumb asses." She flicked raft boy on the head with her forefinger for good measure. She made her hands look like a scale. "Look: big, ugly, well trained army with weapons in this hand. Small starship crew that has been mostly drunk and screwing for weeks—admittedly on my orders—possessed of three hand-held blasters between us, and riding in a rubber raft, in this hand. Big army, boat full of idiots; big army, boat full of idiots. Oh! Oh, oh! Look! I think the fucking scale is tipping, and the boat full of idiots is sinking." She took a deep breath and counted to ten. Life was so much easier when you were too drunk to make decisions.

"Once again. Here's the plan. I'm going to tell them you're going on shore leave. Jurak and I will go to the palace, and I will try to fuck Zarco into submission. In the meantime you will all go to Hepron Station and tell the morons there to put double security on my—as it turns out, not-so-secret—vault. As soon as communications are back up you will send for my old ship, the Garbage Scow. Wait there and hole up. I will call you if I need you. It's a simple plan. You idiots don't have to do anything. Nothing. You can do that, can't you?"

"Yes, my Queen," they all said.

They were about fifty feet from shore when the army boats came out to "save" them. The young captain who addressed her said, "My queen! Thank all the gods that you are alive."

"Good to see you, too. Have we screwed? Because you don't look familiar to me."

After three days locked in a cell, with the three of them sharing the same small bed and toilet, and with no word or sight of Zarco, Stasha had given up all hope.

She sat on the wooden bed and groaned. "We are fucked, we are so fucked."

"Stasha!" Facto said in shock. "You have to quit saying that. Do you even know what it means?"

"No."

To spare his lady wife he walked over and whispered the meaning in Stasha's ear.

"All right, but now I really don't get why it's a bad thing to say," Stasha said with confusion.

Facto looked thoughtful, then confused. "Well, I suppose it has something to do with the way in which you do it." He shrugged. "Or say it."

"We mustn't give up hope, Stasha," Margot said, stopping her pacing to sit beside Stasha on the hard bed.

"Why? Why mustn't we? We have been caged up like animals. Zarco swore that he loved me, and now I have been locked up so that he can pursue my sister."

"Well, she is his wife," Margot reminded her gently.

"Only in name. Drewcila Qwah isn't Taralin. She'd be the first one to tell you that. I can't believe you're defending Zarco. Look what he's done to us...and for what crime?"

"I wasn't defending him. Just, well...he never did really belong to you. You have to look at this realistically..."

"I am. That's why I said we're so fucked!"

"Calm down, ladies," Facto said, although right then he didn't really feel like being the voice of reason. In fact, he had to agree with Stasha. "Let us not lose sight of the real horror. Zarco has started a war. A war in which all the people of our country will suffer and many will die." He turned to face Stasha and his wife, lowering his voice. "Your sister, dear lady, is walking into a trap. A trap from which, as you so rightly stated, even she may not be able to escape."

"Meaning that the whole thing is hopeless, and we are going to rot in this cell until they decide to execute us," Margot said, and started to cry. Facto moved to hold and console her.

"No, no! That's not what I was saying at all."

"Funny, that's more or less what it sounded like you were saying to me," Stasha mumbled.

"My point, though I apparently fumbled rather badly along the way, was that we can't give in to these feelings of self pity. We have many allies among the people. The house staff has not changed, and many of them are loyal to the queen..."

"Do you hear yourself, Facto? We are to be rescued by the cook and the cleaning lady!" Stasha said in disbelief.

"I was merely suggesting that one or more of them might come to our aid. They might find a way to free us. If we got out, if we could only make it to the bar..."

Stasha laughed. "The bar! Facto, I fear you've been working for my sister too long."

"Your sister had a state of the art security system installed on the bar. Force fields on the doors, anti-discharge weapons, the whole works."

"What on Barious for?" Stasha asked.

Facto looked confused. "I don't really know...It's not important now. We must stay strong and convicted. The time may come when we can help. We must stay alert, ready to strike. If our moment comes, we will have but a second to act. The fate of the whole kingdom may very well rest on our shoulders, we must be prepared to move without a moment's hesitation."

"My husband is right, Stasha," Margot said drying her eyes.

"Maybe, and maybe it's way past time to do anything. Perhaps the fate of the whole kingdom has already been written in stone, and we are now impotent to do anything except protest." That said, Stasha got up, walked to the cell door and started yelling.

"Zarco! Zarco, you let us out this minute! Do you hear me? This is insane. It's all insane! Please!" She kept her tirade up till her voice gave out, but no one ever appeared. Not Zarco, not even a guard. Exhausted, she slid down the bars to the floor and started to sob again.

One of the guards, a young man in his early twenties, came around the corner and knelt beside her. "Hey, royal chick."

She looked up at him, a little startled.

"Listen...there are still some people here loyal to Drewcila. We know what they have planned for her, and we have our own plans, see? So just cool your heels for awhile, and everything will be fine." He looked around quickly then to make sure he hadn't been noticed. "For the record, I think the King's a pud. I mean, Drew's all right, but you are one fine babe."

One of the other guard's footsteps could be heard coming their way, so he rose quickly and walked away, leaving a little wake of hope behind him.

Chapter 5

You didn't get to be as rich and powerful as Drewcila Qwah had become because you were slow witted and unobservant. It didn't take a genius to realize what it meant, that she couldn't find a single familiar face among the palace guards, or that they held themselves more like aristocrats than soldiers.

She wasn't surprised. It was more or less what she had expected to find. These men were too stupid to pretend to approve of her, much less give her a friendly greeting. The men Drew had hand picked to fill these positions would have had her on their shoulders by now, carrying her towards the bar.

When she was met halfway through the palace gardens by Zarco and some new ass licker, with no sign of Facto or her sister, she knew that things were even worse than she had anticipated. That, in fact, she might have bitten off considerably more than even she was able to comfortably chew.

"Oh, my darling," Zarco embraced her. "Thank the gods you are all right. When I heard you had been caught up in the fire fight..."

"Fire fight, what fucking fire fight?" Drew shoved forcefully away from him. "What the hell are you talking about? A Lockhede battle cruiser locked on us and opened fire. We fired back. They lost. We won. Yay, good guys! Unfortunately, our ship was buggered up, and we had to make an emergency landing. Not the easiest thing to do on a good day, and made worse because some moron screwed up all the communications on the planet and surrounding space. So, I guess what I really want to know is...Are we the morons that fried all the communications on this planet, or would that be them?"

Zarco turned to glare at Atario.

"Sire...Our ships had been ordered to that sector. I naturally assumed..."

"You're a lying little worm, aren't you, butt kiss? I can call you butt kiss can't I? Me being queen, and you being a flunky and all?" Drewcila said, glaring at Atario with utter contempt. He turned a very gratifying shade of red, and was visibly seething. "That's what I thought." She turned her attention back to Zarco. "All right, idiot, what did you do with Facto, my sister, and for that matter, all my people?"

"You will not talk to me in such a way, Taralin..."

"Oh, you're on that kick again, are you? So let me guess, you have put the whole country at war, ruined my profit margin, and destroyed the economy of our planet because years ago the Lockhedes kidnapped me..."

"The Lockhedes are our sworn enemies."

"It's in our best interest to make trade with them now. They are crippled as a nation. Let them trade with us, and they in fact work for us. We hold all the contracts, we control all the shipping, we tax the living shit out of them, and we take them over slowly, economically, and so painlessly that they don't even know what's happening till it's too late. I say let bygones be bygones, and get on with the business of commerce."

"I will not be party to mollycoddling the Lockhedes. For the gods' sake, Tara..." Drew glared at him. "...Drewcila. These monsters stole you away from me. They tortured you. They took out part of your brain."

"Gee! And what a loss that was! I could have gone on being one of you boring royal fucks the rest of my life. Oh, boo hoo, boo hoo. Get over it, move on, next page already." Drew started to walk towards the castle. "You didn't answer my questions. Where are my sister and Facto?"

"I have sent Facto, his wife, and your sister, as well as your advisors to a place of safety. We can't very well have all the heads of state in one location during a time of war," Zarco answered quickly.

"Gee, now that didn't sound like bullshit at all," Drewcila whispered to Jurak, who nodded silently.

"What's that?" Zarco asked quickly.

"I asked him if, after we go through all this boring formal bullshit, he'd like to ball."

Zarco grabbed her roughly by the shoulder and spun her around to face him. "Damn it...you will not talk this way to me. You will not. You will show me respect!"

His fingers were pressing hard on the flesh of her shoulder, hard enough to leave a bruise, but Drewcila canceled her conditioned response which was to knee him in the nuts. Right now he held all the cards. She didn't believe for a minute that he'd sent Stasha, Facto and Margot off to some safe house, and there was no way he could have forced Arcadia to leave when she knew that Drewcila was on her way. No, he had done something with them, and she had to play this game his way a couple of hands, until she found out just exactly what he had up his sleeve.

Of course, it would be easy for her to play his game, because she knew exactly what his weakness was. It was easy for her to understand, largely because she was sitting on it about half the time.

Instead of attacking him she leaned into him so that her lips brushed his ear. "I like it rough." She moved and winked at him. "I'll be good, daddy." She turned and started walking again, and the others followed.

"Where's your big friend?" Zarco asked, nervously looking around.

"Which one?" Drew asked a hint of laughter in her voice.

"Van Gar."

"He left me to join a religious cult," Drew answered. She didn't have to fake the sad, slightly confused tone that entered her voice.

"Is this one of your twisted jokes? A trick?" Zarco asked a hint of anger in his voice.

"Don't I wish. The bastard stole one of my best ships."

"Why?" Zarco asked curiously.

Drewcila turned, but didn't stop walking, seeming to walk backwards as easily as she walked forward, reminding him of the perfect grace she had once displayed in court. "Why do you think? I started to remember." Her voice dropped to a barely audible whisper. "I started to remember you, being with you. Our love...He couldn't stand it."

Hope bloomed within Zarco, and he knew in that moment that he had his wife back. Oh, she still needed some tutorage on how to act and stay in her place, but if she remembered their great love, then everything else would come easily.

Soon Van Gar had successfully gotten the support of most of the colony. It wasn't actually very hard to convince most of his "brothers and sisters" that they were not actually better off here on Utarus than they had been when they were "strewn across the heavens." The evidence was all around them. In the hard physical labor they did daily, which brought the reward of bowls of green gloppy stuff twice a day. It was there in the constant stench from each other, and in the remembrance of what their lives had been before they had been "saved."

The real problem was that most of them had no place to go. They had given away their worldly possessions and signed over all their property and anything else they had of value. If they left here, where would they go?

That was, of course, how Van Gar had picked up all but a fistful of stragglers, by promising them that if they helped him get off the planet and topple The Reverend Pard Jar, aka the Pride Leader, that he would find them a better homeland. He didn't really figure this was too tall an order. Anything with water and plant life would be an improvement.

This angle had occurred to him one night as he lay staring at Drewcila's name stamped on the plastic-coated cardboard ceiling above him. Most of the Chitzskies had been close, so close to following him, but many were still unsure. After all, even a cardboard box on a planet of dust and rock, and green

glop twice a day, was better than nothing. He'd needed something to convince them.

They'd all understood that the next ship that landed would
be their chance at escape, but it wouldn't hold them all. Most
of them would be forced to stay behind until other ships
could be sent to evacuate them. The ship that landed wouldn't
be empty, either, it would be filled to the gunnels with their
Chitzsky brothers and sisters, consumed with the fever of
the recently converted. They'd have to be deprogrammed.
They weren't likely to give up their dreams of Utopia without a fight.

That was the real rub. Van Gar was asking them to fight
their own people—something he'd learned the hard way was
no small task—to make it possible for some of them to leave
the planet while the rest would be expected to stay behind
with the hope of being rescued. Towards what end? They
had nowhere to go. They had given up everything to be here.

So leaving just didn't sound like such a great idea.

While Van Gar had been lying there trying to figure out
what he could use to tip the scales in his favor, he found
himself asking what Drewcila would do, and the answer
had been clear. She'd feed them a line of bullshit. She
wouldn't stop at just getting off the planet. Oh, no! She'd
find a way to get everything that the good Reverend had
stolen from his people, and she'd find a way to keep it while
making all the Chitzskies believe that she was their great
and unselfish savior.

So he told them that if they worked together they could
get off the planet. He would take all the best fighters with
him. Together they would find the "Pride Leader" and take
back what was theirs. Then Van Gar would take the money
and go in search of a better place for them all while they went
back for the others. It wouldn't be hard to keep his promise.
Property that would be deemed useless by most planets would
look like heaven after Utarus. He'd buy a big plot of land for
the "colony," he'd pocket the bulk of the money, and be half a

galaxy away before they had a chance to realize that they'd been swindled yet again—if they ever did. And he wouldn't feel guilty, because they'd still be a hell of a lot better off than they were now.

This would be a scam worthy of the great one, and he might finally gain some respect in her eyes. Drewcila couldn't possibly ignore such a great swindle, and he'd have riches of his own, be his own man. He'd be her equal.

Of course she'd never see it that way, or at least she'd never let on that she did. But in the end, as long as he knew different, what did it matter what Drewcila or anyone else thought?

Now the plans had been made, the trap was ready, and all that was left was to wait for the ship to land.

Shreta moved to lay beside him, and he cringed. "Can't sleep?" she asked.

"Not yet. I'm trying," Van Gar mustered a smile.

"Worried about tomorrow?"

"Not really. The ship will land. If everything goes as planned, by this time tomorrow we should be half a galaxy away."

"Then what were you thinking about?"

Van Gar sighed. They said it was good to talk about your problems. Who knew? Maybe if he talked about it he could get a handle on things. At the very least, maybe if she understood that he loved someone else, she'd quit her not-so-subtle attempts to have her way with him.

"Her," Van Gar said pointing at the ceiling.

"Who?" Shreta said, looking to where he pointed with confusion.

"Qwah...Drewcila Qwah. Do you know who she is?"

"A salvaging mogul, isn't she?"

"Yes, and Queen of Barious, and a giant pain in the ass, and...the only woman I have ever or will ever love," Van Gar said, his anguish clear in the tone of his voice.

"Oh," Shreta said, looking crushed. "Then it's not just me?"

"No...Well, yes, it's you, too. I like you, but I find you sexually repulsive. Nothing personal."

"Because you love someone else?" Shreta asked hopefully.

"Yes, I suppose so," Van Gar answered kindly.

"If you love her so much, then what are you doing here without her?" Shreta asked gently.

"I...we had a fight. She's basically...well, she's an egotistical little bitch with the morals of a Farak in heat..." He found himself pouring out his soul to her. Even telling her what he'd come home to find. "She doesn't understand why it should upset me," he finished.

"A goat?" Shreta asked.

"She said it belonged to the midget."

Shreta nodded, as if that made perfect sense. "What are you going to do?"

"Clean up this mess and go back to her. Back to my life with her."

"On her terms?" Shreta obviously disapproved.

Van Gar laughed, "That's the nature of Drewcila. There are only her terms. I know that in her own way she loves me. If I just let things go, when I'm not trying to make her behave the way I want her to...Well, we have a really good time. We used to go everywhere and do everything together. We laughed a lot, fought side by side, and there were even moments of great tenderness. Then I...Well, I loved her, so I wanted things between us to change. But Drew was happy with things the way they were, and the more I tried to change things..." Realization suddenly dawned upon him, "the more I tried to make Drewcila do things, the more distance she put between us. The more I tried to keep her all to myself, the less time she spent with me, and the more lovers she took. She's right...Oh, my gods! The bitch was right. She didn't change. I did. I started making demands, and I should know better than anyone else that when you order Drew to do something, then that is the last thing she will be likely to do."

"You're actually blaming yourself for her bad behavior," Shreta said in disbelief.

"It's not bad behavior, Shreta. It's just Drew behavior." Van Gar settled back onto the floor trying to get comfortable. "The way to handle Drew is not to handle her at all. Just let her do whatever she likes, and then she's happy. And when she's happy, I'm happy. Thanks, Shreta."

"Ah...you're welcome...I guess."

Zarco was exhausted. He looked over at Drewcila draped in a satin sheet, puffing on a cigar.

"That was so...professional," Zarco said.

"Thanks. I pride myself in being efficient," Drew answered. "So now...let's get down to brass tacks here. You put us in a war. I don't want the war. I want it over. I want my recycling centers turned back into recycling centers..."

"We just made love," Zarco reminded gently.

"Gee, I said thanks," Drewcila said. "What do you want, applause?"

"You...you don't remember anything!" Zarco accused.

"No wait, wait," she turned and snuffed her cigar out on the bedside table. "I'm remembering something," she turned back around to face him. "You've always been an egotistical, pompous little ass, haven't you?"

"I swear to the gods, Drewcila, you have gone too far this time." Zarco jumped from his bed, grabbed his robe, and slung it on.

"Yeah, all the way. I figure you owe me..."

"Did this mean nothing to you?"

"Now I need a bath," she said with a shrug. "Come on baby, there's no sense in getting all tense now, sit down and let mama rub your shoulders." He sat down, obviously against his better judgment, and she started to rub his shoulders. "Now listen...I have something you want," she licked the side of his neck, "don't I?"

"Yes," he said shuddering.

"And you have the power to give me what I want."

"Drewcila...I thought I made myself very clear. I am not going to trade my kingdom for sex with my own wife," Zarco said.

"Come on...why the hell not? You're screwing the country now. You could stop screwing them, and start screwing me. Seems like more than a fair trade."

"Why must you be so crude? Why must everything be attached to some sort of deal? Is it impossible for you to even try to embrace the idea that I love you? That you once loved me? Must everything with you be made into a commodity?"

"In order: because no one respects a polite salvager; all of life is a deal; you simply aren't my type; I tend to go for exotics; and yes."

He moved out of her grasp, stood up, and turned to look at her. "I thought the worst day of my life was when the Lockhedes stole you away from me, but now I realize that the worst day of my life was when I brought you back. You have destroyed me and brought the kingdom into an age of shame and degradation."

"Yay, me!" Drewcila got out of bed then, and started putting on her clothes.

"Where do you think you're going?" Zarco demanded.

"To the kitchen to get something to eat. I could stroll down the hall buck-naked if you like..."

"You aren't going anywhere. Nowhere, until I have undone what those Lockhede bastards did to you..."

"See...that ordering me around like I'm one of the servants thing that you're doing? That's not a big turn on for me." She finished pulling her coveralls on, but didn't Velcro them shut. "Now...I'm going to go to the kitchen to get something to eat, and when I get back, if you've been a good boy, we can do it again." Drewcila turned on her heel and walked out of the room, slamming the door behind her.

Drew quickly went to the kitchen and made herself a sandwich. Then, carefully checking to make sure she wasn't being followed, she made her way to Zarco's office and entered easily. She munched on the sandwich as she started to hack into his computer.

"Drewcila!"

Startled, she turned to see Zarco standing in the doorway.

"Where is the trust?" she asked in mock despair.

"Just what do you think you're doing?"

"What the hell do you think I think I'm doing? I'm trying to find out how I can undermine all your plans and take over the country again." She stood up and slunk across the room towards him. "But, as long as you're here foiling my plans..." Before she could reach him, two guards entered the room.

"Grab her," Zarco ordered.

"Kinky," Drewcila cooed. The guards rushed her. She dodged them half a dozen times before they finally grabbed her. Her evasion had been mostly for her own amusement. There was no sense in putting up a fight. She couldn't beat every guard in the palace. "I overplayed my hand, didn't I? You know what the problem is? I'm fairly good with bullshit, but when it comes to being as disgustingly nice as I need to be to have you eating out of my hand...Well, I just flat can't stomach it."

"Search her. Unless I'm mistaken, she's armed."

"Well of course I am! I'd look silly with four legs."

They found the small laser she had hidden in the cuff of her pants. Then they pulled her hat from her pocket and held it up.

"Keep it. God only knows what it is," Zarco ordered.

"For shit's sake, it's a stupid hat, and I need it," she cried in mock anguish. "Take my weapon if you must, but please, please don't take my stupid hat!"

"Take her to the dungeon and throw her into a cell...alone."

They started dragging her away, and she made them *drag* her, too. She turned to glare at Zarco as they hauled her away. "You know, Zarco, honey, flowers would have been more appropriate."

They pulled her down to the dungeon, threw her into a cell, and locked the door. "How quaint," she said looking at the metal bars in front of her. The guards started walking away, seeming to pay little if any attention to her remark. "Yeah, well! Expect to hear from my lawyer, Jacko!" She yelled at their backs. "Stupid bastards have no respect for my royal ass. Well, they'll be sorry."

"Drewcila?" a familiar voice called out from the shadows.

"Is that you, God?" Drew answered back, looking up and around.

"It's Drew, all right," Stasha's voice said.

Drew's eyes adjusted to the dim light, and she could make out her sister, Facto, and Margot in the cell across from her.

"Are we ever glad to see you," Facto said.

"Because you think I deserve to be behind bars?" Drew asked sarcastically.

"We were afraid...Well, that they might kill you outright," Facto said. "Zarco has gone quite mad."

"Yeah, and he's pissed off, too."

"Are you all right?" Facto asked.

"Let's see...I'm locked in an antiquated dungeon, and across from me are the only people on this planet who might have actually helped me. Wait, and let me think...Do you know what 'well duh' means?"

"I meant are you physically injured?" Facto asked with concern.

"No. Apart from the effects of the aftermath of really horrible sex, I'm physically fine."

Stasha heard what she said, knew what Drew had proposed, and jumped to all the right conclusions. She ran to the bars and glared at her sister.

"Did you sleep with Zarco?"

"Gee, and all I had to say was lousy sex..."

"You had sex with Zarco!" Stasha hissed.

"I consider sex to be more enjoyable than that. In fact, I consider a root canal to be less tedious."

"Did you have sex with Zarco?" Stasha asked accusingly.

"If that's what you want to call it..."

"Yes or no!"

"Hey! Don't think I enjoyed it. I did it to try and save the kingdom..."

"You did it to try and save your money," Stasha snapped.

"That, too."

"You know how I feel about him, and you slept with him anyway."

"All right, Stasha. I'm not even going to tell you how insane it is that you're pissed off because I fucked my husband. Who, by the way, apparently had your happy ass thrown into jail!" She screamed the last part.

"He...he's distraught. He needs help," Stasha defended.

"He's an inbred mother fucking nut job, who needs serious sexual counseling," Drew said. Then she walked over and flopped on the wooden bed. It had been a long damn day. As if to snuff out yet one more reasonable plan, Jurak was brought into the dungeon and slung into the cell with the others.

"Hey! Hold up there, butt boys," she yelled to the guards, who turned to face her. "How come they all get to be together, but I have to be alone in a separate cell?"

"Whore that you are, I imagine the king feels safer if there is no one for you to have sex with."

"My point exactly. How do you expect me to pass the time of day?"

"Shut up, Queen of Whores! The king may still find some worth in you, but the rest of us certainly do not. Your life hangs in the balance."

Drewcila took a good long look at the man's face, but said nothing.

"What?" he demanded.

"Oh, excuse me. Was I staring? I never actually saw a being talk with his sphincter before."

"Why, you!" he rushed forward, but the other guard grabbed his arm.

"Come on, she's purposely trying to make you mad. It's some trick."

The other guard grumbled, but they both left.

"I shall never forgive you for this, Drewcila," Stasha screamed at her. "Never!"

"For what? Trying to piss the guards off?"

"You know for what! I swear you are the biggest harlot in the universe." Stasha turned on her heel and walked away, moving to stand in the corner so that she wouldn't have to see her sister.

"It's nice to see you again, too, sis," Drew spat back. She looked at Jurak and shrugged. "A clear cut case of sibling rivalry. You have to forgive her. It couldn't be easy to be the younger sister of an overachiever."

They all went about the day's work, seeming to hardly notice the landing of the craft or the arrival of new brothers and sisters as they toiled in the fields moving their loads of rocks. The ship would stay for only a few short hours, then after it had cooled down and re-powered to optimum, it would launch. Except this time it wouldn't be carrying a load of worthless rocks, and it would have a different Captain and crew.

After much thought, they had decided against rushing the ship shortly after landfall, which had been their initial plan. Van Gar had instead decided on a more subtle approach. One with the element of surprise and a lot less risk. They would wait until they were supposed to load the ship. At this point the pilot and crew usually left the ship to stretch their legs and go to the pilots' lounge which was stocked with actual real food and drinks. They knew this because about two days ago they had broken in there and eaten and drunk it all.

Twenty Chitzskies followed the ten man flight crew to the lounge as Van Gar and those who would be going with him made their way to the ship. The twenty Chitzskies descended on the flight crew just as they learned the place had been cleaned out, and before the fighting had stopped Van Gar and the others had boarded the ship.

Van Gar quickly closed the hatches. They all got as secure as the ship would allow them to get, and then without so much as a glance out the port at the planet they were leaving, they lifted off.

As always, reaching escape velocity was less than pleasant, but not any more so than the thought of having to swill down even one more bowl of glop.

As they broke from the planet's gravitational pull, Van Gar felt reborn. He was in space again, piloting a ship. This was where he belonged. Step one of his plan was complete, and they were well on their way to implementing step two. Or would be as soon as he knew what that was.

Chapter 6

"You don't understand, Stasha," Drew cried in anguish. "My life has been left in tattered ruins. When Van Gar left me...he took a little piece of my soul." She covered her face with her hands and just sobbed.

"So...are you really upset, or just putting on a show so that I will forgive your atrocious behavior?" Stasha asked without emotion.

"What? What's atrocious mean?" Drew sniffed.

"Very bad," Stasha answered.

"All right, you caught me." Drew removed her hands from her face and straightened herself. "Damn! I used to be so good at this shit, too."

"I will never forgive you for this, Drew. Do you hear me? Never!" Stasha hissed at her sister, and through both sets of bars and across the hallway that divided them, Drew still got slapped with little bits of spittle.

She made a great show of wiping the spit from her face. "All right, that's like the fifteenth time you've said it, so I'm guessing that you're never going to forgive me...So, now it's your turn to listen to me. All this 'Drew-bad-for-sleeping-with-Zarco,' *is really* not the big issue here. The entire castle has been taken over by the nobility, who, by the way, not only hate me, but hate the entire system of government and commerce that I have put into place. They have detonated an anti-communications device and basically blacked us out from the rest of the universe. For how long, I have no idea, but there's basically nothing to stop them from doing it again as soon as the systems fix themselves. Oh, and if that's not bad enough, we are all in jail, and no one but the people who want to keep us here know we're here! So you can quit blowing the whole my-sleeping-with-Zarco thing all out of proportion at any time now. After all, it's not like I'd never screwed him before, and he's possibly the most boring lover I've ever gone to sleep under, so..."

"Drewcila, have you learned nothing from what happened with Van Gar?" Stasha demanded.

Drew glared back at her sister and thought about it for a second. "Yes, I learned that the people you care about will always let you down, but that Salvage won't."

"There is one man among the guards who says he is loyal to you," Margot said, successfully, if only momentarily, changing the subject.

"I haven't seen him yet this evening," Facto said with real worry. "They might have found him out."

"Leave it to ol' Fucktoad to point out the negative," Drew said, not without a fond smile.

"It's good to see you again, too, Drewcila," Facto said.

Drew laughed. "Ah, we'll turn you into a smart ass yet. So how did you all get here anyway?"

"I'm not talking to you, Drew," Stasha said, and with a huff walked back to the bed and sat down with her back to Drew.

"Then I guess I wasn't asking you, tight ass," Drew hissed back. "Would someone please tell me why everyone seems to be so completely hell-bent on putting all this importance on sex? It's just a simple exchange of surplus body fluids. Shit you aren't really using and aren't even going to miss in the long run."

Facto cleared his throat. "You wanted to know what caused us to be incarcerated?"

"Yeah, yeah!" Drew flopped onto the hard wooden bed and glared at her sister's back. She couldn't understand why Stasha was so pissed off, but worse than that, she couldn't understand why it bothered her so much that Stasha was mad at her.

"Well, Stasha was trying to talk some sense into Zarco's head, and as I'm sure you've seen, he isn't in the mood to hear reason. I wasn't as cunning as I thought I was, and he figured

out that I was working more for you than him. And
Margot...well, if you want to know the truth, as much as anything else I think he threw us all in here because he didn't
want you to have even one friend in the castle."

Drew hated to ask the next question, but she'd looked into
all the other cells, and they were nowhere to be seen. "Where
are Arcadia, Pristin and Dylan?" Drew asked cautiously. Facto
was silent. "Facto, they're not in here, so where are they?"
Drew demanded.

"Drewcila...I'm afraid...Zarco had them killed."

Drew's features crumbled. "They're dead?"

"Yes, I'm afraid so."

Drew took in a deep breath. It was too much. For the first
time in the part of her life that she could remember she felt
completely and totally alone. She choked down the ball of
tears in her throat, flopped back on the bed, and covered her
face with her hands. She didn't know how long she just lay
there like that, but it must have been a fairly long time, because the next thing she became aware of was Facto screaming urgently.

"Drewcila! Are you all right!"

"No, I'm not all fucking right." She sat up, drying her eyes
with her fists, and didn't look at Facto as she hissed through
clenched teeth. "He's going to pay. The bastard is going to pay
with his blood, or my name isn't Drewcila Qwah."

"Actually, it's not," Stasha said spinning on her sister. "Your
name is Taralin Zarco, and you're in no position to talk about
getting revenge on anyone. Because, as you keep reminding
me, we are locked up in jail!"

Drewcila suddenly lost any cool she might have had left.
"Why don't you go fuck yourself, you damn self-righteous,
tight assed little bitch!" She stood up, looking for something
to throw. Finding a small rock on the cell floor, she picked it
up and chucked it into her sister's head.

"Ow!" Stasha yelled. Holding her head, she started sob-
bing as the blood trickled from under her fingers. Margot tried

to move Stasha's hands to look at the wound, but Stasha's hands weren't budging, as if she thought she was holding her head together and if she let go for even a second her brain might unravel.

"Let that be a lesson to you. Don't ever piss me off, and don't ever, ever count me out of the game." Drew started pacing and mumbling. "If only those bastards hadn't gotten my stupid hat, I would have shown them a thing or two."

General Frater Tryte of the Lockhede Air Force looked at the data rolling in, and his conviction was deepened with each name that rolled across the screen.

This time the Barions had gone too far. Communications were back up across the world, and he now gleaned as much from what the Barions were saying as what they had learned from the wreckage. It painted a picture he found hard to believe.

He himself had given the orders that their space fleet was to fire upon any Barion ship which came near their air space. No doubt when the Admiral of the Artvail saw the imperial ship, one that they were more or less sure was carrying the Barion Queen—once transmissions they had intercepted from Barious before the blackout had implied the Queen was on her way—he had crossed the lines and opened fire.

What happened next was as unforgivable as it was inconceivable. That small and inadequately armed imperial "salvaging" ship had utterly and completely destroyed the Artvail, the largest of their three star class battle cruisers. It was something that could not and would not be forgotten. Eight thousand of their best and their brightest had gone to their deaths, while the Barion Queen had apparently walked away unscathed and triumphant.

Of course, how bright could they have been, seeing as they had let a relatively small, non-military ship blast them out of the sky? Still, people hadn't been taking the war effort seriously. The people were hungry and unhappy, and as such they didn't feel like going to war yet again. They needed a reason to fight, a good reason. And they needed a villain.

Now they had a rallying cry. *Remember the Artvail!* Now they had a villain, and what a villain! A salvaging whore with a taste for Lockhede blood.

Now this broken, destitute people would come together. The Barions had just given them a good reason to fight, and they would fight to the last man and take no prisoners. They would convince the people that their bad luck and poverty was somehow the fault of the Barion's extreme good fortune and affluence. They were greedy and evil.

They had started the war, and now they would finish it. They would stomp the Barions back to prehistory. Now there would be no trade agreements, no talk of peace.

"General," the news woman prompted.

"I'm sorry. It is so hard to tear myself away...the list of names. Our best and our brightest, atomized in the destruction of the jewel of the fleet." He sounded choked up, and it wasn't all an act. "What did you ask?"

"Rumor has it that the vessel which actually took us down was that of the Barion's Queen, and that we fired on her ship first."

"Scandalous lies," the general declared, pounding his fist into his console. Then he told not only a 'scandalous lie,' but a really well-rehearsed one as well. "As you know, our enemies detonated an anti-communications device. Our ship was on patrol. We saw the ship marked with the imperial seal of Barious in our air space, but disregarded it, assuming it was harmless. We, of course, had no way of hailing the ship since all communications had been knocked out: in fact, only minimum communications have been restored at this time. Our brave fighters had no reason to believe that they were in any danger, or that this small ship was in fact any threat at all. Of course, that's exactly what the Barions wanted us to think. This ship only *looked* like a simple imperial "salvaging" vessel. It was in fact a mach fifty-seven class frigate with a full cache of weapons. The Barion Queen is indeed a very devious, and dangerous woman.

"By the time our people realized the danger they were in, it was too late. She had fired her large cache of weapons and run away like the coward that she is. This is what we are fighting. A cold, calculating people who want to starve us out economically. A filthy rich populace that wants to be rid of us so that they can have the entire planet to themselves. They are selfish, greedy, dangerous, and they won't rest until they have killed us down to the last child."

No one seemed too worried about the fact that with communications between the destroyed battle cruiser and the planet's surface completely blocked out, and with the remains of the ship still on fire and sinking ever steadily into the Galdart Desert, there was no way he could know what actually happened.

That just flat wouldn't have been newsworthy.

"Pisst! Hey, *pisst!"* a voice whispered.

Stasha quietly climbed out of bed and made her way in a sleep filled daze through the dark to crouch by the bars. It took a second for her eyes to adjust, and then she saw him.

"Where did you go?" she asked quietly as she rubbed her eyes.

"I thought someone was wise to me, so I ducked out for awhile. You sure are hot. What's your sign?"

"Excuse me?" Stasha was sure he was talking in some sort of secret code.

"Dylan?" A whispered question from the cell across the hall.

Dylan left Stasha quickly and crawled across the space. "Drew!" He hugged her through the cell bars. "Damn! Word had it that you were with the king, not that you'd been locked up."

"Dylan, what the hell? They told me you were dead."

"No. Just hiding. My coloring's close enough I can pass for a Barion if they don't look real good..."

"Arcadia?"

"This was all Arcadia's plan. I thought we were going to get out...See, we created this big diversion, and then we killed the guard at the back gate, but instead of leaving we stayed inside. But just like she said, they quit looking for us inside because they figured we got away. We knew you'd come here, see? And..."

"She's all right then?"

"Yeah, she's fine." Dylan laughed and punched her on the shoulder. "Well, you old dog, you! You *do* care."

"Pris?" Drew asked.

Dylan's face dropped, and Drew had her answer before he said, "He didn't make it. They just killed him. Would have killed us, too. They changed the palace guard."

"So I have noticed. I'm so sorry, man. I had no idea any of you were in danger. That he'd do something that bum-fuck crazy."

"It's not your fault. None of us knew he was that bent, and we've been right here watching him." He lowered his voice even more. "I mean, he's been ballin' your sister for what? Like years? And he just had her locked up. That's pretty fucking cold. Hey, you think I got a chance with her?"

"Go for it, dude. She could use a really good fuck."

"So...what's the plan, boss?"

"Here's what I want you to do..."

"Her tongue is covered in blue and yellow spots," the guard said in a panic.

"She did that to herself," Zarco said. He was exhausted. He'd had trouble going to sleep after all that had happened, and had hoped for a few hours of blissful oblivion. Now he was being awakened far too early on the morning after. He could still smell her on his bed and still feel her touch, and all his convictions to deal with her as she should be dealt with were washed away by the thought of holding her in his arms again.

And he just didn't want to be feeling any of this. Certainly not when he hadn't had enough sleep.

"There is nothing wrong with her. She is faking it so that I will let her go," Zarco said, and no doubt if he saw her he would.

"The doctor has said that she may have been hurt in the crash. She threw up her breakfast and is complaining of abdominal cramps."

"Tell them that no one is to open the cell till I get down there. Grab Atario. Tell him to meet me here. We will go down together."

His servant started to dress him even as the page left his presence. Atario met him in the hallway still pulling on his clothes.

"Do you believe that she's ill?" Atario asked.

"Not for one minute," Zarco said.

"Yet you rush to her side. Sire, surely after last night there can be no doubt…"

"She is my wife. Your Queen. I have to be sure."

When they arrived in the dungeon, Drew was lying on the floor. Her color was bad, and there was vomit all over her cell. She seemed to be unconscious.

"You! You have to do something, Zarco!" Stasha cried. She was mad at her sister, but she certainly didn't want her dead.

"Open the door slowly and keep a close eye on her." They did, and Zarco ran in, carefully skirting the piles of puke. It had a foul odor, even more so than normal bile. He knelt beside her and took her wrist in his hand. Her pulse was strong, but her skin was cold and clammy. Zarco motioned for the doctor to come and check Drewcila out. "What the hell happened here?" Zarco demanded of the guard.

"I brought them their food. She ate like all the others. The next thing I knew she was complaining of stomach cramps, and then she was throwing up."

Jurak was obviously distraught, and he accused the guard through the bars of their cell, "Just last night I heard that man threaten the queen. He even moved to strike her."

"But I didn't, I…"

"She's been poisoned," the doctor said. "Quick! We have to get her to my office. We need to find out what poison was used and deliver an antidote before it's too late."

"Grab him!" Zarco ordered, pointing to the guard. "Take him at once to an interrogation room. Atario, you see to it personally."

"But, sire, I swear..." the guard started, but fell silent when the cold blue eyes of his sovereign locked on his. Drewcila was rushed off to the surgery as the guard was manhandled off to the interrogation room.

"Zarco, please I implore you," Stasha cried from her cell. "She is my sister, my only sibling. I had harsh words with her just last night. Please let me go with her."

"Let her out, but watch her," Zarco ordered one of the guards. Stasha was released, and she followed Zarco and the doctor.

The medics were pushing Drew along on a gurney. Stasha ran to catch up with the stretcher and took Drew's hand. "Drewcila, please, you can't die. I love you. I'm sorry for all that I said."

The doctor shoved her gently out of the way as they entered the surgery, and the medics skillfully moved Drew from the gurney to the bed.

The doctor hooked Drewcila up to a computer medic.

The doctor sighed, though it was hard to tell whether he was relieved or disappointed. "All right, we can all relax, the poison was triple phosforin."

"It's not deadly, then?" Zarco asked.

"Oh, no, it's lethal enough, but it would have had to be fully digested to do any real damage. It wasn't in her system long enough for that since she threw most of it up. I'll simply program a dose of the antidote, Radiol 16." He punched some buttons on the apparatus. "She should be just fine in two to three days with bed rest."

"Slut!" Stasha screamed in Drew's face. She glared at Zarco. "All right lock me back up."

"Stasha...must there be all this ill will between us? I will release you, and you may go to your parents' house if you will only apologize," Zarco said.

"Apologize! For what? Giving you the best years of my life? Wasting my love and my time on you? I've done nothing to you. You locked me in jail, you bedded my sister. You have completely discounted my feelings for you, and now you expect me to apologize to you! I'd sooner rot in jail."

"That can be arranged!" Zarco glared at her. "Guards! Escort my sister-in-law back to her cell."

The guards grabbed Stasha. She shook off their hands, and holding her head high, walked off towards the dungeon. Zarco watched her go and almost told her to come back, almost decided that he should be the one to apologize. Tell her that he understood now that he belonged more with her than he did Drewcila. However, before he could open his mouth to speak, the doctor interrupted his thoughts.

"Whoever our assassin is, he doesn't know much about poison," Doctor Sortas said conversationally.

"Why do you say that?" Zarco asked, his curiosity piqued.

"Triple phosforin is a slow working poison. If you wanted to kill someone with it, you would administer it in small doses over a long period of time. Giving someone enough to actually kill them all at once, well, more times than not you get the reaction Drewcila had. It causes intense stomach cramps, and they throw it up before it can do any real damage."

"Where could they find this poison?" Zarco asked, hoping to narrow his list of suspects.

"Just about anywhere. For instance, it's the main ingredient in most organic toilet bowl cleaners."

"There is deadly poison in an organic product?" Zarco said in disbelief.

"Sire, just because something is organic doesn't mean you should eat it," the doctor explained.

"Are you mocking me?" Zarco asked hotly.

"Why, no...Not at all, sire. I didn't mean to offend."

"I'm sorry, doctor. I'm a little edgy lately. I know you said she should be fine in two or three days, but how long will it take her to come to?"

"Her system's had quite a shock, this is her body's way of coping with it; still, she shouldn't be out more than an hour, two tops."

"I know she's sick, but you had best keep an eye on her. She's a tricky one. I will leave two guards outside the room." Zarco hesitated at the door, and turned to face the doctor. "How do you feel about Drewcila?"

The doctor swallowed hard. That was a double edged question. On the one hand, the king had purposely removed anyone with loyalty to the queen from the castle. On the other, he obviously didn't want his wife killed. Sortas chose his words carefully. "I don't agree with her politics, but I also believe that she, more than any of us, is a victim of the Lockhedes. I certainly don't want to see any harm come to her. I believe she can be fixed."

"All right. Don't leave her side," Zarco said again.

"I shan't," Sortas promised. Of course he didn't promise to actually do anything to *help* Drewcila, either

Drew opened one eye carefully and looked around the room. The doctor was looking at her readouts, and she knew that meant he must realize that she was awake. Damn monitor.

Well, she might as well talk to him. "Doctor!" she croaked out weakly. "What happened to me?"

"Someone tried to poison you. They weren't very successful. You should be your old self in a day or two."

"Great. It sucks to be in poor health when you're in prison." Drew laughed weakly. "Who...who did it?"

"They suspect a guard. He's being interrogated." The doctor turned to look at her for the first time. "The King does love you so very much. Couldn't you at least try to be a proper queen?"

"You know, doc, I feel like warmed up dog shit, and I'm fresh out of patience for even one more lecture. I wouldn't expect a doctor—possibly the group that bitched most about my maximum wage law—to understand what it's like to be a monarch who cares as much for the poor as they do the rich. To think that an unlucky man deserves medical care and a decent life as much as the privileged."

"You make it sound as if I am without compassion. I wouldn't be in this profession if I didn't care about people..."

"Yeah, that's why you'd be the king's physician, where you maybe treat what? Twenty or thirty people a year? Mostly kitchen burns and scraped knees. Save your crap for someone who'll buy it. All you rich fucks are alike."

"No one is quite as rich as yourself, majesty," the doctor reminded.

"True. But unlike you I haven't gotten rich off peoples' pain. In fact, I have gotten rich by stopping that pain. By giving jobs to people who didn't have jobs, by giving medical care to people who couldn't afford it before. By shrinking the giant gap between the haves and the have-nots. This is the real reason the nobility hate me. Not because I'm a salvager, or because I'm a whore, or even a drunk—although I'm sure all those things piss them off to no end. No, they hate me because there are far fewer people for them to be better than. Not as many people for them to push around. And not nearly as many people who have to kiss their asses. That's my big crime—I'm actually fair."

The doctor laughed then. "My, my! You are indeed the consummate public speaker. I had forgotten just how eloquent you can be when you're sober, and you set your mind to it. Save your speeches for the peons, my Queen, you shan't sway me."

"I wasn't actually trying to sway you. I was just trying to keep you distracted long enough for my associates to take out the two guards at the door and sneak up on your ass."

"What?" The doctor felt the needle sliding into the flesh of his butt, felt a slight sting, and then he was out.

"What took you so long?" Drew asked with a smile.

"You ever try to carry a Valtarian lizard woman in a garbage can?" Dylan asked with a grin. "She's heavy, and her tail kept sliding out from under the lid."

Drew got out of the bed and stumbled. Arcadia caught and held her, and Drew threw her arms around Arcadia's neck and kissed her on the mouth. "I am so incredibly glad that you aren't dead."

"I wouldn't be nearly so much fun that way," Arcadia said.

"You just would not believe the shitty week I've had."

"Me, too. How are you feeling?" Arcadia asked.

"Horrible," Drew said. "Like I've been hit by a truck. But I've had worse hang-overs, so let's get the hell out of here."

"For the record, I thought this whole crazy-assed plan was a big mistake," Arcadia said.

"Yeah, not actually my very brightest moment," Drew said with a smile. Her legs were weak and would hardly hold her. "For one thing, I feel a lot worse than I thought I was going to. I really figured that with all the booze I've consumed over the years, I'd be more or less immune to most poisons."

Arcadia helped Drew into the palace guard's uniform that Dylan handed her. Drew was feeling a little better by the time Dylan checked the hall and they walked out. She leaned against the wall, laser in hand, and kept guard as Dylan and Arcadia dragged the two very dead guards into the infirmary. One had obviously wound up with a tail spike through his head. The other'd had his neck broken. So Drew guessed that Arcadia was as pissed about Pris as she was.

"Hey! Look what we just caught," the guard announced.

"Thought we were supposed to shoot them on sight," the gate keeper said as he rose with his ring of keys to open the door to the cell block for them.

"The king changed his mind."

"He seems to do that a lot these days."

"He thinks he can use this one to sway the queen. Rumor has it that this one is one of the queen's lovers."

"This ugly lizard thing?" The guard laughed as he opened the door. "You've got to be kidding me."

Jurak watched the exchange with obvious interest. The others seemed to be too depressed to notice much of anything now. They had brought them their lunch a few minutes before, but for obvious reasons none of them had eaten.

He watched as the gate keeper and the other two walked in with their prisoner.

"That's Arcadia," Facto whispered in despair at his shoulder. "We are quickly running out of hope and options."

Jurak nodded his head silently.

"Which cell?" the gate keeper asked.

"That one. She's dangerous, and we need to keep her separate from the others," one of the other guards answered. The gate keeper opened the cell door across from them. "You know, you would think we could get a little more high-tech than this. Install computer door locks and laser bars and such. Even an alarm might be nice. Maybe some security cameras. This whole system is so antiquated."

"You know the king and the higher-ups. They want to keep everything in the castle as authentic as possible."

"Yeah, well, that's too bad for you."

Jurak watched in confusion as the guard released the prisoner and fell against the bars of the cell, barely holding himself up. Arcadia grabbed the keys from the gate keeper and shoved him roughly into the open cell, shut the door and locked it.

Arcadia then threw the keys to Dylan and turned to peel Drewcila from the bars of the cell.

Drew addressed the guard in the cell. "Now, fat ass...You don't mind if I call you fat ass? No, of course not. Anyway, fat ass, here's the score. Now I'd just as soon kill your worthless rich ass as look at it. So if you don't want me to smoke your butt, you'll get very quiet...Ah, fuck it." Drew raised her weapon and sent a bolt through the guy's head, then turned to look at Arcadia, who was still holding her up. "I'm having a really bad day, and it's just easier to shoot him than it is to give the speech. Besides, why take chances, right?"

"He called me an ugly lizard thing," Arcadia added with a mock pout.

"God! I hate rude people," Drew said. "Don't you hate rude people?"

"Dead people are rarely rude," Arcadia said conversationally. Drew nodded her agreement.

Dylan unlocked the door to the crowded cell, and the others ran out to join them.

"Now what?" Facto asked Drew expectantly.

"We make like a baby and go," Drew said.

They started moving, but Drew stumbled, and if Arcadia hadn't been holding her up she no doubt would have fallen. "Sorry," Drew said.

"No problem," Arcadia said with a smile.

"Are you up to this, Drew?" Facto asked.

"Not really. I mean, I ate poison, but we aren't working in the 'have a whole lot of options' column here. At lunch time all the guards but the fat ass left the dungeon area. When the guards get back from lunch, I think even those lame-asses are going to notice that you're all gone. That is if they don't figure out that I'm missing from sick bay first. We have a relatively small window of opportunity, so we have to keep moving. Margot...you're a dresser. Where do they keep the spare uniforms? And don't tell me in the barracks. That isn't going to help."

"The palace laundry room is just at the top of the stairs leading out of the dungeon," Margot said.

"Let's go then."

They got into the laundry room without incident, which meant that so far no one had noticed that any of them were missing. No doubt because of that lovely antiquated security system.

"Wait a minute," Stasha said as she pulled on a uniform. "You said you ate poison. That means..."

"Yeah, yeah. Dylan slipped the poison into my food. I knew I was eating it. That's why I started hurling it up so quick."

"Are you crazy! What did you do that for?" Stasha asked hotly. "And why the hell didn't you tell us? We thought you were really dying."

"Gee, I'm sorry to disappoint you," Drew hissed back, growing more tired of her sister's misplaced anger as the day progressed. "I didn't tell you because you would have blown it. As to why I did it—three reasons, actually. First, it got me the hell out of the cell. Second, no one's going to expect someone whose just been poisoned to stage a prison break. Third, and this is my favorite one, the guilt factor. Zarco put me in jail, therefore he put me in danger. He has purposely hired guards that hate me, so now they're all suspect, and it pits them against him. Everyone's walking on eggshells, afraid of being accused. We need to get our happy asses in gear and get the hell out of here. I'm thinking we tie a shit load of sheets together and go out one of the second story windows which open onto the city streets. Out there in the streets, that's where our allies are."

"Drew, you're in no condition to make a climb like that," Arcadia reminded.

"We can lower her down first," Dylan said as he worked with Margot tying sheets together.

When they had their make-shift rope, they made their way down the hall and up to the second story with both Drewcila and Arcadia shoved into a laundry cart which they pushed along.

Looking like palace guards, and with no alarm having yet been sounded, they were able to walk through the halls and use the elevator with no one giving them a second look, much less stopping to question why guards were handling the laundry. No doubt they thought it was some new war-time thing that called for the palace staff to do more "double tasking."

Their luck didn't hold. As they exited the elevator on the second floor, the alarm bell was sounded. Dylan looked at his watch. The guards must have gotten back from lunch and noticed that they had a jail full of...well, nothing. They started to move a little faster.

Three guards rounded the corner in front of them.

"You there! What have you got in that cart?" Then they all started to run, no doubt having recognized Facto and Stasha, whose faces would have been well known in the castle and to the nobility.

"A pissed-off Valtarian lizard woman," Dylan screamed, raising his laser and firing.

Arcadia erupted from the laundry cart, sending the sheet ropes that had been concealing them all over, and opened fire on the guards

All three fell.

Arcadia and Facto helped Drewcila from the laundry cart as Margot and Dylan gathered up their rope.

They started running again, but when they turned the corner, there blocking the hall was a large troop of guards. When they turned to retrace their steps there was another troop closing behind them.

"Surrender!" a familiar voice said as Zarco waded out of the sea of guards. "You're ill, Drewcila, and you're badly out numbered. Put your weapons down." Feeling cocky, he moved still closer to the escapees.

Drewcila glared back at him defiantly. "You killed Pristin," she accused.

Zarco looked confused, and Atario moved through the crowd to whisper to the king.

The king nodded, and then said, "You actually expected me to take orders from an ugly blue dwarf with three legs?"

"That wasn't a third leg, you dumb ass!" Drew hissed. She flung her head wildly.

"I'm giving you one chance to surrender, then I'm going to order my men to open fire."

"You shouldn't threaten me, Zarco. You should never threaten me. NOW!"

She fired her weapon, putting a bolt through the nearest guard's head as Arcadia slapped out with her tail, taking Zarco's feet out and sending him falling right into Dylan's waiting arms. Dylan quickly twisted the king's arm behind his back with one hand, and held a blaster to his head with the other.

Drew laughed maniacally. "Now who's winning? Back the fuck up, all you flunky-nobility pieces of shit! The common folks will always kick your asses, and do you know why?" she asked Atario, who only shook his head silently. "Because the poor have nothing to do to pass the time but fuck, so there are always going to be more of them. And because they're always going to be trying to get all the cool shit you have."

Zarco glared at Drew. "Drewcila, I demand…"

"Zarco, darling," Drewcila drawled, "you really should have gone for the flowers. We are way past the point of you demanding anything from me. Gee! You give a guy the best years of your life and a big chunk of your brain, and how does he repay you? By locking you up." She looked at the guards as a group again. "Now I'm going to tell you one more time. *Back the fuck off!*"

They did then. As a group they ran down the hall in the opposite direction.

"Pick a door, any door on the right side of the hall," Drew said. Her vision was blurred, and she was having trouble keeping up, even with Facto and Arcadia all but carrying her.

Jurak swung a door open on the right side of the hall, and they ran in, slamming it behind them and locking it. Then Jurak, Stasha and Margot moved a huge dresser in front of it just for good measure.

Dylan set the king roughly in a chair. "Don't move." He picked up another chair and slung it into the window. It bounced off and started careening around the room.

"What the hell!" Dylan screamed, barely jumping out of the way in time.

"The windows are made of bullet proof glass," Facto said.

"You might try just opening it, moron," Drew said in disbelief. She swung her head around to look at Facto. "I feel like a bad death warmed up. How do I look?"

"Not much better, I'm afraid," Facto said, smiling at her fondly.

"Listen, all of you!" Zarco screamed.

"Screw him and get that fucking window open now," Drew ordered. Then turned to Zarco, "You just shut up and look pretty. We wouldn't be in this mess right now if you'd remembered that in the first place. Everything was just fine as long as I did all the thinking, and you did all the sitting around looking pretty crap."

When Dylan couldn't seem to get the window open, Jurak went to help him. It wasn't budging.

"People, this is high treason. If you release me at once..."

"Actually, it would be high treason," Facto walked away from Drew, leaving Arcadia to hold her up alone, "if we were defying *both* the king and the queen, or if we were doing something to destroy the country. But the only one who has defied the queen and done anything to destroy this country lately has been you." Facto's voice had risen in volume and in pitch. "So indeed I say that when the history books are written, and they talk of this day, it shall be *you* who is remembered as a traitor."

"Wow! Ol' Fucktoe's really pissed," Drew whispered to Arcadia, who just nodded.

"It's stuck," Dylan announced.

"Then blast it. Come on, we're running out of time," Drew ordered.

"It's bullet proof. I'm assuming that means laser proof," Dylan said looking at her like she was a moron.

"The fucking window seals are wood. Try blasting those, dumb ass."

"Oh, yeah." Dylan started firing his laser at the wood frame as someone started pounding on the door.

"We will give you exactly five minute to release the king, and then we will break the door down," Atario said from outside.

"Oh, God! Please don't do that! I love that door. Please, father, pray for the door," Drew whined back. "Gee! All we have is your king, and you have our door. Whatever shall we do?"

"The doors are also bullet proof, and the locks are made of Taligite steel. They can stand against anything," Facto reported.

Then they heard Atario scream. "Get a battering ram and knock it down!"

"Except maybe that," Facto said.

"Battering ram. That's a damn good idea," Drew said thoughtfully as she looked around the room. Her eyes landed on a large trunk. "Dylan. Jurak. Grab that trunk and use it to batter the window. Maybe now that you have weakened the sill it will bust out."

They grabbed the trunk and started pounding on the window at the same time as the guards started pounding on the door.

Stasha, Margot and Facto worked at moving still more furniture in front of the door.

"Stasha, surely you..." Zarco started.

Stasha looked at him and shook her head no. "After what you did to me and with my sister, the Whore of the Spaceways..."

"Wow! I've got another title," Drew said, letting her head bob up and down.

Stasha more or less ignored Drewcila as she continued glaring at Zarco. "I'm the last person you ought to be asking for any kind of help."

Zarco moved as if to get up, and Arcadia's laser leveled on him, "Ugh," she said. He sat back down.

The window popped out just as the door made a cracking sound.

"Tie the sheets to the footboard of the bed, and let's go," Drew ordered.

Dylan tied off the sheets, and threw the end of their rope out the window. "Man, like we made way too much rope, dudes."

"Better too much than not enough I always say," Drew said with a smile, looking at Zarco with meaning.

"Drewcila...you had better listen to me..."

"Don't bother me right now, Zarco, I'm trying to remember something important. One last thing I have to do before I go. Now what was it? Oh, yeah! I remember." She turned to glare at Zarco. "Kill you." She leveled her blaster on him. "You killed my friend, cheated on my sister, and had me thrown into jail. I can't just let it slide."

"Drewcila, no!" Stasha screamed. The bolt hit Zarco in the leg instead of the chest, and he let out a scream of pain.

"Damn! My aim must be off," Drew started to re-aim, and Stasha grabbed her arm.

"Drew, don't kill him," Stasha pleaded with tears in her eyes.

"Damn! There is just no pleasing some people. First it's don't screw him, and now it's don't kill him. I wish you'd make up your mind what it is you want." Drew watched him writhing around the floor in pain, and decided it was good enough for now. Stasha ran to his side and tried to help him. "All right, I'll let him live, but don't ask me for any favors for awhile."

The door made another cracking noise. "Drew, we have to go," Arcadia said. Margot and Dylan were already on the ground, and Facto was well on his way.

"You next, Stasha," Drew said.

"Don't you dare order me around," Stasha screamed up at Drew, tears streaming down her face.

"Go out the fucking window on our little sheet rope that Margot and Dylan worked so hard on, or I'm going to throw you out the window and use you as a landing pad for my fat ass. Now go!"

"You'll be all right, Zarco," Stasha promised. Then she got up, ran to the window, and with Jurak's help started down the rope.

"Drewcila...I'll make you pay for this!" Zarco screamed.

"You're pushing it, Zarco," Drew hissed back. "My sister's gone now, and there is nothing at all to stop me burning a hole right through your freaked out brain. Then I'll be queen." She laughed maniacally. Arcadia dragged her to where Jurak had hauled the rope back up. They tied it around her, just under her shoulders, and then quickly lowered her to the ground. By the time they had done this, the guards were almost through the door.

"You go," Arcadia ordered abruptly.

"No, you...I'll be fine."

Arcadia didn't argue with him. As the door and its barricade started to move, she shimmied over the sill and down the rope.

They had determined that the rope probably wouldn't hold more than one of them at a time, so Jurak reached quickly into his pocket, pulled out his silly hat, and stuck it on his head. Then just as the door and barricade noisily gave way, almost drowning the din of his monarch's cries of agony, he went out the window and down the rope only a few feet behind Arcadia. The rope gave a little, but didn't break. As they both reached the ground safely, Dylan hurried them away from the rope and shot the top of it with his laser. The rope fell in flames to the ground. Jurak and Arcadia helped Drewcila, and together they ran as fast and as far into the city as they could get.

The door broke, and there was enough room for one man to squeeze past. From inside they could hear someone screaming in pain, and while they'd heard the argument between the queen and her sister and knew Zarco had been wounded, they couldn't be sure that he was alone.

Atario pulled his laser and looked at the others. "Stay here. We don't know what we might face. I may be able to negotiate."

The guards all nodded. Though it was no doubt more because they were glad to be staying out here away from danger
than because they thought Atario had a good idea—or even
that they understood. There was something that Atario hadn't
considered when he had talked the king into changing members of the palace guard for members of the nobility. The nobility were a bunch of out of shape desk slugs who had no
training or natural ability for the job. They were ready to pull a
trigger, but they weren't really ready to actually get hurt, and
now that several of them had easily been killed by the queen
and her rabble, they were less and less willing to put themselves in the actual line of fire.

So Atario walked carefully into the room himself. He saw
the broken window and the king clutching his leg on the floor.
He ran to Zarco's side. "Sire, are you all right?"

"Do I look all right? The bitch shot me. She shot me, Atario.
She wanted to kill me. My great love, my wife…"

Atario had heard enough. All of this trouble had come
from one source, and he could easily kill two birds with one
stone. He pressed the business end of his laser to the king's
head.

"Oh, sire! What has that traitorous whore done to you!"
he cried out.

"What the…" the laser beam seared through Zarco's skull
and brain, killing him almost instantly.

Chapter 7

Finding the Reverend Pard Jar hadn't been very difficult. Especially since the on-board computer came complete with a schedule of all the Reverend's appointments, and the programmed flight plan would take them right to him.

It was really a no-brainer. Pard Jar held a revival meeting, got a bunch of converts, then shipped them off to the planet before they had a chance to realize how stupid everything he said was and change their minds. Van Gar pretended like he'd known this all along, because he just felt too stupid that it hadn't actually dawned on him until he looked at the travel log.

After they had cleaned up in the flight crew's quarters and fought over who got to wear the crew's clothing, Van Gar and his recruits, for the most part, blended right in with the rest of the Chitzsky mob that had surrounded Pard Jar in the middle of the station.

He listened to Pard Jar spout his drivel and let it feed his already large stock of righteous anger. Shreta nudged him.

"You can stop kicking yourself now. I'm listening to him and wondering how any of us could have bought what sounds now like a three-day dirty Chitzsky smells," Shreta said in a whisper at his shoulder.

Van Gar turned to her, baring his teeth in an evil grin. "I wasn't kicking myself. I was thinking of the many and varied ways I am going to kick his ass."

"...A man looks at a mountain. It is very tall, but he will climb it one step at a time," Pard Jar said.

"Why?" Van Gar yelled out.

"What, my brother?" Pard Jar asked.

"Why does he want to climb the mountain?" Van Gar screamed back.

"Because it's there, my brother," Pard Jar said with a smile. "Every great journey starts with a single step…"

"Isn't that sort of stupid? I mean, why climb a mountain if there's nothing at the top? Now if there was a really great bar up there, or a strip club, it might be worth the trip."

Pard Jar painted on a patronizing smile before he went on as if Van Gar hadn't interrupted him. "So, we as a people put our first steps upon our new homeland. Through our hard work and our conviction our world shall bloom, one step at a time, one dream at a time. We are all our own power, we feel and are felt, heal and are healed, love and are loved…"

"What the fuck is that supposed to mean?" Van Gar asked with a laugh. "Let me get this straight. You're like this superior enlightened dude, and you can't say anything more relevant than vague shit like, *We are all our own power. We feel and are felt, heal and are healed, love and are loved.*"

He'd finally managed to rub the Reverend's fur the wrong way. "Perhaps, my brother, this is not the path for you."

"Got news for you, Jack, this ain't the path for anyone. See, me and my friends bought your pretty line of bullshit. We've been to your promised land, and we feel like you screwed us out of our shit. Healing…that's what you're going to need after we get done beating you to a bloody pulp. And love, well we'd simply *love* to shove your crappy home planet right up your lying, cheating, thieving ass."

Pard Jar and his two "assistants" tried to make a run for it, and Van Gar's people—who had been positioned strategically close to the "Pride Leader"—grabbed them. No one in the crowd moved to help the good Reverend. In fact, they had started growling and screaming profanities at him.

Whatever spell he'd held them with had been broken, and he had instantly gone from the dimpled savior of their race to the scourge of their universe in a few short seconds.

After a few gratifying moments of them begging, pleading, and denying any knowledge of what evil Pard Jar was involved with, Van Gar decided to release the two assistants, even though he was pretty sure they were full of shit concerning their lack of involvement. He didn't want any distractions. Van Gar wanted to focus all his anger and energy on the self-proclaimed "Pride Leader."

Van Gar grabbed Pard Jar by the short hairs on the back of his neck and started dragging him back towards the ship, stopping every few feet to kick the good Reverend in the ass with his heavily booted foot. "You are going to give us all of our shit back, and if you do that, I might just let you live. With a heavy emphasis on *might.*"

"My brother, all of that money has gone back into the colony," Pard Jar cried.

"Hey! Dumb fuck!" Van Gar stopped long enough to haul Pard Jar to his feet. He knocked on Pard Jar's head with his fist. "Is anyone home in there? We've all *been* to the colony, remember? And we've seen the ship's manifests. Not only have you got all the shit you took from us and others like us, but that stupid shitty rock we've all been hauling around is actually worth some fucking money to the Yorgites, who apparently need a mineral in the rocks as a food additive. We want all that money, too. Since we hauled all the rock, it seems only fair."

Security ran in from all directions, saw what was going on, threw up their hands to show they had no intention of interfering, and then quickly ran away again. There was no way they were going to take on an angry mob of Chitzskies, especially when they seemed content to torture one of their own.

Drewcila and her entourage walked to the nearest safe haven, a bar. It took the clientele a minute to realize who had walked into their space, but when they did, the bowing and scraping started.

"Get up, guys," Drew said as Arcadia and Facto helped her sit in a chair close to the bar. "Listen, dudes, the shit has hit the fan up at the palace, and I need your help."

"Anything, my queen," the bartender said with a bow.

"I need a vehicle large enough to carry me, my two ambassadors, my councilor, and my sister."

"You can use mine," the bartender said, wading forward and putting the keys into Dylan's outstretched hand.

"I need someone to take Margot and Jurak to the nearest TV station. The people must be warned about the coup."

"I'll do it," a client said, stepping forward.

"I need your loyalty now more than ever, and I desperately need a beer," Drew said.

"Our loyalty to the queen forever!" The patrons of the bar said in unison, as the bartender opened a bottle quickly and started to pour it into a glass. Drewcila shook her head, and he handed her the bottle.

"Ah, you guys are the best," Drewcila said with a smile. "I knew you'd come through for me."

"My queen, if I may…What has happened?"

"The nobility…isn't it always those assholes?" Drew took a long swig of the beer. While she was trying to keep her stomach from slinging the offering out at a high rate of speed, the patrons of the bar and the bartender all mumbled their agreement that the nobility were indeed a lot of assholes. As soon as she was sure she wasn't going to hurl, she continued. "They tried to kill me with poison. They shot the king. We barely escaped with our lives."

Stasha opened her mouth to knock holes in her sister's story, and Drew shot her a look which was backed up by Dylan's hand on her elbow.

Drew set her beer down without finishing it, and got shakily to her feet. Arcadia moved quickly to steady her, and Drew looked at her with a smile. "You just want to touch me, don't you?"

"That was never a question," Arcadia answered.

"I'd love to sit and chat with you, but we're awful busy. You know, saving the country, and little shit like that. Thanks for all your help, you will be adequately repaid for your service to the crown. Drinks are on me, I believe we have a fund for such things."

They started to leave, Margot and Jurak going with their ride and their instructions, as the bartender showed the queen and her entourage to his car. Behind them the bar yelled out choruses of "Long live the queen!"

Drew looked up and saw Jurak and Margot walking the other way. Jurak still had his silly hat—a rainbow colored beret—on his head.

"Wait!" Drew screamed, stopping short. "Jurak, come here."

Jurak trotted over happily, thinking that perhaps he was after all important to her mission. He was feeling a little left out, and wasn't enjoying at all being treated as a common errand boy. Surely the woman could do this job without his help. His rightful place was at the queen's side.

"My queen?" he said.

"Give me that hat. I think I need it more than you do," Drew said.

Jurak looked dejected, and reluctantly pulled the hat from his head and handed it to Drew, who put it in her pocket.

"What's with the hat?" Facto asked as he watched the young man walk away with his shoulders slumped.

"I'm afraid it's over your head."

They had tied Pard Jar to a chair with self bonding duct tape.

Van Gar had let him stew there and think about what they were going to do to him for several hours. Now he paced back and forth in front of Pard Jar, a look of concentration on his face, the neck of a beer bottle in one hand and a cigar in the other. Except for Shreta, who he still didn't seem to be able to shake, the other Chitzskies were making up for lost time spending the large amount of cash they'd found in the good Reverend's hotel room on the space station to buy food and booze and anything else money could buy.

Pard Jar looked at him, tears running down his face and matting his fur. "I swear to you, brother, I did none of this for my own personal gain. There is no other money! All of the money has gone to buy things for the colony and to pay for the use of the ships, for food and..."

"Before you go on lying out your ass, I think it's only fair I tell you that I've spent the last few hours thinking of different ways of torturing the information out of you..."

"Brother, what was in my room...That was all the money that there is, and..."

Van Gar stopped in front of him and stuck his cigar to the fur of Pard Jar's face, holding it there in spite of the man's thrashing until it had burned through his fur and into his flesh.

"You crazy son of a bitch!" Pard Jar screamed in pain.

Van Gar removed the cigar and took an experimental puff off it. He smiled appreciatively and took a longer drag before he spoke. "Let me explain something to you. I am Van Gar, and before a moment of insanity in which I actually bought the line of crap you were selling, I was a salvager. Not just any salvager, I worked with Drewcila Qwah, I was her right hand man. In fact, I gave you one of the bitch queen's ships, and here's the thing, see? I can't go back to Drew without that ship, and if I don't get to go back to Drew soon, I'm going to get very, very cranky. I have seen the shipping manifests. You've made a small fortune off the damn rock. More than enough to buy a gazillion recycled domes. You haven't used even one ninetieth of what you've taken in on that one project alone. So you can quit wasting my time, and your breath, lying to me. I want all the money—every last cent of it. And I want my ship back, and I want it now."

"I'm telling you..."

Van Gar bent over, putting his face right in Pard Jar's and growled, "You better tell me what I want to hear, or I'm going to wrap my rather large fist in barbed wire and shove it up your ass!" he straightened. "And that's just for starters."

Pard Jar wet his pants, giving Van Gar a whole new smell to hate. "Your ship's at the end of the docks," he sobbed.

"Do I look like an idiot? I know you must have sold the ship by now and pocketed the money."

"No, I swear. It was so much better than my ship. Besides...have you ever tried to sell a Qwah ship? Why is everyone so afraid of your boss, anyway?"

"Because she's very rich, very powerful, and completely crazy. And she's not my boss, she's my...girlfriend," Van Gar growled angrily.

"Oh."

"And the money?"

"That's another reason I kept the ship." He sobbed louder. "It had room for the big safe I wanted."

"You mean...the money's on the ship?"

Pard Jar nodded.

"All of it?" Van Gar asked in disbelief.

"Hey!" Pard Jar defended. "When you're scamming your own people out of all their money, and sticking them on a stinking hole of a planet, you know there's a good chance someone's going to get pissed off and come after you. And when they do...Well, you want the iggys with you, don't you? Besides, if I had put the money in a bank, even several banks, someone would have figured out what I was really doing long before now. Damn! I can't believe this shit. I should have quit long ago, but no! I had to get greedy. I kept thinking, just one more space station, what could it hurt? I mean, I've been doing this shit for two fucking years! I kept deciding it was time to stop, and I'd almost do it, and then I'd remember just how God damn dumb our people are. Then when the bastards just kept mining the rock, trying to actually terraform that piss hole, and I found out that some other idiots would pay a small fortune for worthless rock...Well, it was just so damn easy, wasn't it?"

"And being every bit as stupid as the rest of us, you just didn't know how to quit when you were ahead," Van Gar snarled. He would have liked to argue with the bastard on behalf of their race, except that it was something he had just recently learned himself.

"What now?" Shreta asked.

"We take the *Pride Leader* down the dock and see if he's telling the truth. If he isn't, we buy a roll of barbed wire."

As they rattled down the road in the bartender's kindly offered, if slightly dilapidated, vehicle, Drew suddenly lurched over Dylan, slinging the top part of her body out the window. Dylan quickly grabbed onto and held the belt of her pants. Drew heaved violently, threw up the beer, and then threw up things that she was pretty sure she hadn't finished using yet.

She crawled back in the window looking pale, and wiped the puke and spittle from her face on the sleeve of Dylan's shirt.

"God damn it Drew!" Dylan yelled, and Arcadia jetted her head across Drew to bare her teeth at him and hiss, making him jump. "I should have sat up front with the really stiff guy and the hot chick," he mumbled.

"She shouldn't still be sick," Arcadia said in a worried voice.

"Maybe it's guilt," Stasha twisted in her seat to give Drewcila a heated look.

"Oh, I doubt that," Arcadia said simply.

"It's that rich fuck doctor," Drew said sickly. "He didn't give me the antidote. He probably gave me some damn placebo."

"Or more poison," Dylan said.

Facto suddenly turned the vehicle around.

"What are you doing, Facto?" Drew ordered.

"Taking you to the hospital."

"He wouldn't have poisoned me," Drew said. "Go on to Hepron, I can get medical aid there."

"NO!" Facto yelled firmly. "As much as it pains me to say this, you are our country's only hope now, and we can't afford to take chances with your health..."

"Damn it, Fatroad..." she jumped back over Dylan and threw up again.

"Take us to the hospital." Arcadia said.

It was decided that Facto and Drew would enter the hospital alone, hoping to draw as little attention to themselves as possible, while the others waited in the vehicle.

The emergency room crew recognized Drew at once, and when she fed them her bull shit story, they immediately started to treat her. A tox screen determined that there was no way the doctor had given Drew the antidote.

"See, my people, how none of the nobles are to be trusted? How even a doctor trained in the ways of healing will take a hand at killing the queen to stop equality? Why, you're a doctor, can you believe that one of your own profession could do such a thing?"

"No, my queen," he said stiffly.

"Tell you what, doc. You look like a busy guy. Lots of sick people in here and shit. It's a simple shot, one of the nurses can do it..."

"My queen, it's not a problem, but an honor..."

"To see my butt? You bet it is, but seriously, one of the nurses can do this. I'm sure you have lots more important things to do than to stick me in the ass."

"As you wish, my queen." He bowed and left, obviously in a huff.

The nurse smiled a knowing smile and went off to get the antidote. Nurses had done very well under the laws of the new queen, and their loyalty had therefore been bought and paid for. Drewcila Qwah was no one's fool.

They were almost out of the hospital when the screen in the emergency room waiting area lit up with a news flash. It was that weasel Atario, and he was shedding big crocodile tears.

"The queen has assassinated the king..."

Drew didn't wait to hear more. "Let's get the hell out of here," she whispered. Facto was more or less carrying her, and he doubled his pace. Outside the hospital he asked in an angry whisper.

"Did you kill Zarco?"

"I most certainly did not," Drew said with righteous indignation. "I shot him, but I didn't kill him. No doubt that snake Atario did it. Damn! I should have seen that one coming."

"Drewcila Qwah, I know you, and if I have learned nothing else I have learned that most of the time when your lips are moving you're lying. Now you and your two alien cohorts..."

"I have co-whores?" Drew asked with a smile.

"I said cohorts..."

"Whatever the hell those are."

"The lizard woman and Jurak..."

"He's Barion..."

"But he works for you...Damn it, Drewcila." He stopped short, grabbed her chin and forced her to look at him. "Did you wait till Stasha couldn't see and then kill Zarco..."

"Damn! Now why didn't I think of that?"

"Did you, Drew?"

She looked him in his eyes without blinking. "No, I did not. Am I sad he's dead? No. Would I have killed him to avenge the death of my friend and make my life easier? You bet your sweet ass. But my sister begged me not to, so I didn't."

Arcadia was suddenly running up the sidewalk towards them, Dylan not far behind her. Their lasers were pulled, and when Drew turned around to see why, she saw two large security guards coming down the sidewalk after them. However they quickly dropped their weapons and threw up their hands when they saw the two armed aliens, proving—at least in Drew's mind—that their hearts weren't really in it. Arcadia took hold of one of Drew's arms, Facto had the other, and Dylan watched their backs as they made a run for the vehicle. Arcadia pulled Drew in the back seat with her. Dylan gently but quickly shoved Facto towards the back seat as he took the driver's seat. He started the beast and took off at a high rate of speed as two police cars came roaring up the driveway towards them. He expertly maneuvered the vehicle around them and through the parking lot filled with miscellaneous vehicles, barely making it out the main entrance before two more police vehicles rolled in. He punched it, and was pleasantly surprised to find that there was so much life left in the old girl. As he drove like a mad man, avoiding the police cars that seemed to materialize from nowhere, he leaned towards Stasha, "So, babe, you have got to be getting tired, because you've been running through my mind all day."

Atario looked with total disdain at the report that filled his screen, then back at the doctor.

"She has managed to slip through our hands. It's as if she simply vanished...You say you didn't give her the antidote?" Atario asked with a hint of disbelief.

"No, sir," Dr Sortas reported.

"It doesn't appear to have slowed her down any."

"With all due respect, Chancellor, she had thrown virtually all the poison up, so it wouldn't have done any real damage anyway," The doctor smiled a wicked smile then. "I didn't want to actually kill the trollop, just teach her a lesson. I am a physician after all..."

"If you had a doctor's ethics, you would have treated your patient. As long as you didn't, you should have given her a lethal dose of something and saved us all the headache of having to deal with Drewcila Qwah..."

The doctor feigned being shocked. "She is our queen!"

"She killed the king!"

The doctor glared at Atario. "Now, I doubt that seriously. Remember that I was in the hallway just outside the door waiting to tend any wounds the king might have. I heard the confrontation between the king and the queen just as you did, and I know that she did indeed shoot him, but that the blast was not fatal. I saw the injuries. I did an autopsy on the body. Blasters leave a signature mark, and there are two very different signatures on his wounds. Now the blaster that Drewcila was carrying was rather large. That would match the wound I found on his leg, but not the other one. So as you can see, I have no reason to believe that she shot him in the head." He looked right at Atario then. "After all, an execution style killing? Well, that hardly seems our good queen's style, does it?"

"One of her thugs, then..."

The doctor smiled and shook his head. "No, that doesn't make sense, either. They had apparently been on the castle grounds all this time. If their intention was to kill Zarco, they could have done it at any time..."

"Just why did you request this meeting?" Atario asked raising his eyebrows.

"I think we both know. And we also both know that I can easily prove when I have finished the autopsy who actually fired the blast that killed our good king..."

Atario smiled widely then. "You must have a price, or you would have gone to the press instead of coming to me."

"Before you decide it would be easier to kill me as well, I think it's only fair I tell you that I have sent my findings and conclusions off as a closed attachment to my attorney with the instructions to forward it to the nearest news agency upon my death. Further, you should know that I do not condone what you have done."

The smile faded from Atario's face. "Just tell me what it is you want."

"Since there is no bringing Zarco back, what I desire is a piece of the action. With the nobility firmly behind you, and without Drewcila Qwah to stop you, I have no doubt you will be our new king. As such, you will have the power to make me your chancellor. I want power and position. I want to get back everything I had before that dubious whore stole it away from me...and then some."

Atario smiled again. "Ambitious and ruthless, a man after my own heart. I can use someone like you working for me...Chancellor."

Even with Dylan's skill as a driver, they had barely made it out of Capital without being captured, and the vehicle had taken considerable damage when one of Dylan's maneuvers forced it into a fight with the side of a building. The vehicle lost rather badly, and it was now losing power and making an unhealthy wheezing noise. Dylan knew pursuit couldn't be far behind them, so he pulled off the road and into some bushes where the car sputtered and died.

"Beautiful, fucking beautiful!" Drewcila groaned, then leaned out the window and threw up again.

"I can't believe that Zarco would call the entire army down upon our heads," Stasha said, and then turned to glare at what to her dismay turned out to be Drew's ass. She continued anyway. "But, oh wait... YOU TRIED TO KILL HIM!"

Dylan noticed that Facto was very quiet, and catalogued the fact somewhere in the back of his mind. Drew crawled back in the window and glared back at her sister while wiping vomit off her mouth onto her sleeve, which made Dylan have to swallow hard to keep from hurling himself. There was something about seeing a beautiful woman puke that almost, but not quite, had him thinking about something other than his perpetual stiffy. It had been entirely too long since he'd had sex—at least a week!—and he was more than certain that he could bed Drew's sister. Now what was her name again?

"Get off my back, Stasha!" Drew growled.

Oh, yeah, that was her name. Chicks liked it when you remembered their name.

"We're all a little uptight right now, Stasha," Dylan said putting a hand on her shoulder and gently kneading her flesh. She didn't jerk away, so he kept doing it until she finally did move away, turning towards her sister again.

"None of this would have happened if you hadn't come back in the first place," Stasha started to cry then, burying her face in her hands.

"No, the country would have collapsed in economic ruin. There would have been a war between the classes, and if you didn't all get killed in that, you most assuredly would have been killed when the Lockhedes jumped on the dilapidated condition of the kingdom and took over. And now it's going to happen anyway unless we can get to Hepron Station, which isn't going to be very easy with the whole of the Barion army and police force trying to frag our asses, not to mention the broken vehicle. So, if you'll excuse the hell out of me, in between bouts of puking up what's left of my internal organs, I'd like to spend my time trying to formulate a plan out of this mess instead of fighting with you about shooting Zarco. Who, by the way, IS THE REASON WE'RE IN THIS MESS IN THE FIRST PLACE!"

Tired from the exertion of yelling at her sibling, Drew flopped back in the seat. Her color was almost nonexistent, and she was sweating, which considering it was actually a little cold in the car wasn't a good sign.

Dylan smiled broadly at Stasha and opened the vehicle door. "I'm going to get out and have a look around, want to go with me?"

"I'd do practically anything to get away from her," Stasha hissed.

"Fine!" Drew retorted.

"Fine!" Stasha hollered back and followed Dylan out of the vehicle. He walked carefully towards the road they had come from, then stood in the shadow of a tree and watched. When he was sure it was clear, he grabbed a tree limb and started towards the road.

"Tell me if you hear or see a vehicle."

Stasha nodded silently. Dylan went down towards the road and tried to wipe out their tracks by rubbing them with the limb. It wasn't working very well because a recent rain had left the ground muddy, and they had left huge ruts which weren't going to be covered by rubbing a weak branch that kept snapping and breaking over the trail.

"I hear something," Stasha warned.

Dylan threw his branch onto the ruts in hopes of obscuring at least part of the trail, and then ran up into hiding, successfully reaching the tree line and Stasha just as first a civilian vehicle and then an armored troop carrier went roaring past. They had brought out the big guns, and no doubt the high tech shit. So even though these stupid bastards rolled right past the obvious damage, it couldn't be long till they found their trail now.

"Come on, we've got to get moving." Dylan grabbed Stasha's arm and started dragging her along back towards the vehicle. "God, I hate all this outdoors shit. Look at the glop sticking to my boots, and my hands are covered in *shmutz...*"

"Do you trust her?" Stasha asked in a small voice. Dylan didn't stop.

"Who?" he asked.

"Drewcila Qwah, my sister. Do you trust her?"

"Of course I do. Drew's a good friend, a loyal friend...mostly. So she slept with your boyfriend. Big f'in deal. You act like she did it to hurt your feelings, and she didn't. It probably didn't even occur to her that you'd care. She did it to try to get control of Zarco. Salvagers...Well, we just don't live by the same stupid rules that the rest of you do. And Drewcila, well she's the Queen of the Salvagers, ain't she?"

They had reached the vehicle. Arcadia got out and walked over to him.

"Well?"

"We've left a trail a blind monkey could follow, and they've sent out armored transports to look for us. We'll have to get moving."

Arcadia nodded, stuck her head into the air and sniffed, turning as she did so. "I smell civilization this way." She pointed, then reached in the open vehicle door and dragged Drewcila, who was mumbling incoherently and limp as a rag, out of the car, and promptly dropped her. Drew's head hit the car door.

"Ow!" She rubbed at her head.

"Oh, baby...I'm so sorry," Arcadia said as she and Dylan lifted her up off the ground.

"Key-rist! It's like she has no bones in her body," Dylan whispered to Arcadia, who nodded.

Facto got out of the vehicle and started talking. "We'll have to make some sort of carrying..."

Arcadia easily tossed the limp, mumbling woman over her shoulder and then started all but running in the direction she had pointed earlier.

Dylan motioned with his head that they should follow her, saying with a smile. "Valtarian lizard people are very strong...and fast. We'll have to run to keep up." He grabbed Stasha's hand. "I'll help you."

They were only able to catch up with Arcadia because she stopped to sniff the air again.

Dylan was out of breath and had a stitch in his side, so he knew the others had to be near to the dropping point.

"Arcadia...do you think you could slow down a little?"

"Drewcila...she's running a fever. It's almost dark. The temperature will drop..."

"How can you be sure she's running a fever?" Facto asked, not seeing how anything so alien could know anything about a Barion's physical condition.

For answer Arcadia swiveled so that Drew was even with Facto.

"I have a butt, you have a butt, we all have a butt. This is my butt, and I'll do what I like with it," Drewcila said, and then started laughing hysterically.

"Because she's been talking out of her head like that for over twenty minutes," Arcadia answered, turning back around to glare at Facto as if it was somehow his fault.

"Maybe we should stop and try to make a camp for the night. Build a fire," Facto suggested.

"You mean stay out here in...all this nature?" Dylan asked, pulling a face.

"Yes, it won't be comfortable, but..."

"No! Absolutely not! Are you mad!" Dylan yelled.

"He may be right, Dylan, we are probably still an hour away from the civilization I smelled, and who knows but that it might be hostile territory," Arcadia said thoughtfully. "I grow very tired, and I can see that the rest of you aren't doing any better."

"We could make some sort of stretcher to carry Drew and help you," Dylan insisted. "If you would just slow down we could make it."

"But even then there is no guarantee of help," Facto said. "It would be better to get some rest and tackle it first thing in the morning when there is light, and we are rested."

"Arcadia can see in the dark," Dylan was now in a near panic. "How much rest can we possibly get out here in the middle of nowhere with God only knows what sort of murderous animals and...and plants."

"We'll be fine Dylan, help me lay Drew down," Arcadia ordered. He did so reluctantly.

"We're laying her on the cold ground. That couldn't be good for her fever," Dylan insisted. Arcadia just smiled at him, knowing exactly why he was protesting. She rose to her feet and patted his shoulder in a comforting way.

"Don't worry. I wouldn't let anything happen to you, little brother."

Dylan nodded his head, resigned to spending yet another night in the great outdoors. The courtyard grounds had been bad enough, but out here there were no walls. Nothing but woods and trees and...other stuff, and it was all that other stuff that he wasn't quite sure of.

He was in hell.

Arcadia took off her jacket and lay it over Drew, than grabbed Dylan. "Come on. Let's go get some wood."

Dylan nodded, resigned.

When they were out of ear shot of the others he said, "All right, I didn't want to say this in front of the chick, but," he continued in a whine, "I'm cold, I'm hungry, I'm thirsty, and I just want to have a nice hot bath, crawl into a warm bed with her ladyship, get my groove on, and get some real sleep."

"Help me get some wood, and I'll see what I can do about finding some water and getting some food."

Dylan groaned, "Oh, I don't even want to know what that means."

The wood was still damp, and even with Arcadia's wonderful camping skills and the help of a laser, it took them a good hour to get a real fire going. During this time Drewcila's fever had broken, and she had started to sweat again, so she pulled Arcadia's jacket around her and moved closer to the fire. Even if she had her senses back, she obviously still didn't feel like talking.

Arcadia knelt beside Drew and whispered something to her. Drew forced a smile and nodded, so she must be feeling better. Arcadia rose and went into the woods—no doubt to hunt. She came back with her blaster holster filled with water and some small fur-bearing creature impaled on one of the spikes of her tail. She handed the water to Drew first. She drank half of it and handed it to Dylan. Dylan looked at the water reluctantly. It was dirty looking, and he imagined Arcadia had gotten it from some mud puddle. Still, he knew all about the effects of dehydration, so he swallowed hard and took a drink. It didn't taste too bad, a little gritty but all and all palatable. Before he realized what he was doing he had greedily drunk the whole thing.

"Oops!" he said, looking with guilt at Stasha and Facto who were glaring at him.

"It's all right, there's more where that came from," Arcadia promised. She was using her knife to skin and gut the animal, something which none of the others seemed to be up to watching, much less doing. When she was done she put the animal on a stick and held it over the fire, telling Dylan "Hold it here, any closer and it will burn on the outside without cooking in the middle. Any further away and it will never get done. Turn it every few minutes."

Dylan nodded, taking the stick as he handed her his holster to fill as well. He sat down next to Drew.

"So, how you feeling?"

"Mostly stupid," Drew answered in a whisper. "I had no idea it would make me this sick. And how could I not have known that eating poison was probably going to make me sick? I guess I really do believe that I'm something more than Barion. At least it looks like the water's going to stay down. Maybe if I can eat something and get it to stay down I'll start to feel humanoid again."

Dylan realized something then. "Being out here...it doesn't bother you at all?"

"Honey, compared to other places I've been, this is a fucking picnic. Hell, Van Gar and I used to do this sort of thing just for fun."

"What happened with Van?" Dylan asked carefully.

"If I told you, you wouldn't believe me. Suffice it to say he thinks a little too much like my rather uptight little sister over there."

Chapter 8

Van Gar paced the deck of the bridge, making a face as he looked around at all the gaudy decorations Pard Jar had encrusted on the ship. Drewcila wouldn't be pleased. Filth and garbage was one thing, bad taste quite another.

He'd had time to check on Drewcila's plummeting stocks and the reasons for them. In the last few hours, with communications restored to Barious, he had been able to learn all of what was going on. Drewcila was in trouble, and the time of his redemption might very well be at hand.

He grinned happily, for now he was a very wealthy man in his own right, with something to trade. So he took half of his crew with him, and sent the other half off with Pard Jar and a half dozen of Pard Jar's ships to the "home planet," where they would retrieve the others and leave Pard Jar there with whatever idiots still wanted to follow him. Forcing Pard Jar to live on the planet he'd told so many others was so wonderful seemed to them all to be a perfect and altogether fitting punishment.

Now Van Gar just needed to make some sort of plan. Problem was that he just really wasn't a plan man. Drewcila was the big game player, she was the one looked at all the data and came up with the answers. Van Gar just occasionally came up with a missing piece that helped put the big picture together.

If only he could have contacted Drew, but everything he had tried had failed dramatically. After he learned that she'd killed Zarco and escaped from the palace, he figured she'd head for Hepron Station. But while he'd managed to reach a member of her crew there, and had learned that she had plans to meet them there, they weren't able to tell him where she might be or what sort of condition she might be in. Rumors were that she'd been poisoned or drugged, and since she had been accused of killing the king, the entire military had been called out to search for her. In fact, Hepron Station was swarming with police and military, so he and her people obviously weren't the only ones who expected Drewcila to put in an appearance there.

Still..."Unless she just can't get there for some reason, Drewcila will head for Hepron Station," he mumbled to himself.

"What's that, Van Gar?" Shreta asked.

"Navigator, plot a course for the planet Barious, Hepron Station," Van Gar ordered.

"I thought we were going to go in search of a homeland for our people?" Shreta said with a frown.

Van turned to her and forced a smile. "And that's what we're doing. We'll kill two birds and only get stoned once." He made a face, knowing he didn't exactly have that right. "We need land, and I've got an in with the Barion queen, remember?"

Dylan couldn't bring himself to eat the roast beast on a stick, and he noticed that neither could Stasha. That left Arcadia, Facto and Drew to eat it on their own, which they did. Drew was obviously well on the way to recovery, because she was keeping it all down. Dylan was more than a little surprised to see that Facto actually knew something about surviving in the great outdoors, and seemed to be rather enjoying their little adventure.

"My life used to be rather quiet and uninteresting," Stasha said with a sigh as he sat down beside her.

"I can't tell whether you're disappointed or relieved," Dylan said with a smile.

"It's just an observation. Look at her..." she slung her head towards Drewcila. "Everyone falls at her feet. And I don't mean because she's queen. She has a presence now that she never had before. Though she was always strong willed, and— I'll admit it now, even if Zarco never will—manipulative. We are of the same blood, we look so much alike that I have for years, with very little effort on the part of make up, passed myself off as her when the need arose. Yet she and I are nothing alike. All men fall under her spell, and I could not hold the love of even one. What is so special about her?"

Dylan shrugged and smiled. "She's Drewcila Qwah."

"What sort of an answer is that?" Stasha asked angrily. "She's not really Drewcila Qwah. Drewcila Qwah is just a made up person..."

"Aren't we all just 'made-up people'? Aren't we handed an identity at birth that we then feel compelled to fit into? She's Drewcila Qwah, whether that identity was made up for her or not. She became the role, just like I became mine, and you became yours. We all waste our whole lives trying to become what we think we're supposed to be. What makes Drewcila so powerful and so attractive is that she knows exactly who she is. She isn't trying to be anyone, she just is. She lives in the moment. How many people actually do that?"

Arcadia moved to wrap herself around Drewcila, and Stasha sighed. "I don't have a single friend who would do for me what that alien has done for Drew today."

"I wish you wouldn't say alien like it was some dirty word. After all, I'm just as alien to your world as Arcadia is."

"I'm sorry, Dylan, I don't mean it to sound like a slur. Just that she's so different. Must have different ways and different customs, different loyalties. And yet she's obviously so devoted to Drew. I mean...what's in it for her?"

Dylan sighed wistfully. "I imagine some really great sex."

"What!" Stasha exclaimed. She looked at her feet as the other three turned to stare at her, and didn't speak again till they had all turned away again. "Are you saying...?"

Dylan chuckled, "I thought it was pretty obvious. Arcadia and Drew, well, they've been lovers for a long time."

"But, but it's a lizard, and...well I thought...isn't it female?"

"Oh, yeah! Arcadia's all girl. It's not like she's a cold blooded reptile, and she's bipedal. Some people...they get into the exotics. Why do you think Drew was with Van Gar, and he with her for that matter?"

"But they're both women! What on earth could Drewcila get from her that she couldn't get from a man?"

"Hey, Arcadia!" Dylan screamed. Stasha cringed as the lizard woman turned to face them. "Show Stasha your tongue."

Ten inches of forked tongue rolled out of the alien's mouth and just as quickly back in before she turned away again.

"So?" Stasha asked in confusion.

"You're fucking kidding me, right?" Dylan laughed.

Stasha shook her head no.

"What a backwards planet. No wonder I'm such a big hit with the local girls."

Atario had been named provisional regent, the "provisional" being a formality until the queen could be captured and brought to trial. As such, his new chancellor, Doctor Sortas, and he were desperately going over maps trying to figure out just where the queen might be.

"Figuring on her love affair with the press, I would have thought she'd have made a bee-line for one of the television stations. But we set up blockades, and no one's seen anything," Atario said.

"She's not a moron, Atario," Sortas said with a sigh. "Would you walk up to a building surrounded by huge military road blocks if you were her? No. No doubt by now she knows that you have framed her for the king's death, and since you've blocked her from going to the news media with her own story..."

"What would you suggest I do, Sortas? Just let her walk into a television station and take over? The people, the vast majority, love her. If they are asked to choose her word over mine, they will choose hers every time. That's why she must not be allowed to live to go to trial. That's why we must capture her quickly, and she must meet with a quick and unfortunate accident."

"I just think it would have been more expedient to have a less noticeable presence at the stations, that's all. You know, something a little more covert than concrete barriers and armored tanks, which by the way, are needed for security. We cannot afford to keep pulling our forces away from strategic areas that must be secured to go after the queen. The Lockhedes have quit pushing our forces at the borders, which means they are planning something. Probably something big in retaliation for..." he couldn't remember the name of the ship, "that...that really big ship that we blew up."

"The Artvail. It was their largest star class battle cruiser, and we didn't blow it up. Drewcila Qwah did," Atario hissed.

"Its name and who actually did it, is immaterial. We now have the war you wanted, but we're not prepared to actually fight it. Add to that the fact that you keep removing necessary forces from sensitive areas to go in search of Drewcila...we're just asking for a catastrophe. We know her ship the Garbage Scow has been called to Hepron Station, and that her crew is there. Perhaps we had best concentrate our efforts on catching her there, and return everyone else to their positions. We must be prepared to counter the Lockhedes attack when they make it."

Sortas was starting to really annoy Atario. As if it weren't bad enough that he had insinuated himself into Atario's reign, he seemed to be constantly saying things that were really distressing. Mostly because they made a great deal of sense and therefore couldn't be easily dismissed.

"What do you suggest I do about it, Sortas?" Atario made it sound flippant, but actually hoped the smart-assed bastard had an answer, because he sure as hell didn't.

"Make a strike against another major target while they're trying to do whatever it is that they're planning to do. Something that will force them to pull troops or whatever away from their planned objective in order to clean up the mess we've made. Hit a main population center. An air strike at a heavily populated city, perhaps even their capital, ought to do the trick. Crank it up a notch, as the salvagers are fond of saying. They want a war, give them a war. We already took out their battle cruiser. Hit them again before they have a chance to retaliate, and we keep the upper hand," Sortas said smugly.

Atario glared across the table loaded with maps and snarled out. "As if I hadn't already thought of it and wasn't just waiting to ask you what you thought of my plan. In fact, I have already implemented the action."

Sortas gave him an arrogant, all knowing look, and Atario decided to see if Sortas' lawyer couldn't be bribed into giving over the information so that Sortas could be done away with, and the sooner the better. Maybe just take the easy way out and kill the lawyer first.

Margot and Jurak had made it to the television station way before the military did, and they'd told their story.

The most celebrated reporter in Barious was assigned to the story, and they flew him back to the station from where he'd been reporting from a craft hovering over the Galdart desert. He hadn't been told why he'd been summoned for security reasons, and for this reason he entered the producer's office screaming.

"This had better be good, damn good! We damn near got our asses shot off up there to try and get those shots of the Artvail sinking into the sand, and..."

"Dartan, I'd like you to meet Jurak and Margot. Jurak is first mate of our queen's ship, Margot is the queen's personal servant, and is married to Chancellor Facto. I think you want to hear what they have to say."

They told their story, and Jurak ended with, "...the queen has ordered you to meet with her at Hepron Station and be her personal liaison with the media and the people through this crisis."

It took Dartan a minute to comprehend what he was being told, and then a couple more minutes to quiet the urge to jump up and start dancing and squealing like a giddy school girl. For all practical purposes, he had just been assigned the job of queen's press secretary. When he had managed to quell his uncharacteristically spontaneous reaction, he started barking out orders. He wanted this camera man and that sound man. He wanted this kind of equipment and that kind of gear. He wanted this, that, and all at once. He also wanted to use the network's hovercraft.

In fifteen minutes, equipment and staff were loaded into the waiting hovercraft, and they were lifting off just as the military arrived in force.

"What the hell!" Dartan quickly donned communicator head gear. "What the hell's going on?"

"We've been scooped by BOB network, the new Chancellor Atario Biggin has just made a broadcast accusing the queen of killing the king."

Dartan relayed the message to Jurak and Margot.

Jurak shook his head violently. "That is not possible. I was the last one out of the castle, and the king was very much alive when I left him. He was wounded, too badly wounded to follow us out the window, and he begged us to go on without him. But his injury wasn't even close to life threatening. If the king is dead, then it is the nobles who have killed him."

"You hear that?" Dartan asked his boss.

"Yeah, I heard it…"

"Give us about ten minutes to get out of sight of the military below, and then I want to go live…"

"Dartan…if the queen did kill the king, and we help her…"

"Jesop…listen to me, man. Who watches the news?"

"The general public?"

"And if the general public has to make a decision between believing some noble who they have just now learned is the new Chancellor, or the Queen who brought them into the Golden Age of Salvaging and gave their lives meaning, who do you think they are going to believe?"

"We go live in ten minutes."

Sortas rushed into the room without so much as the courtesy of a knock, and flipped on the TV.

"Who do you think you are?" Atario snapped.

"Shut up and watch," Sortas ordered.

"I'm in the air, flying away from the capitol on my way to a secret destination where I will meet with the queen. With me are two of the queen's emissaries, who have quite a different take on recent events than the one that you have just been told by Chancellor Atario. Who is this man any way? Isn't your husband, Facto, in fact chancellor, Lady Margot?" The camera moved to show the woman.

"He was until the castle was taken over..."

"They slowly removed the normal guards and replaced them with members of the nobility." The camera moved to the man called Jurak. "Neither the king nor the queen wanted a war with Lockhedes. They wanted to sign trade agreements, because they knew that such agreements would lead to a lasting peace and a better economy. So the nobles imprisoned the king and Chancellor Facto, and lay in wait for the queen..."

"They poisoned her," Margot reminded.

"Yes, they tried to kill her..."

"Fortunately two of Drewcila's people had evaded capture, and they came and rescued us..."

"Unfortunately, in the fire fight the king was hit..."

They were giving the poor camera man whiplash going back and forth between the two.

"We were lucky to escape with our lives."

Atario had seen enough. A long, throaty growl echoed from his lips. "Get a battalion in the air. I want this reporter and Drewcila's lackeys shot out of the sky."

"That's going to be very hard to do," Sortas spat back. "Most of our air force is currently pounding the Lockhede capital even as we speak, and the others...when they hear this...their hearts weren't in capturing her before. They want to believe her, and so they will. We'll be lucky if we can escape with our lives. I don't think we're in any position to order anyone to do anything. By morning it will be a whole new world."

Chapter 9

General Tryte looked at the incoming data. Just after nightfall the Barions had started pounding their capital. Their own plans to bomb Hepron Station were thwarted as they pulled their planes and ships back in an effort to save their homeland. But even as their planes got into a position to defend against the attacks, the Barion planes turned and ran away like the cowards they were. They hadn't chased them for fear of leaving the air space over the city unprotected, fully expecting and waiting for a second wave of attacks which never came.

After they had intercepted several newscasts from Barious, Tryte began to wonder whether this was just brilliant war tactics on the part of the Barions, or if Barious was as completely politically crippled as the reports would have them believe. Their king was supposedly dead. Either killed by his treacherous, salvager wife, or the greedy self-serving nobility, depending completely on which channel you chose to watch.

Whatever the case, he as General of the Air Force couldn't afford to drop his guard.

His aide walked into the room, "General Tryte."

"Yes?"

"President Ralling wants to see you in his office."

"I figured he would." He rose from his chair and followed the aide out of his office and down the hall.

They had made all military decisions together—he, the president, the president's advisors, the General of the Army, and Admiral of the Navy. However the "elected"—a term used lightly since every one was well aware that the social elite chose a candidate and then bought him into office—official had a habit of assigning blame to someone other than himself. Since it had been Tryte's idea to bomb Hepron Station, he was sure it was going to be his fault that they'd had no way of defending their own capitol against that first wave of attacks when they'd come.

Tryte didn't really care. He could roll with the punches. He had no respect at all for this president, whose election seemed even more suspect than elections of the past. The social elite had for generations bought the candidates they wanted, but in the last election the common man had come out in force and refused to vote with the upper classes. The people's candidate had won by a popular landside. That was when the rich started to bring out antiquated laws and dust them off. Before the common folks could say "screwed," their candidate had been thrown out on a technicality, and this joker Ralling had been placed at the head of their country.

Ralling was the idiot offspring of some rich politician. He was Teflon-coated, and crap simply didn't stick to him. However, even if Tryte didn't respect the president, he was glad he'd won, and didn't really care how. As was their law, the loser of the election was their vice-president. Trailings was a highly intelligent man with the people's best interests at heart, and he scared the living shit out of Tryte.

See, Tryte wanted the war. It proved they needed a strong military, and gave him job security. More importantly, he wanted to finally stomp the Barions' asses. In the past they had usually lost wars, just like the last one. But the Barions had gotten soft, and being fat and well fed they weren't in a fighting mood.

Trailings had wanted to make trade agreements with the Barions. It was what he had promised in his campaign, and was the main reason he had won the popular vote so easily. Trying to gain his constituents' approval, Ralling had agreed to work on trade agreements as well. Of course, at the first sign of Barion rejection, and at the general's not-so-gentle urging, he had threatened the Barions with military retaliation, something which the general knew would cause Zarco to go on the attack. When they declared war on Barious, it was way too late for any kind of agreement.

No matter what any of the reports said, and whether he was dead or alive, Tryte knew one thing for a fact. There was no way that Zarco would ever willingly make peace with them. Tryte knew what losing Zarco's wife had done to him. He knew, because he was the one who made and executed the plans to capture, torture, and mentally mutilate the Barion queen. And it was he who had given her to Eric Rider, who had then turned her into Drewcila Qwah.

Now that same Drewcila Qwah had shot his battle cruiser out of the sky, and it looked like there was a very good chance that he was going to wind up going toe-to-toe with her militarily. A deeper man might say that he was reaping what he had sown. General Tryte just wished he had killed the bitch when he'd had the chance.

When he entered the president's office, the other generals and the vice-president were already there.

"Glad you could make it, General," Ralling said in a voice dripping with sarcasm.

"Sorry I'm late," Tryte said, although he couldn't really see how the hell he could be late since he had come as soon as he'd been summoned. It was always a good idea to kiss a little political ass. The president waved him into a seat, and he sat down.

"What the hell happened?" the president demanded.

All the generals and the vice-president started talking at once.

"One at a time!" Ralling screamed. "You," he pointed at Tryte. "What went wrong? We were supposed to be bombing Hepron Station last night, and instead they're bombing our capital. The capitol building has taken extensive damage. My wife and I barely escaped with our lives. Six skyscrapers were hit. They're saying an estimated twenty thousand people are dead. The whole country's screaming."

Trailings didn't give Tryte a chance to answer, which just proved to Tryte what a rude bastard he actually was. "I told you. I told all of you that it was wrong to attack the Barions. They have slaughtered us out right in the last three wars. That has left our country in financial and military ruin..."

"With all due respect," Tryte bit out. "The Barions are in a very vulnerable position. They have scrapped out most of their military equipment..."

"So you've said. Meanwhile they are stomping us, and our people are going hungry and getting killed, for what? We aren't going to force them to do anything. We need the trade agreements."

"When we totally annihilate them, we will have their trade agreements," Tryte said, his face getting red.

"What are we going to annihilate them with?" Trailings demanded. "The only attacks we have successfully deployed are a few minor border skirmishes and a lot of idle threats."

"There is nothing idle about our threats." Tryte could now feel his heart racing in his chest. "We are militarily superior. While we have continued to build our war machine, they have been tearing theirs apart."

"I see no proof of that," Trailings said.

"Well I do," the president said with conviction. The stupid bastard knew nothing about the military, and had no doubt been going to ream Tryte out good 'til he saw that Trailings was attacking him. Since Ralling hated Trailings, Tryte suddenly found himself in the pleasant position of being—at least temporarily—the golden haired boy. "What should our next move be, Tryte?"

"You're actually asking this moron?" Trailings said in disbelief. "So far he's managed to get one of our battle cruisers destroyed and our capital bombed."

"Everyone has a bad day," Ralling said.

Trailings threw up his hands and left the room, which suited Tryte just fine.

Drew woke up with a slight throbbing in her head, which meant she was more or less back to normal. She shook Arcadia till she woke up and then put a finger over her mouth. She got up and motioned for Arcadia to follow her a little out of camp. When they were a sufficient distance away, Drew stopped. At which point Arcadia proceeded to wrap herself around her.

"Honey, I've got puke breath, Drew protested.

"I don't care, Drew...it's been so long, and I've missed you so much."

Drew kissed her gently on the mouth, then pushed her away. "I promise you that as soon as we get to Hepron Station I'll make it up to you. Right now I need to fill you in on what's going on, and then you can tell Dylan..." Drew relayed the news cast to Arcadia.

"But you didn't kill him..."

"You think my sister's going to believe me?"

"But I was there! I know you didn't do it."

"And you think she'd believe you any sooner than she'd believe me?"

"I suppose not." She saw the way Drewcila was looking at her, and mistook an attack of gas for accusation. "I swear to you, Drew, that I didn't..."

"I know that. Jurak would have had a fit if you did. I also know he didn't do it, because...well, he just wouldn't."

"Then who?"

"I imagine the evil Atario. Power hungry and stupid...He killed Zarco and blamed it on me, which really pisses me off, because I wanted to kill Zarco and blame it on him. It's just so unfair."

"So that's why all the police and military are after us. They think you killed the king."

"And so will Stasha. Like I said, she won't believe you, and she certainly isn't going to believe me. She might believe Jurak, I don't know. At any rate, I don't want her to find out Zarco's dead just yet. She's bitching enough now when she thinks all I did was screw and shoot him. Besides...the dumb ass actually loved the bastard."

"So did you...once," Arcadia reminded.

Drew smiled and looked back towards the camp and her sister. "See...I just don't believe that for a minute. I don't think a person could change that much. They might have removed my memories, but they didn't remove *me*, and I just never felt *anything* for him but contempt."

"And Van Gar?"

"What about him?"

"Do you love him?"

Drew smiled and ran her hand down the side of Arcadia's face. "Are you jealous?"

"You know that I am."

"Well, do yourself a favor and STOP IT! Don't you start that sentimental bullshit, too, I just can't take it right now. Van Gar left because he couldn't live on my terms. Why does everyone have to get so damned serious? Doesn't anyone just want to have fun anymore?" Drew laughed then and popped Arcadia on the back. "Hell, girl! Isn't life throwing enough crap at us right now?"

Arcadia nodded, although she wouldn't look at her.

Drew took Arcadia's claw in her hand. "Come on, let's get this show on the road. The sooner we get to Hepron the better."

"They will be waiting there for us?"

"Most probably. However, I'm hoping that by then Jurak and Margot will have gotten to the news media. If so, I'm expecting a rather uneventful arrival."

"And we'll be together?" Arcadia asked carefully.

"Of course we will," Drew answered enthusiastically.

Dartan woke early, which turned out to be a total waste of time because there was still no sign of the queen. Over night, news had broken that they'd bombed the capital of Lockhede, and that there was a huge demonstration outside the castle. It was reported that several nobles had committed suicide rather than face the wrath of the population outside the castle walls should they fall.

Of course he wasn't reporting on any of that; in fact, all the things that were news-worthy he wasn't being allowed to report on at all. Hepron Station was run by Salvagers, most of whom were alien. Everyone here was an employee of Qwah-Co, and as such all highly loyal to the queen. No one was going to allow him to report that the queen was still missing or where she was heading. Any of that might give away where she was. And although it seemed that the military, which had arrived in force sometime during the night, was currently awaiting orders—not from the reigning regent, Atario, but from their queen—no one was willing to take any chances.

Vehicles, both land and air, were being prepared, and it was obvious that a reconnaissance mission was being launched. However, no one was telling him anything. He sighed. He had been sure he'd been handed the assignment of his life, and now the news seemed to be happening everywhere but here. It just wasn't fair.

Arcadia continued to play with her wrist com. "Well, it's obvious that communications are back up."

"But?" Drew drawled, standing close to the fire to warm her freezing ass.

"I haven't been able to get an open channel to Hepron Station yet."

"Keep trying."

"Drewcila, we had a plan. A plan to go to civilization and seek help. I think that was a good plan," Dylan said.

Arcadia laughed and looked at Drew. "Little Dylan's afraid to stay in the big dark woods another night."

"Bite me, Arcadia," Dylan snapped. "I don't care what any of you say, something big was breathing on my neck last night, and something with way too many legs to be anything but creepy was crawling on my face when I woke up this morning. If God had meant for us to live in the woods, he would have given us shells like turtles so that we could carry our home with us."

"And no doubt your shell would contain all the modern conveniences of a space station," Arcadia teased.

"A little piece of heaven for him and his blow-up doll," Drew laughed.

"Fuck you, Qwah!" Dylan said angrily. "I'm tired, I'm hungry, and I'm cold. I don't think either of you pathetic bitches are particularly funny this morning. I surely-to-fuck never had to resort to screwing some blow-up plastic piece of shit."

"I'm guessing Stasha wouldn't screw you," Drewcila said.

"Most certainly not!" Stasha said, her head snapping up from where she'd been sitting staring at the fire. "Unlike you, I don't bed everything with legs."

"Neither do I...That thing that crawled across Dylan's face? I don't care what that lying bastard says, I didn't fuck it," Drew said with a laugh.

"She's never screwed me either," Dylan said with a pout.

"I told you...you're too normal," Drew said.

"I'm not having any luck getting a link with Hepron Station," Arcadia sighed.

"May I?" Facto asked holding out his hand. Arcadia handed him the communicator.

"Why not give it to my sister? Maybe she could have sex with it," Stasha said.

"All right, but you have to set it on vibrate mode, and I don't know how good an antenna I'm going to make." If Drew was at all upset by Stasha's obvious jabs it wasn't showing.

"I vote we start walking," Dylan said.

"I say we stay put and let our people find us," Drew said.

"And I think it's more likely that the army guys will find us," Dylan insisted.

"Quiet, I think I've reached Hepron Station," Facto reported.

Dartan heard the commotion, and he and his camera men moved towards it. A hovercraft landed on the pad just outside the door, and armed Qwah-Co soldiers climbed out and took up position, followed by the queen and her retinue, and the word that jumped immediately to Dartan's thoughts was 'competent.'

It was evident in their movements and in those of their queen's. These were people who understood who they were and knew exactly what they were doing.

"Can we please start filming now?" Dartan asked the angry looking gray alien who had spent the better part of the night before and this morning telling them what and when they could and could not shoot.

"Knock yourselves out."

"Jesop...bring us on live now," Dartan ordered into his head set. And then the words just flowed as they had never flowed for him before. "I'm here at a secret location where the queen and her retinue have just arrived." They were digging their way through the crowd as he spoke. "In the face of tragedy and treachery, our queen stands tall. All our hopes, all our fears rest on her shoulders and hers alone, and looking at her now surrounded by those she trusts most, I personally have no doubt that we as a nation shall surely triumph over any adversity. She saved us before, and she shall save us again." The queen suddenly stumbled, and was quickly caught by a man he recognized immediately as Chancellor Facto. "I don't know if you can see her clearly, she just stumbled, and Chancellor Facto caught her. Her color is very bad, and she appears to be very weak, which would seem to confirm the reports that she has been poisoned. She was supposed to have met us here last night, and she is just now arriving with a reconnaissance team that was sent out earlier to locate and retrieve her. The gods alone know what horrors she has endured through the night, and yet despite her obvious physical weakness and her crushing loss, she's here. And I have to believe that she will be able to sew our troubled nation back together. We are almost through the crowd now." He forced his way past the last few bipedal obstacles in his way, and found himself face to face with the queen, who looked at him and smiled.

"I'm glad you could make it," she said.

"My Queen...so much has happened, and your great personal loss..."

"Someone please give my sister a sedative. She's very distraught because of our ordeal," the queen ordered quickly.

"I'm wha...?" Stasha collapsed into the arms of the medic who had given her a shot, and was hauled quickly away towards the medical facility with Margot right behind them.

"My sister...she's a delicate flower, and she's been through a great ordeal." Drewcila stumbled again, and Dartan found himself supplying a supportive arm to the monarch.

"My Queen...are you ill? What happened to your tongue?"

"Ah...There's something wrong with my tongue? Must be the effects of the poison. I sure ain't feelin' in the pink if you know what I mean. Atario had me poisoned, and I have just a few moments ago learned that he had my dear husband killed. Then the bastard had the nerve to try and frame me for it! His attempt at a coup shall not, will not, succeed. My sister and my husband...they were very close, and I'm afraid she just completely lost it. I'm still very sick, and it's been a very long, stressful night. You'd be surprised to know how much one person can puke...

"I have much to think about, and consume, and I'm a little overwhelmed right now. I'm not going to lie to you: the nobles have put our country in a position of grave peril. Give me a few hours to rest, time to eat a warm meal and absorb all the data, and I will better be able to address the problems we all face." She nodded her head, and the Valtarian lizard woman took the queen from him, and started mostly carrying her towards what Dartan assumed were her chambers. The rest of the queen's entourage followed.

"Cameras off," Dartan ordered. For the moment all his reporter's instincts were on hold. He motioned for the camera men and his crew to stay behind as he rushed to catch up with the queen. "May I help you, my Queen?"

She smiled broadly at him. "Whatever floats your boat."

He took her other arm and helped to move her along. "My Queen..." words which had flowed so easily just moments ago momentarily left him. "...I have heard so much about you."

"Ah, you can't believe everything you hear," she warned.

"Most of what I've heard has been very good," he assured her.

"That's exactly my point," she said laughing out loud. They had reached the door to her chambers and stopped. She raised a hand and gently patted the side of his face. "Don't get too far off. I just need to get a shower, recharge my batteries, and figure out just what in hell's name is actually going on. When I know all the details and have made a plan of action, I'll want to address the nation. Four hours," she looked briefly at the lizard woman and smiled, "five tops. In the meantime, extol my virtues and make damn sure you don't allow anything in a frame that would give away our position. Hepron Station is a prime target for our enemies as it stands, and with me here...well, that's just bonus points if you know what I mean, and I'm sure you do. You look like a sharp guy. Oh, and see if you can't incite the people to riot on the castle, start kicking some noble butt-boy ass. Those guys have really started to piss me off, and it would be nice if they had been crunched by the time I woke up from my little nap. Something to look forward to in these darkest of times."

"As you wish, my Queen." He bowed low and departed. Drew opened the door, and she and Arcadia entered. The others started to follow, but Drew held up a hand. "Where the hell do you yahoos think you're going?"

Jurak, Dylan and Facto just shrugged.

She sighed deeply. "My brain is tired! Why do I always have to do all the thinking?"

They shrugged again.

"Great. All right. You," she pointed at Jurak, "keep an eye on the reporter and his crew. And you," she pointed at Dylan. "Damn it, Drew, I'm tired and I'm hungry..."

"And you whine more than my fucking grandmother. Get something to eat, and then make sure Hepron Station is secure, that all our early warning systems are intact, and that all our anti-aircraft guns are operational. Make sure my ship is actually here, or at the very least on its way. We're a prime target for the Lockhedes. I wasn't just bullshitting him about that. I want to be able to jump planet if I have to." This got her a dirty look from Facto, which she mostly ignored. "I want the station put on the highest possible alert..."

"What would that be?" Dylan asked curiously.

"How the fuck should I know? Call it ugly-puppy-delta-red-six-alert for all I care. I just want to make damn sure that if any Lockhede bastard thinks it's a good idea to attack us, we show them real quick that it's not. And you," she pointed at Facto. "You make damn sure that my sister talks to no one, and that she doesn't find out that Zarco's dead until I get a chance to talk to her."

"Why can't I do that job?" Dylan whined.

"Because I think in your fragile, hungry, tired state, it might be a good idea if some of the blood actually got back to your brain. When you put us on hair-pie-beta-blue-five-alert, go and get some sleep. You can return to your quest to bone my sister when you wake up."

Dylan snapped a salute, "Yes, sir!"

Drew looked at the three of them and sighed again. "Keyrist! What the hell are you still standing her for? Get your asses in gear, and do my bidding."

Drew walked the rest of the way into the room, and Arcadia shut the door. Her chambers here were large and lavish, fit for a queen or the galaxy's leading salvaging mogul, and she was, of course, both. Truth was she had rarely used them, and yet had still spent more time here than she had at the castle. She looked at Arcadia and smiled. "Gee, I thought they'd never leave." She walked over to the bar and started mixing herself a drink. "So...let's see. Jack Be Nimble with a shot of Barcadian Rum."

"I'm surprised you remember," Arcadia smiled. "These days I'm mostly drinking Hurling Monkeys."

Drew looked momentarily surprised. "Me, too. I like mine with a twist."

Arcadia laughed. "Well, I didn't expect you'd drink it straight." Arcadia sat on the couch, moving her tail out of the way. Keeping her spikes from puncturing things had become as natural to her as a human not sitting on their hands. Of course there were times when she had to actually remind herself that she was permanently attached to a dangerous weapon. Safe sex for her meant corking the tips of her spikes. Drew mixed the drinks, walked over and handed Arcadia hers, and then flopped on the couch next to her, successfully spilling both drinks. She mumbled curses and wiped her hand over the liquid on her jumpsuit and then licked it off.

"I'd never actually heard you speak on camera before. Very impressive with all the shall-nots and big words and all."

"It's just like bullshit, only a little more formal. You have to be just stiff enough that you sound like you know what you're talking about, yet honest enough that the common folk buy your line of crap."

"So...what was with the act? I mean...you hardly seem worse for the wear right now."

Drew leaned against Arcadia and sipped at her drink. "Sympathy. Besides, I need a little time to think about everything that's happened and go over all the events of last night as reported on all sides. Find out just where my ship's at." She pointed at her head. "Work up a good getting all the people over to my side speech."

"Oh..." Arcadia said a hint of disappointment in her voice.

Drewcila laughed at her. "Arcadia...my planet is in chaos, my business is falling into the toilet, and I'm a widow, which means I'm now the reigning monarch if I can get those noble rich fucks out of my castle...My castle. That has a nice ring to it, doesn't it? I'm a little hurt, though. I thought you knew me better than that. Of course I wouldn't think of tackling any of that shit without a good stiff drink and a really good tumble first."

Stasha woke to a strange whirling sensation in her head.

"You're all right," a familiar voice was saying. "We're safe, you were a little over-wrought." It was Margot. If she squinted her eyes a little she could put the face with the voice.

"Margot...what happened to me?"

"You were very upset..."

Memory flooded in as the fogginess left her head. "No I wasn't. I wasn't upset at all. My sister had me drugged. She had me drugged so that I wouldn't tell the reporters that she's the one that shot Zarco. That's it, isn't it?"

"Now calm down, Stasha. Getting upset isn't going to help anyone." That was Facto.

She was alone in a dark room with Margot and Facto. She tried to get up, and found that she was strapped to the bed. "What madness is this? How long does my sister think she can bind me here like this?"

"Calm down," Facto ordered, moving to undo the straps. "You aren't being restrained. The straps were only to keep you from rolling out of the bed."

"Don't lie to me, Facto. Why would I roll out of my bed? Do I normally roll out of my bed? No." She rubbed at her wrists. "Where is she? Where is the Queen of Whores now?"

"She's sleeping."

"Alone?" Stasha asked in an accusing way.

"No, I don't think so," Facto said.

"But I'm alone, all alone..."

"We're here for you, Stasha." Margot said in a comforting tone that was wasted on Stasha.

"No you're not. You're here because she ordered you to be here. You're not my friends, you're my guards, and I'm not the idiot my sister thinks I am."

"You're just talking nonsense now, Stasha," Facto said throwing up his hands.

"Oh really? Well here." She sat up and slid her feet off the bed. "I'm getting up, and I'm..." she started walking towards the door, "...going to leave!"

Facto quickly moved to stand between her and the door. "Stasha, you aren't thinking clearly."

"Why's that Facto? Could it be because I'm trying to leave the room, where you've been ordered to keep me so that my sister can weave whatever lies she's going to weave? Would that be why you'd say I'm not thinking clearly?"

"No, actually, I was thinking you were confused because you're naked," Facto said gently.

Stasha looked down, noticed that she was indeed naked, ran back to the bed and covered herself with a sheet.

"Where...where are my clothes?" she demanded.

"They were very dirty and torn. The medics cut them off you and gave you a bath. We all thought you'd rest better this way," Margot explained.

"No...no you didn't. You took my clothes to make me vulnerable...To make it so that I can't leave without making a spectacle of myself." Stasha pulled the sheet more tightly around her. "I want to see Drewcila. I demand to see her at once."

"Your sister has been sick, and there are matters which need her attention. She needs her sleep," Facto objected.

"Facto...you get me my sister, or I swear I will walk out of this room naked and scream until the reporter finds me."

"You will not do that," Facto said sternly.

"You watch me."

"You will not do it, because I will not let you do it."

Her comlink was making that god awful noise that comlinks make when someone was patching an emergency call through. Drew pulled a pillow over her head and tried to ignore it.

"Drew," Arcadia started rocking her body. "Drew, you'd better get that, it's a distress call."

"What? A distress call in the middle of a coup and a war? Unthinkable!" Drew sat up and slung the pillow aside. "All right, hand me the fucking thing." Drew ran her hands down her face as Arcadia grabbed the buzzing comlink and handed it to Drew. Drew opened the channel. "What! What the fuck do you want?" she screamed into the receiver.

"It's Stasha. She's out of control," Margot said in a panic.

"I told you not to let her find out that Zarco was dead."

"We didn't, she doesn't know that Zarco's dead," Margot said.

"Dead! Zarco's dead! Oh my gods!" she heard Stasha cry out.

"Oops," Margot said.

"Yeah, big fucking oops, Margot."

"She killed him! Drew killed him, didn't she? Oh, gods..."

"Where are you?"

"Med unit, room six," Margot answered.

"Don't let her leave. Sedate her if you have to. I'll be there as soon as I get dressed."

Dartan was waiting with his crew outside the queen's chambers, hoping she would emerge soon, since he had exhausted all other possible newsworthy venues within the station. The door opened, and she walked out wearing tight black leather pants with zippers where zippers shouldn't be, and a dark blue shirt with no sleeves which didn't quite hit her belt and was open all the way to her navel. A huge blaster in an elaborate black leather holster hung on her right hip. She looked well, awake, and ready for action. Out the door behind her came her bodyguard, the Valtarian lizard woman, wearing the plain blue sleeveless jump suit with the Qwah-Co logo that most Qwah-Co employs wore. Her blaster was also prominently displayed on her person.

They were battle ready, and he said as much as they followed them down the hall with their cameras.

"My Queen, you look as if you are ready for anything..."

"Can't talk now. Busy," Drewcila said waving her hand in the air dismissively.

"But, my Queen…"

The lizard woman turned on him and hissed, at which point he threw up his hands and backed away.

"My sister is having a breakdown. I will call for you when I'm ready to address the nation. In the meantime, color some pictures, or study flash cards…you know—busy work."

Surprisingly, Dartan, who normally would have thrown a fit over being treated in such a manner, wasn't upset at all. "As you wish, my Queen."

Atario looked out at the sea of angry citizens rioting outside the castle walls. He had just made yet another speech on TV, discrediting Drewcila and trying to defend all his recent policy decisions. He had even replayed the speech Zarco had given, telling the people that he wanted them to take up arms and smite—that was the word he used—the Lockhedes. If they were watching that channel at all—and from the mob outside he doubted anyone was watching anything but the long line of propaganda Drewcila and her people were feeding the other station—they weren't listening. And if they were listening, they weren't buying it.

He could tell that the news crew he had with him were close to bolting. They didn't want to be forever seen as the network that had helped the hated nobles in their attempt to take over the kingdom. The head reporter had said as much, at which point Atario had him carted off to the dungeon.

"You'd better think of something, Atario, and you had better think of it fast," Sortas hissed at his shoulder. "Several nobles have been dragged from their homes and beaten to death in these riots. Many of those who stood with us fled before we raised the gates in an effort to distance themselves from us and to save themselves. Several others have hanged themselves rather than face the wrath of the mob. The gates—even the walls—will not hold forever, and there's word that the military is standing down, waiting until they have orders from the queen…"

"You act as if this is all my fault. It is not. It is yours. You had a chance to kill her. If you had killed her, she...none of them would have escaped, and my plan would have worked brilliantly. If anyone is to blame, it's you...only you," Atario accused.

Sortas laughed, though he was obviously not amused. "Like the people, you give this salvaging whore way too much credit. She was slowing her friends down in their escape. Without her, they still would have escaped, and we'd be facing a mob angry because we'd killed both monarchs, not just one. How would you have explained it away? If both of them were dead, who would you have blamed then?"

"If she was dead, there would have been no reason for me to kill Zarco."

Sortas smiled smugly then and whispered to Atario. "I believe the salvagers call it saving my own ass." He looked back towards a closet in the back of the room. "You boys get that?"

The reporter that Atario had locked up and a camera man stepped out of the now open closet door. "Every bit of it, and it went out on live feed."

"Why you!" Atario launched himself at Sortas, and felt something hot and painful pierce his chest. He hit the floor with a thud. Looking up, he saw the blaster in Sortas' hand.

"I thought he had a gun," Sortas said in an agonized voice.

He might fool them, but he didn't fool Atario, at least not this time.

Atario died, and Sortas and the newsmen used his body as part of the barricade they stacked against the door to save them from the remaining nobles. Once the door was secured, the news team went about trying to save their own asses.

By the time Drewcila reached the room, Stasha had given up her fight—although it was clear by the shiner and the ripped clothes hanging on Facto's sweat covered, scratched-up body, that she had put up quite a fight—and was just sitting in the middle of the floor in a huddled mass, crying.

"Ah," Drew said, not without real compassion. She knelt beside her sister and put her hand on her shoulder. "I'm really sorry, Stasha. I know you loved him…" Stasha shoved her, and because of the way she was perched on her feet, Drew fell right over, landing unceremoniously and very un-monarch like on her butt. Arcadia rushed to help Drew to her feet.

"I hate you! I hate you! You killed him. You said you wouldn't, and then you did," Stasha said accusingly.

"Facto! My sister is upset. Quick, go now, draw from the pool of assholes, and bring her someone to flog!"

"How can you make jokes after what you've done?" Stasha cried.

"I didn't kill him. I shot him a little, but I didn't kill him," Drew defended.

"I know you murdered him. You don't have to lie about it. Just get away from me, or murder me, too, and have it over with."

"That's a little dramatic, even for you, Stasha," Drew said, losing patience with her sister. "I didn't murder him. You ought to know me well enough by now to know that. If I'd killed him, I'd crow and do a little dance about it. I might lie to the public, but I wouldn't lie to you…Well, I would, but not about this. I mean…come on! I shot him right in front of you! That's got to mean something."

"Exactly! And as soon as I wasn't looking, you killed him."

"Drewcila left before Jurak and I did, and he was still alive when Jurak and I left," Arcadia said helpfully.

"You…Why on earth would I believe you? Like every male creature who falls within her aura, you are completely and totally infatuated by her. You'd kill for her, so why on earth wouldn't you lie for her?"

Drew looked at Arcadia. "She's got you there, chick."

"I tried," Arcadia shrugged.

"Come on, Stasha, use a little common sense. This guy was a bastard. He wanted to treat me like a possession. He treated you like dog shit. He didn't give a flying donkey dick about the country. And as if all of that wasn't bad enough, the guy was a lousy lay. I guarantee, you get you one good fuck..."

"You killed the man I love, and now you find it necessary to remind me that you had sex with him."

"Gods! Is there no winning with you?" Drew sighed deeply. "I screwed him, and I shot him, but I sure as fuck didn't kill him. If you keep screaming that I did, then someone's going to hear you, and there's a very good chance that you'll wind up helping the person who really did kill the egg-headed bastard. I have to go save the country now. You just lay here and wallow in your self pity. I have better things to do...Arcadia?"

Drew turned and left, and Arcadia followed her out, not that Arcadia really needed to be ordered.

Facto secured the door behind them. Margot got the sheet, brought it over and covered Stasha with it. Stasha buried her face in Margot's shoulder and just cried.

Drew sat down behind her desk in her office. She started keyboarding as Arcadia sat in a chair on the other side of the desk and just watched her.

"Finally a little good news. The Garbage Scow has just docked. Atario's dead. Good. The bastard poisoned me and killed Zarco."

Arcadia cleared her throat. "Ah, Drew, you poisoned yourself."

"Oh yeah, but it was his fault."

"Actually, it was Zarco who locked you up."

"Yeah, that's right."

"Atario killed Zarco, but since you wanted to kill him, he sort of did you a favor."

"Ah...poor Atario," Drew said. She looked across the desk and smiled at Arcadia. "Now stop it. It works better if I actually believe my own lies."

Chapter 10

Van Gar patched the communication through with a trembling hand. It could be very bad news. Last time he had talked to Hepron Station they still had no news about Drew. His fear turned to adulation when Drew's face appeared on the screen.

"Drewcila! You're alive!" he said stating the obvious.

She smiled. "Really? Do you think the others know?" She frowned then, seeming to remember how and why they had parted. Her eyes narrowed to slits as she hissed. "Do you have my ship?"

"Yes, yes I do. It's so good to see you…"

"Is that my ship you're flying?"

Van Gar swallowed hard. "Yes."

"What the fuck did you do to it? Looks like a Hepelon drag queen threw up in there."

"It's a long story…It runs fine, no worse for the wear. This can all be fixed, a little paint, a little wall paper." He laughed nervously then added. "I'm on my way to Hepron Station, I figured with everything that's going on you could use my help…"

"We don't need him here," a familiar voice hissed out.

"Arcadia!" Van Gar answered in a voice dripping with acid.

"Van Gar," she said in an equally disgusted tone.

"Knock it off!" Drew ordered. "So…what happened with the religious cult? God and goodness and shit not all it's cracked up to be or what?"

Apparently Drewcila was not yet ready to let bygones be bygones, and he wasn't ready to tell her the whole truth. He lowered his voice to a whisper. "Drewcila…I can't talk about it right now, but I have run the scam of scams, and if you help me out, I'll help you out and split the profit with you seventy-thirty."

"Seventy for me, right?"

"No. Damn it, Drew! Seventy for me, thirty for you."

"Sixty-forty."

"Sixty for me?" Van asked carefully.

"Oh, I guess so," Drew said reluctantly. She smiled. "How fast can you be here?"

"Twelve hours tops." He swallowed a little more of his pride. "I shouldn't have left. I've missed you, Drewcila."

It looked like she was about to apologize to him, or at the very least tell him she'd missed him, but no such luck. "No, you sure as fuck shouldn't have left me, and stealing one of my ships...well, that was totally uncalled for!" Drew snapped back and closed the transmission.

Van Gar sighed and relaxed into his chair.

"She's a very beautiful creature," Shreta said behind him, making him jump. "I can see why you love her."

Van Gar laughed. "Well, I'm glad someone can. Right now I have half a mind to turn this tin can around and go anywhere else in the galaxy."

"But you won't." She walked around to face him. "I can see it in your eyes when you talk to her, and I could see it in her eyes when she looked at you." She sighed longingly. "No male will ever look at me that way."

"Don't say that, Shreta. You're a nice girl. You have a great personality. Someday some man will..." Van Gar looked at her, and the words died on his lips to be replaced by: "They make some really great sex aids. I've heard they're just like the real thing."

"We don't need him here," Arcadia said with a pout.

"Don't start that shit, Arcadia. I want him here," Drew said. "No one's hanging a 'property of' sign on my ass. Not him, and not you."

Arcadia nodded silently. "I'm sorry."

"Don't be sorry. Just don't do it," Drewcila said. "You know how I feel about him."

"Yes...What I don't know is how you feel about me."
Drew smiled at her. "Yes, you do."

President Ralling sat in his office with his chief advisors, thinking how unfortunate it was that the vice-president had decided to attend this meeting. This seemed like about the twelfth strategy discussion they'd had that day, and he wasn't really a strategy kind of guy. He was more a sitting-on-his-ass-reveling-in-the-power-and-passing-stupid-assed-laws-that-only-he-gave-a-crap-about sort of guy.

The vice-president was yelling that they needed to try and negotiate a truce, while all the war-mongering military heads were calling for a blood bath. He was inclined to agree with the military guys, just because they sounded like they knew what they were talking about, and because he hated that idiot Trailings. He was about to tell them all to shut up because he was tired of listening to them, when his aide walked in, bowed then straightened.

"Mr. President...The Barion Queen is on line one."

There was a sudden hush in which they all just stared at each other. Finally Trailings said, "We'd better listen to what she has to say."

Ralling nodded and hit the button on his video phone. There she sat, the reigning Barion Queen, flanked by some strange reptilian alien and their country's High Chancellor, Facto.

She was examining her nails, and took several moments to make eye contact. Her way, he supposed, of showing utter contempt for them.

When she spoke she said simply, "Fellows, we've got us a little problem."

"What we've got is a war," Ralling said hotly.

"Hey...you started it."

"We asked for trade agreements, and you tossed them in our face," Trailings said.

"Now see, that's the shit right there. Our country...Well, we've had a wee little problem with our upper class. It was our—mine and my dear departed husband's—every intention to sign trade agreements with you. Unfortunately, we weren't aware that the nobles were attempting a coup until it was too late. We will shortly have things back under control..."

"You attacked one of our battle cruisers..." Ralling started.

"Hey, don't interrupt me, rat fucker. Your cowardly battle cruiser attacked me, and your bullshit about me being in a frigate fully loaded with weapons and all that crap is just that, bullshit. I was in one of my friggin' salvaging vessels, an imperial class salvaging barge, but a barge all the same. Your people fired on me. I defended my ship and my crew. If your people hadn't been damned inept, and if I wasn't the best fighter pilot in this galaxy—ah, screw the humble crap—the fucking universe, I'd be in pieces in the Galdart Desert instead of them. As it was, I had to crash land in a lake, which was really messy."

She obviously wasn't intimidated by his lofty position, but then why should she be? He was only a president who had lots of people to answer to; she was queen, the king was dead, and as such she had no one to answer to for her actions. As soon as this whole war thing was over, he was going to see if he couldn't get them to make him king.

"How dare you speak to me in this manner!" he said, thinking of nothing else to say.

"Ah, let's cut through the crap. We don't want a war. If you will call off your war, we will sign treaties and trade agreements with you. We will even send advisors to teach your people how to set up for recycling..."

"Why should we make deals with you?" General Tryte said. "You attacked our capital. Tens of thousands were killed..."

"I didn't do shit. I told you already that was the nobles. I'm back in command now, and I have the power to call off the attacks..."

"We are militarily superior to you..."

The queen laughed loudly at Tryte's suggestion. "How do you figure that? Our economy has been thriving. We're taking in billions in tax revenue monthly. What do you think we have been doing with all that money? Maybe shoving it up our asses?"

"We've done many reconnaissance missions, and we know that you have scrapped out much of your weaponry. We know that we are militarily superior, and that there is no way that you can win a long term war against us."

"Apparently more money buys better spies as well, because the way we understand it, we are by far militarily superior to you. If you insist on continuing this idiocy, we will stomp your butt into oblivion." She never even blinked.

"Thousands of our people are dead...they must be avenged. We will not back down. We know your reputation well, and know that you lie as easily as most people tell the truth," Tryte said.

"Ah, now that hurts," she said in mock agony. Then she glared back at them, no hint of fear in her cold blue eyes. "This is one bluff you don't want to call. No one shall win in a battle between our two countries, and many shall lose. You more than us, but I prefer to stop the death now and get on with the business of commerce."

Tryte bent down and whispered in Ralling's ear. "I know it looks like we are losing so far...but I swear to you that there is no way that we can lose this war. When we win, then all that they have will be ours. Why should we share when we can have it all?"

Ralling nodded and glared back at the Barion queen. "There will be no truce. We cannot and will not let our dead go unavenged. We will totally smite you, and to the victor go the spoils."

Trailings bent down and whispered in his ear. "Don't do this. It's in our best interest to make a truce, to go for the trade agreements. There is no way of knowing whether we are militarily superior or not. She's right on at least one count: in this war no one will win."

Trailings' objections more or less sealed the deal for him. He looked at the queen again and addressed the smug look on her face. "In my country we care about more than just profit. We are a proud people, and when we are victorious, we shall no longer walk cowed, but will hold our heads up high..."

"Yeah, what ever. Don't say I didn't warn you." She closed the transmission, and he was looking at a blank screen.

"What the hell have you done to us?" Trailings asked, literally tugging at his hair.

"I have insured that the future of our country is one of wealth and prosperity instead of poverty and despair." Ralling glared at Tryte, and said with meaning, "Isn't that right, Tryte?"

Tryte nodded emphatically.

"So what now, military idiots?" Trailings demanded.

"We attack. We attack hard and fast while they're still dealing with their internal problems. We make a giant hole in their landscape and even the score," Tryte answered. "We hit Hepron Station as we planned to, only with even more fire power."

"Well?" Facto asked. Dylan had taken over the job of babysitting the queen's sister, and he was once again doing his actual job, head Councilor to the Monarch.

"Well what?" Drew asked, taking a drink from the beer bottle she held in her hand.

"Are they militarily superior to us?"

"You're head councilor. You know this shit. What do you think?" Drew asked hotly.

"That while we've turned much of our weapons of mass destruction into scrap and sold it, and turned many of our munitions plants into recycling venues, they have continued to build their war machine..."

Drew took over from him, probably just to prove that she was up on what was going on. "However, the weapons we have replaced some of those with are bigger and better. Our military manpower is as large and far better trained. We would win the war, but it would be a long and bitter uphill battle, and an economic nightmare. Many of our people would be killed, both military and civilian. Not at all a very profitable endeavor. Well, send in the news guys, and let's get this over with."

Facto nodded and left.

"So what we going to do?" Arcadia asked when he was gone.

"I'm going to give a very good 'Let's go kick their asses speech,' and then you and Dylan and I are going to empty out the safe and get the hell off this rock. We'll meet Van Gar in space and find another location for our salvaging operation, and then we'll evacuate all our people from this planet," Drewcila said.

Arcadia looked a little shocked. "You'd really do that? Leave these people without leadership? Take away their livelihoods?"

"Hey...they're fuckin' up my business!"

"Give me ten more," the queen addressed them from behind her desk. She was on a comlink, so they could only hear her side of the conversation. "I just saw the report where ol Atario first admitted to killing Zarco and then bought the big one. I am now sole ruler of Barious. As such, you are now under my command, General...I tried, the Lockhedes will not back off...First, I want you to launch an attack on the nobles in the castle. Shoot to kill. I want every last one of them out of the castle, my staff returned to their posts there, and a mint on my pillow by sunrise tomorrow morning. Second, I want you to put the military on the highest possible alert, with double man power around the capital and all the spaceports and major recycling centers. The real bone of contention for the Lockhedes is that we live so much better than they do, so they're going to target our economic areas...I'm glad to be back, too. Now go kill some nobles and make me proud."

She hung up the phone and put a cigar in her mouth. Arcadia almost tripped over her tail to light it. The queen took a long drag on it and let it out, making smoke rings as she did so. "You there," she pointed at one of the grips who then pointed at himself and said: "Me?"

"Yeah, you. You're sitting on my ice chest."

He jumped up like his butt was on fire. "A million pardons, my Queen."

The queen smiled broadly. "It's all right if you sit on my ice chest, I was just wondering if you'd bring me a beer. My throat gets awful dry when I'm smoking and giving a 'Here's how we save the planet' speech." The man opened the chest, reached in and pulled out a beer. He brought it carefully to the queen and handed it to her. "Thanks...Arcadia?" she asked holding up the beer.

"No thanks," Arcadia told the man, who then sat upon the ice chest as if it were a great honor.

Drew popped the cap off the beer on the corner of her desk and then took a long drink before she looked up at Dartan. "All right, let's get this trash out of the can."

Dartan nodded and said, "Going live in five, four, three, two..."

"Are we on now?" Drew asked. To which Dartan nodded anxiously. "All righty then. Here's the shit, gang. Zarco and I wanted to sign trade agreements with the Lockhedes. This would have helped to stabilize their economy, made us a shit load of money, and brought us a lasting peace. The nobles— what a bunch of bastards—am I right? Well, of course I am, being right is what being queen is all about. Anyway, these rich fucks, they forced Zarco to give some speech about how he wanted us to go to war, and a bunch of other flowery crap about returning the glory of our country, yada yada yada. Well, I knew that was shit, so I came back here, and, well, you more or less know what went down, since that rat Atario just confessed on the other network...Sorry about that one, Dartan."

Dartan smiled and shrugged.

Drewcila continued. "Our troops even now are moving to attack the nobles still holed in the castle, and the governor general has assured me that they will all be dead by morning. Our real problem is that they have already started this war with the Lockhedes. I personally shot down the Artvail, and I hope the people of Lockhede can hear and see this, because they are being fed the same sort of misinformation that you were. They are being told that our vessel fired on their battle cruiser. My people, this was not the case. I mean...do I look fucking stupid? It was a battle cruiser—the biggest in their fleet. I'm flying in one of my salvaging ships with minimal armaments. They fired on us, and it's only by luck that I was able to avoid being shot out of the sky and save myself and my crew. It was never my intention to bring down their ship, merely to defend my own. It was a freak accident that their ship went down the way it did. My own ship had to crash land. So why on Barious would I have attacked that big battle cruiser? No, they attacked me. They attacked me because they were big, and they didn't know who they were messing with." She paused a moment for effect, then continued.

"I called the leaders of Lockhede and tried to offer them a peace agreement and the trade agreement they originally asked for. They wanted none of it. The Lockhede people are not our enemies, it's only their leaders. Leaders that, like our own nobles have done to us, force their people to do things they know are wrong. Still...like it or not, we are going to have to pull out the big guns and start kicking some Lockhede butt. They don't really understand what they are up against. They fight us because they have nothing to lose. Their country is a poverty stricken cesspool, and their people are starving.

"We on the other hand, have a standard of living worth fighting for. We aren't the mollycoddled pampered pussies they seem to think we are. We took out the largest of their battle cruisers and decimated their capital, and we weren't even really trying. Imagine the devastation when we actually go after them! If they so much as fart in our direction, we will be going after them with everything we've got, and we won't stop till they either surrender or Lockhede is nothing but a smoking hole. I will be moving from one location to another in order to keep the Lockhedes from attempting to kidnap me as they have done in the past, or kill me as the nobles tried to do. You may not see or hear from me for weeks at a time. But do not lose heart. Just because you can't see me, doesn't mean I'm not here. Good night."

"My Queen, there are questions about the current state of our military. Can we really trust them? Are they on our side, or are they working for the nobles?" Dartan asked.

"Our military took orders from the head of the country. Not an easy thing to do when no one's really sure who's running things. They will take my orders, they will do what's best for the country. They are not now, and never were, part of the coup attempt."

"Are you afraid for your own life?"

"We are at war, people. Every man, woman, and child should be in fear for their life tonight. This isn't a game. They have weapons of mass destruction, but so do we. The sooner we can talk some sense into their stupid leaders' heads, the better it will be for everyone," Drewcila said.

"What arrangements will be made concerning the king's burial? Will there be a national service? A quiet family one?"

"A dead body is a dead body. The king's problems are over. We are at war, and I hardly think it's a good idea to bring myself and large numbers of our statesmen and the heads of our military together for such a thing. Might as well pull our pants down and paint bullseyes on our butts. A service will be held when and where we think it's appropriate. No prior knowledge will be given out. It will be small. The people should grieve in their own ways, maybe light a candle."

"My Queen..."

"I'm sorry, Dartan, but I have places to go and things to do." She stood up and started out of the room with Arcadia and Facto following behind her. She stopped at the doorway and turned to look at them as a group. "Ah, nothing personal, but you guys need to get out of my office. You know...I'm leaving, you should leave."

Dartan nodded. "It will take us a minute."

"Lock up when you go."

Drew stopped the disk and turned towards her sister. "See, you see, now I think some one owes someone else a little thing called an apology."

"Zarco's still dead, Drewcila. No, you didn't actually kill him, but you wanted him dead. If you had brought him with us, he might still be alive. You heard what Atario said, if you were dead he wouldn't have killed Zarco." Stasha, who had stopped crying, started all over again.

"Screw you then. I give up. There's no pleasing you. You'd rather I was dead than Zarco? What a hateful thing to say. Why, if they were talking to me—and if they didn't love you better—I'd call our mother and father and tell on you," Drew said nodding her head. She was trying to sound flip, and hoped she had succeeded, because it was in fact bugging the living shit out of her that Stasha was so mad at her, that she had said she hated her. To add to her problems, Van Gar had been very suspicious when she had asked him to stay in orbit instead of landing, and Arcadia was trying so hard not to look like she was pouting that it was obvious to everyone that she was. Although she hadn't told Facto her plans, it was obvious that he'd figured out from her speech that she was planning to bolt, and he just kept giving her this 'very disappointed' look, which seemed to have the ability to make her want to confess to crimes she hadn't even committed.

Everyone seemed to be hell-bent on judging her for something, and the truth was that she really didn't understand why. Maybe when they were taking out the part of her brain that held her previous memories, they had also removed the part that was able to comprehend why everyone she had any personal relationship with immediately became completely and totally unreasonable.

She found that their obvious disapproval, anger, and indignation was making it incredibly difficult to be wantonly selfish and self-serving, which was putting her completely off her game. She had this strange, unusual urge to somehow try to please them all, and that just wasn't like her at all.

It must be some residual effect of the poison.

An uncomfortable silence had fallen over the room. Everyone seemed to be looking at her, as if waiting for her to rationalize and make excuses for her actions, both in recent and ancient history. Except she didn't think anything she had done was really wrong, and even if it was she certainly didn't care...except that it was driving her crazy that they were all varying degrees of pissed off at her. She glared around the room at them for several minutes, daring one of them to say...well, anything at all. Nobody said anything. They just stood there, silently bombarding her psyche with varying degrees of displeasure till she could stand it no longer.

"Screw all of you!" She threw up her hands and stormed out of the room. Arcadia and Dylan followed her out and ran to catch up with her as she stomped down the hall. She stopped suddenly and turned on them, causing them to crash into each other. "You can only come with me if you think you can quit judging me."

"Judging you? Shit, Drew! What the fuck are you talking about? I ain't judging you," Dylan said in a confused tone. She glared at him as if trying to read his mind, then she swung on Arcadia. "But you are...!"

"I think maybe you're judging yourself, Drew," Arcadia said calmly.

Drew spun back around and started back down the hall with purpose. "What the fuck is that supposed to mean? Why would I judge myself? I'm not doing anything wrong. This operation has become unprofitable. At any moment we could be bombarded. I'm leaving, and I'm taking my money with me. There's nothing bad or evil about it. It just makes good plain sense."

"I didn't say it didn't. I also didn't say that I was the one with morals and ethics. I implied that perhaps you were," Arcadia said, a hint of laughter in her voice.

Drew stopped and spun on her abruptly. She stood nose to nose with Arcadia, and punched Arcadia's shoulder with her forefinger. "You wash your filthy mouth out this minute."

"Sorry," Arcadia said with a smile and a shrug.

"Come on, let's get this show on the road," Drew said spinning back around and walking faster this time.

"If you say so," Arcadia said.

"Damn it, Arcadia! Quit doing that," Drew said over her shoulder. "I don't care. I don't care about my stupid sister or the stinking country. All I care about is my money and my empire, and I'm not going to let these idiots ruin all that I have worked and grifted to get."

"I know that."

"I said, knock it off!"

"All right, I will."

"If you keep it up, I'm going to leave you here."

"If you have to."

"Dylan, smack the shit out of her," Drew ordered hotly.

"No, she'll hurt me bad. I don't know what the hell you're actually even fighting about, so leave me the hell out of it," Dylan said.

Drew ignored them both. She knew what she had to do. If her sister knew her "secret" vault was at Hepron Station, so did other heads of state. If other heads of state knew, it was a sure bet that the Lockhedes knew. And if they knew, they'd figure out she was here, and they'd aim every bomb they had at them. She and her money weren't going to be here when that happened. None of this was her fault. She hadn't caused any of this shit, why should she have to suffer for it?

Putting the vault in her chambers would have been too obvious. The vault was hidden under a sliding panel in the farthest of the six loading bays of the station.

She ordered the area cleared, and by the time they got there they were alone. She opened the secret panel and punched in a code. The floor opened, and when they had walked through, it closed behind them. Six doors and six codes later they were standing outside the main vault.

"How does it open?" Arcadia asked, seeing no recognizable panel.

"Ah! Now you see, people, that's the beauty of it." She found the secret panel, flipped it open, and punched some buttons on it, which caused a long thin panel with thousands of points of light to pop out. "A retinal scan can be very easily duplicated, finger prints are the same way, and voice activation is a joke. But did you know that each tongue has its own unique signature?"

"I knew yours did," Arcadia answered with a smile.

Drew smiled back, then continued to explain. "You can get a cold in your eye. A scar can screw up your fingerprints, but what the hell could happen to your tongue?" She stuck her tongue on the pad, and nothing happened.

"Oh, I don't know, Drew," Dylan said angrily. "Some idiot drunk could let some alien whore paint God only knows what on it."

"This can't fucking be happening!" Drew tried it again and again and again, until her tongue was completely dry, and still nothing happened. Then she went completely ballistic. She started kicking the vault door and screaming, "You stupid worthless forty-hundred-thousand iggy piece of crap! Give me my fucking money! You hear me? I said give me my fucking money!"

Arcadia turned to Dylan as they both ignored Drew's rampage. "Look on the bright side, now you can continue to try to bed Stasha."

"Oh, I am sooo over her. I tried to help console her after she heard about Zarco's death, and she called me a perverted pig. Hell, I might be perverted, but I ain't no pig."

"How were you trying to console her?" Arcadia asked with a knowing smile.

"I dove between her legs."

"Hell, that always works with Drew."

"Do you think you two assholes could stop with your little tête-à-tête and come help me?" Drew yelled.

Arcadia and Dylan looked at each other, shrugged, then walked over and started kicking the safe and cussing.

Drewcila was less than amused.

"I'm not leaving without my money, Van Gar!" Drew screamed at his picture on the viewing screen.

"Any idea when that crap on your tongue is supposed to go away?"

"None at all, but I'm pretty sure it's fading."

"Well, I hope the shit at least did what they promised it would," Van Gar laughed.

"It's not fucking funny, Van, and for the record, no. Not as far as I could tell. What a fucking mess!"

"New game plan?"

"Yeah, meet us in Capital. We'll be leaving here within the hour and taking up residence in the castle. After all, that's the last place those Lockhede bastards will think to look for me. I've got to find a way to win this fucking war. Quick."

"Tell the truth, Drewcila, you're sort of glad you have to stay there and save the country," Van Gar needled.

"I wish everyone would just get off my back!" Drewcila spat back angrily.

"So you're alone now. No one to show off for. Did you miss me at all?"

"When did I have time?"

"Ah, come on, Drew..."

"All right! Damn! What the hell is happening to me? Yes! Yes, I fucking missed you."

"And do you love me, Drew?"

"You're pushing your luck, Van Gar." She closed the transmission.

Van Gar looked at the blank screen and smiled.

"So?" Shreta asked from behind him.

For answer he addressed the com. "All hands, prepare for entry. We're going planet side. We will be landing in the Barion capital port Ionan."

Drewcila moved quickly now. Her ship was fueled and ready to go. A short planet hop was a simple maneuver, and she'd be piloting.

Stasha pitched a bitch and said she was not going back to the castle with Drew, so Drew had her sedated. Stasha, Margot, and Facto were already on the Garbage Scow. Drew left final orders for the station, grabbed her computer, and she, Arcadia, Dylan and Jurak followed Dartan and the news team, who were filming their departure.

Arcadia stopped suddenly and grabbed Drew's arm. "I hear something."

"Everyone stop!" Drew ordered.

Arcadia's head swung around and up to their right. As they followed her movements, everyone saw the missile coming through the clear domed ceiling above them.

They ran, scattering in different directions. Drewcila, Arcadia and Dylan dove behind a huge rock planter as the missile hit. The dome held against the impact, but blew into a million pieces with the explosion.

Drew covered her head to protect it from the debris that rained down on top of them. She yelled into her comlink. "We are under attack! Repeat. The station is under attack! Man all battle stations! Stomp these fuckers' asses!"

She pulled her side arm, although she wasn't sure what she thought she was going to do with it. This was an air strike, so there was really nothing to shoot at. Still, how could you feel battle ready if you weren't armed? Arcadia and Dylan must have felt the same way, because they had both pulled their weapons as well.

She could hear the sounds of the station's defenses as the anti-aircraft guns started firing steadily.

"They must have sent everything they had," Drew said.

Arcadia nodded.

Drew looked around at the devastation, looking for a safe passage way to get them to her ship, and saw Jurak lying amidst the rubble. She ran up to him with Arcadia and Dylan following behind her. They grabbed him and pulled him into a more protected area. He didn't look good. In fact, it looked as if his chest had been flattened. He didn't seem to be in any real pain, which was of course the worse sign of all.

"Hey, Jurak, what were you trying to do? Catch that thing?" Drewcila asked, moving a bloody strand of hair away from his face.

"I'm dying."

"No, no, you're not, Jurak. You're a little squished, that's all. Here," she reached in her pocket, pulled out the hat, and stuck it on his head. "There. Now that ought to do it."

"Not this time." The life left his eyes, and his body went into spasms. Drew tried to hold him still. When he stopped jerking, she was still holding him.

"Drew," Arcadia said putting a hand on her shoulder. "He's gone. We have to get out of here."

Drew nodded, let go of Jurak and stood up. "Now I'm pissed off! This way. Let's go!" She took off running through, around, and over the debris. Arcadia and Dylan followed with Dartan and the news crew not far behind them.

"Incoming!" Arcadia yelled, and again they scattered and hit the floor. This time the devastation was immediate since the dome was already broken. As soon as the dust began to clear, Drewcila screamed.

"Move! Move!"

"Drew, I don't see Dylan."

A quick search found him lying unconscious with his right leg stuck under a large piece of fallen ceiling. The whole place looked like it could come down with one more direct hit.

"Dylan, can you hear me, man?" Drew asked.

There was a muttering sound that echoed from his lips.

"What did he say?" Arcadia asked at her shoulder.

"Sounded like, go on, leave me here, save ourselves." Drew started to leave, and Arcadia grabbed her arm and shook her head no.

Drew sighed, and she and Arcadia put their shoulders to the chunk of rubble. "Hey, you think some of you stupid media fucks could stop filming long enough to help us out here?" Drew ordered.

They slung their equipment down, still running—after all, they didn't want to completely lose the moment—and helped. Arcadia pulled Dylan out as soon as his leg was free and slung him unceremoniously over her shoulder. They started running again. They finally made it out of the building and onto the loading bay. Above them was an air fight of epic proportions, and it was impossible to see who was winning. Not that it really mattered, because down here on the ground, where they all were, all that really mattered was that all the shit that was being shot off machines above them was falling around their heads.

They made a run for the Garbage Scow. When they were all in, Drew closed the hatch and ran for the flight deck. "All hands prepare for escape velocity."

"What?" Arcadia asked in a near panic.

"Hang with me, chick, I've got a plan. Everyone strap in, secure the wounded." Drewcila launched herself into her seat, punched some buttons, and the ship's engines came on line and started powering up. "Take off in ten, nine, eight..." She punched the launch button, and they shot up in the air like a cat with a firecracker up its ass. Debris and a small ship or two bounced off their hull, doing little or no damage.

"You skipped a bunch of numbers, Drew!" Arcadia accused, hanging on for dear life to a seat she hadn't had time to fasten herself into.

"Well, here they are. Pulling the warp engine off line in seven, six, five, four, three..."

"Are you fucking crazy!" Arcadia forced herself into the seat, and quickly fastened her harness.

"...two, one." Drew took the warp drive off line, and the ship stopped abruptly, and then started falling. She put the interplanetary engines on line, and their decent slowed. They finally stopped just a few thousand feet above the dog fight below.

"Arcadia..."

"Can't talk. Stomach in tail," Arcadia said with a gulp.

"Take command of the weapons console."

Arcadia nodded, silently unstrapped herself, got up, staggered to the appropriate console, and strapped herself in, double-checking her harness.

"Van Gar, this is Drewcila. Where are you?"

"I was on my way to the capital. What in hell's name are you doing? Trying to rip your ship in two?"

"It would take a hell of a lot more than that to blow my ship. I'm in a fucking planet of trouble here, Van. Hepron Station—you know, the same Hepron Station where all my iggys are?—is under fire. I swear, it looks like the Lockhedes sent their entire fleet. I blew out of there quick because I wanted to be on top of the bastards, not under them."

"Well, that at least makes sense."

"I'm going to attack."

"Are you fucking nuts?"

"I didn't know that was ever a question. Get your ass over here and back me up."

"Drewcila..."

"I'm going in. Are you going to come back me up, or leave me blowing in the wind?"

"I'm coming, but at least wait for me."

"No can do. They killed my favorite lackey, and I'm royally pissed," Drew said simply and started the ship moving again. She looked at Arcadia, who was silent now. "Well, aren't you going to tell me that we don't need him here?"

"No. I know you well enough to know that whatever you're planning probably is insane. We definitely do need Van Gar now. His skill was never in question." She smiled then. "If it had been, he wouldn't have been any competition whatsoever."

Dartan had forced his crew to follow him to the bridge where the queen had said they could stay, but that they would have to find something to strap themselves to, as she fully intended to join the battle. Dartan had never stopped reporting, and his crew had never stopped shooting, and they were running live all over Barious. This was the story, this was the moment for which he would be remembered throughout the history of Barion journalism, and since he might very likely get killed in the next few minutes, he was going to make it count.

"The queen has moved her ship into a position where she can very easily see the battle going on below us and over Hepron Station. Our forces are obviously taking a beating. But the queen's ship is a large class freighter with a very thick hull, and we are told it carries more weapons than it's legally allowed to carry..."

"Hey, idiot boy!" Drew screamed. "Did it ever dawn on you that the Lockhedes might actually watch TV, too? Why don't you just go ahead and tell them exactly where we are and how to kill us!"

"Sorry," Dartan said sheepishly.

"Don't be sorry, be smart."

Dartan nodded. "Cut the audio. For now stick with visual."

The queen stuck a cigar in her teeth and lit it with her laser side arm. The ship seemed to have momentarily stopped. The Queen took a long draw on the cigar and holstered her side arm. Leaving the cigar clenched between her teeth, she puffed the smoke out and then announced through her teeth. "Hang on, boys and girls. It's party time!"

She punched it, and the ship went screaming into the battle. It hit two small enemy planes, and they blew up. Apparently the ship was big enough and strong enough that such impacts did no damage at all.

Then the ship seemed to spin completely around.

"Targeting frigate," Arcadia announced. The ship lurched with the recoil as the guns fired a large missile. The frigate exploded in a ball of fire, and Drewcila pulled the nose of the ship up and over the burning wreckage.

Dartan figured out what was happening. The queen was maneuvering the ship into the best firing position, and the lizard woman manning the weapons station was targeting and firing at the precise moment that it would do the most damage. To do this as successfully and as seemingly effortlessly as they were doing it, it couldn't have been the first time. Drewcila moved the ship through the corridors of both enemy and friendly planes and ships, targeting the bigger and more dangerous Lockhede ships. The Valtarian aimed and fired, picking them off with deadly accuracy. But they were starting to take hits themselves now, and the computer was squawking about where and to what extent the ship was being damaged. It looked like they had met their end when they came nose to nose with a large frigate that had her canons aimed right at them. If they both fired, they'd both get hit, and one of them would go down. The other ship didn't seem as damaged as theirs sounded like it was. Then suddenly the ship in front of them exploded.

"What took you so long?" Drewcila asked with a hint of laughter in her voice.

"I hit traffic," a strong male voice replied.

Dartan looked at her, and longed to tell the people what he was seeing. She wasn't afraid. There was part of her, perhaps the larger part, that was actually enjoying this. There was no fear on her face, nor in the voice of whoever had just ridden to their rescue.

"Target?" the male voice asked.

"Ship eight," she answered, and Dartan assumed they had some grid that marked the ship's locations and numbered them to make it easier to target. "You go starboard."

"Got you. On your command."

"Now."

The entire complexion of the battle changed in that moment. No longer were they the defenders; they had become the aggressors. As he had watched the queen and Valtarian work together as if one, these two ships and their crews now worked together—creating a greater unity. Two ships moved as if with one mind, zeroing in on targets, watching each other's backs, and totally crushing the enemy. All around him he could see the ship's crew—he guessed they were techs—running around making repairs even as the ship lurched and bucked and changed speed. They were on long harnesses which he assumed gave them some protection from the ship's lurching, but didn't keep them from being knocked down. They would get knocked down, get right back up again, and continue the work they had been doing as if nothing had happened. This ship's crew was a strange mixture of Barions and aliens from every corner of the universe, and at least for this moment it was only their appearance that was different.

It seemed like hours, but it probably wasn't more than fifteen minutes before the Lockhedes turned tail and started to run. They were retreating, and Dartan was sure they would be allowed to retreat.

"Run them down and destroy them!" Drewcila ordered.

"But, my queen...they are retreating," Dartan objected.

"Then it will be harder for them to fire on us, won't it?"

And it was. In minutes the remaining Lockhede vessels were blown out of the sky.

"Hepron Station, do you read?" Drewcila asked as they turned to head back in the direction of the station.

"Aye, aye. The tower's hit, but still standing," a female voice replied.

"Good...Call all ships back to the station. Remain on Dirty-Red-Dog-Alpha-6-Alert until told otherwise. Start repairs at once. If they have intelligence anywhere near, I want them to think that they have done minimum damage. Get rid of the bodies as quickly as possible. We want morale to stay high, and there is something about dead bodies that just brings down the spirit of the whole place."

"Sorting the bodies from the rubble alone could take weeks," the voice answered.

"Then don't sort the bodies from the rubble. Find an empty canyon. Shove all the debris, bodies and all, into piles. Cart it off and dump it in the canyon. I don't even want you to worry about the recyclable materials. Right now image is everything. If they think they have lost a huge chunk of their fleet and haven't given us more than a scratch, their morale, which was already low to begin with, is going to plummet."

"But Drew...people will be asking about their loved ones. They'll want to bury them..."

"They're going to be buried. I don't have time for a whole lot of sentimental bullshit. If I can throw away perfectly good trash, then they can deal with losing a few bodies. If someone doesn't call home, it means they're dead. When we get done cleaning up the mess we'll cover the debris with dirt, and I'll have a huge memorial erected there with the names of all the dead on it to commemorate those who fell because of Zarco's absurd stupidity."

"Zarco's?" Dartan asked in confusion.

"Did I say Zarco? I meant to say Atario. Their names sound alike. Don't you think they sound alike?"

"Ah...I guess so," Dartan said.

Drew smiled broadly at him. "Oh, I do so love a man who humors me."

Chapter 11

Van Gar lay in the huge bed, stared up at the ceiling, and didn't even try to pry the stupid grin from his face.

Drew lay with her head on his chest, almost but not quite asleep, and at least for the moment all seemed right with his world.

"You suppose blue blood is going to be any harder to get out of the carpets than regular blood?" Drew asked sleepily.

Van Gar laughed. "Could you have really just run off and abandoned them?"

"If I could have gotten my iggys? In a fucking heartbeat. This kingdom is like a bad investment, if you can't sell the son of a bitch you grab all the liquid assets and walk away. Unfortunately, I couldn't get to my liquid assets."

"If you say so, Drew," Van Gar laughed.

"Don't you start with me. I'm ruthless and self serving, and I like me that way," Drew said emphatically. "I wish everyone would quit insinuating that I've grown some kind of conscience! Why the very thought makes me want to vomit."

Van Gar wrapped his arms tightly around her and kissed the top of her head. "I was...it was stupid for me to leave you, Drew, over something so trivial..."

"As four guys, two chicks, a midget and a goat," she supplied.

"For any reason," he said through gritted teeth.

"It certainly was. And joining a crack pot religious cult run by some second-rate grifter...well, that was just fucking priceless," Drew said with a laugh. "Next time you're going to punish me, you might try something less masochistic."

"Well, I did turn all that around," Van Gar reminded her quickly.

She picked her head up and turned to look at him momentarily. "Oh, do tell?" She kissed him, then lay her head back on his chest.

She sounded genuinely interested, so he told her the whole story, adding special emphasis to the parts where he had been particularly clever, brave and/or tough. Skipping over the part where he was stupid enough to actually believe Pard Jar, instead insisting that it had been his plan to take everything away from the religious freak all along. He completely left out the part where he'd gotten his ass kicked by the foremen and had been forced to work for green glop.

She was quiet throughout the telling, and so he was sure that she was completely enthralled with his tale. That was until the bitch started snoring.

He was more than a little put out. He was sure that he'd never tell the story quite as well as he just had, and he had no way of knowing just how much she had actually heard.

He knew he should be exhausted, but he just wasn't. The castle was a mess, but apparently the cleaning and maintenance staff had knocked themselves out returning the queen's quarters to their normal pristine state. Of course, Van Gar doubted a bunch of disgruntled nobles or even an angry mob could do much more damage than Drew did when she was on a really good toot. No doubt the staff had developed a system for removing the debris from Drew's room, quickly patching holes in the walls and covering them over with well-placed pieces of the wall paper.

He yawned. He was a very rich man, and Drew would have to respect him now.

Except...now that Zarco was dead she was sole ruler of a whole fucking country. Damn it! The bitch had stolen his thunder.

Dylan was none too happy. His leg was broken, and the only doctor in the castle had been dragged up from the dungeon, and turned out to be the same one who had done such an absolutely nothing job on Drew. Of course when he'd finished working on Dylan's leg and taken care of a couple of other minor injuries suffered by the crew, they'd locked the bastard back in the dungeon. So if he hadn't done what he was supposed to have done, they'd know right where to find him. Of course, the bastard had kept saying he knew nothing about alien anatomy the whole time he was working on him, so he might have screwed up accidentally. Didn't really matter; if he didn't heal quick and right, he was still going to kill that bastard.

The doctor had cleaned Dylan up, which sucked, because if he was going to have a sponge bath, he preferred he get it from some pretty nurse instead of some gnarly looking old guy. After he'd cleaned Dylan up, he'd given him some sort of pain killer and set his leg. He must have really given him the pain killer, too, because if he hadn't, with the pain Dylan had already been in, he was pretty sure that he would have crapped himself if he'd had to feel his leg pulled back into place. He was now laying in bed in one of those stupid gowns with no back in it, with some light shining on the leg which was supposed to cause the bone to repair itself in forty-eight hours.

Of course, as the doctor had said some twenty times, Dylan wasn't Barion, and he couldn't be sure that he would heal the same. Dylan still couldn't really feel his leg yet, so he had no idea whether the little light thingy was working or not.

He felt like a dork laying there under a fucking light. Like some hot house flower in that stupid gown with no back. He wondered why he couldn't have some boxer shorts and a T-shirt.

He supposed that was too damn much to ask for.

It was funny when he thought about it. It seemed that no bipedal people had been able to construct a hospital gown which actually covered your ass. He understood that the gowns were constructed this way to make it easier for the doctors and nurses to care for you, but was there some reason that they couldn't invent a gown that could cover your ass that opened easily enough that it didn't inhibit treatment of the patient?

In fact, if Dylan really put his mind to it, there were a whole lot of things that he was really surprised hadn't been invented. For instance, couldn't someone somewhere find a way to make a tube of lubricant so that it didn't sound like a big juicy fart when you dispensed the product? When you were all revved up and in the moment, there was nothing quite like having to stop everything to explain that you didn't do it, that it was just the tube.

And hemorrhoids...what the hell was up with that? Hundreds and thousands of scientists all over the universe, and several hundred different species all suffered from the damn things. Yet no one had found a really good way to treat them that didn't leave you feeling like someone had stuck a slimy candle up your butt. Made you feel like you must be leaving a slime trail like a slug. Seemed like there ought to be a better way.

As soon as he got better, he was going to put his mind into inventing some of these items. Fellow could make himself a damn fortune.

"Dylan?" a soft voice called out, interrupting his thoughts of industrial conquest.

Dylan turned towards the voice and saw Stasha in the doorway. Seeing that he was awake, she walked in.

"How are you feeling?" she asked.

"Like someone said my dick was too short. I'll be fine. How 'bout you?" Dylan shifted in his bed, trying to get more comfortable.

"It's hard...being back here. Knowing he's not here." She sniffled a little, then started to cry in earnest. "Knowing that he's never coming back," she sobbed.

Dylan guessed he shouldn't have asked. "Stasha...you have to pull yourself together, girl. This dude...I mean I know you loved him, but let's face it, sugar, he was sort of a jerk. He sure as hell didn't appreciate you."

"I know." She sniffed hard and seemed to be making a real effort to quit crying. She pulled a handkerchief from her pocket and wiped her nose. It was then that he noticed that she'd lost the Qwah-Co jumper she'd been forced to wear when they'd left Hepron Station, and had changed into a beautiful red silk dress that was almost...Well, for Stasha it was indecently short. She was wearing—he recognized the scent, and smiled—Ode To Salvager, Drewcila's normal fragrance.

"You all right, Stasha?" Dylan asked.

"No...I'm tired of it. I'm tired of always living in my sister's shadow. It was bad enough before. Before when she was just Zarco's queen, happy to stand behind him and wave at the people every once in awhile. Bad enough when she was gone, and we all thought most probably dead, and I knew I was nothing more than a replacement to him. But then she came back, and she's...well, she's magnificent. Look what she did! She saved the country and made herself rich at the same time. She took stuff that no one wanted, stuff that was thrown away, and she built an empire. The nobles and Zarco tried to wrest that empire away from her, and she took it back. And today I came to, and the ship was under fire. Margot told me what was happening, and I really thought we were all dead, that we'd breathed our last. Drewcila never even flinched..."

"You didn't see her when she couldn't get into her safe," Dylan said with a laugh.

Stasha ignored him. "She turned what could have been one of the darkest days in our nation's history into a military triumph. Everyone loves her. She treats everyone horribly, and yet they all love her. Our people, the salvagers, Van Gar, Arcadia, Zarco loved her..."

"Is there a point to all this, or would you just like to come over here close enough so that I can kick you with my good leg so you can take a break from kicking your self?" Dylan asked with a smile.

"The point is...I'm tired of being me. I've been thinking about what you said about everyone just pretending to be someone, and well it dawned on me that the only time I have been truly happy in years was when I was pretending to be my sister. When I would dress like her, and walk like her, and talk like her, and read the speeches she'd written for the public, and they would applaud and throw flowers. I keep damning her, but the truth is I *liked* being her. People respect her, they love her. No one loves me, and they surely don't respect me," Stasha said. "I'm sick to death of being nice, proper, and highly forgettable Stasha."

Dylan smiled charmingly and incanted the magical-getting-laid words as they had just been revealed to him, "Stasha...there is nothing forgettable about you. If I had the choice between you and Drewcila, why I'd pick you any day."

She ran to him and hugged him. He grabbed her head and kissed her. She didn't object. In fact, she hungrily kissed him back. This was a woman who was long over-due for some serious attention, and gimped up or not he was going to give it to her. He thought of it as sort of his civic duty. His mind was racing, trying to figure out how he was going to get his groove on with his leg broken and strapped under the "all healing" light.

As it turned out, he didn't have to figure out anything at all, because Stasha already seemed to have given it quite a bit of thought.

He didn't hate that hospital gown near as much as he thought he was going to.

Having momentarily lost her "toy of choice" status, Arcadia had gone down to her old quarters to see what damage had been wreaked upon her space. She expected the place to be completely wrecked, but it was worse than she had anticipated.

The "ambassadors" had been given a suite of rooms at the end of a long corridor, one which had originally been built for traveling dignitaries. As Drewcila's ambassadors, she, Pristin, and Dylan had split their time between the castle—dealing with the state-run part of the salvaging operation on Barious—

and the various stations, factories and recycling venues that belonged to Qwah-Co.

They'd each had their own bedrooms here, but had shared a large common room with all the latest in high tech entertainment. That room was now completely demolished. The view screens, computer games, and holographic projectors had been smashed to pieces.

It was hard to say when the rooms had been trashed. The nobles might have done it when they were looking for Dylan and Arcadia. Or they may have done it at any time just for shits and giggles. The rooms might have also been trashed by the horde of rioters who had apparently beaten the military into the castle and killed many of the nobles—mostly by beating them to death. They had trashed other areas of the castle, and there was a good chance that they might have thought that these rooms had been inhabited by the hated nobles.

Somehow Arcadia doubted it was the latter. They were now a salvaging country with a salvagers' mentality, and whoever had done their rooms had broken or ripped everything to pieces. The commoners weren't likely to have done damage to anything that might have resale value. They just didn't think that way anymore. The total devastation of the rooms, and the fact that she could see some of Pristin's clothing strewn around, just strengthened Arcadia's belief that the nobles had committed this crime. After all, Pristin's clothes were definitely an "alien's" clothing, and the common man on the street had no beef with the aliens. In fact, most commoners saw them as the bringers of a new and prosperous era for them all. Only the nobles had hated the alien presence the recycling trade had brought to their planet.

Pristin was dead. That was a hard pill to swallow. She'd worked with Pristin long before she'd ever been associated with Qwah-Co, before she'd ever even meet Drewcila. In those days she'd just been a simple salvager. Digging through piles of trash and picking out the good stuff. Pristin had been her buyer. He bought the crap she found and then shipped it to people who needed it. Drewcila hauled the stuff across the galaxy. That's how Arcadia had met Drewcila Qwah. Drew was on the docks one day hustling a bunch of workers along to hurry and load her trash, no doubt in an attempt to get them so rattled that they would load stuff that she hadn't actually paid for. For Arcadia the attraction had been immediate, and Drew must have felt the same way because they'd been in bed before they'd finished their second drink.

Drewcila had been in her life in one capacity or another ever since.

When Drew put Qwah-Co together, she'd been looking for people she could trust, as well as people who were competent, and she'd hired Arcadia and Pristin to oversee the operations on Barious, a position that had given them both power and money. Dylan had come a year later, when the workload got to be too much for Arcadia and Pristin to handle on their own.

Arcadia liked to think that Drew had moved her here to have a reason to at least occasionally spend some time with her. A notion which was fed by the fact that normally when Drewcila came to Barious, Van Gar wasn't with her.

Arcadia realized that she wasn't finding any of her clothing. Not a stitch of it, not her personal clothing or her Qwah-Co uniforms. Which didn't make any sense, because even though she had spent a small fortune on clothing and accessories, no Barion woman could wear her things. She started sifting through the rubble, getting more pissed off by the moment that some asshole had stolen her stuff. After forty minutes with no luck she gave up and decided to take a shower and go to bed. She cleared her bed off then made her way to the bathroom. Of course when she opened the shower door she found her clothes. Some fucker—actually probably more than one—had thrown her clothes in there, and no doubt took great pleasure in pissing on them.

It was just too much! Pris was dead. Drewcila was in her room with Van Gar doing things Arcadia didn't want to think about, and now some asshole had filled her shower with pissy clothes. And not just *any* clothes but *her* clothes.

She let out a deep, throaty growl and decided to go kill something.

Sortas wasn't an idiot. He knew that his life had only been slightly lengthened when he'd sold Atario out. The news crew had barely been able to save him when the unruly mob of commoners had stormed the castle. They had stuck him in the dungeon, thinking that it was altogether fitting that they should leave him for Drewcila to deal with. There were a few of the other nobles they had imprisoned instead of killing as well, no doubt because it was hard to kill a man when he had thrown down his weapons and was on his knees begging for his life. But none of them had escaped a serious beating— including Sortas.

He hurt everywhere, making it very hard to concentrate, and he desperately needed to concentrate. He had horribly miscalculated the situation. He had withheld treatment from the queen and had allied himself to Atario, a man who was destined to go down in the history books as the country's greatest traitor. When the commoners had come across Atario's body, they had literally ripped it to shreds.

The fact that Sortas had killed Atario and patched up a few of her crew wasn't likely to appease the queen's wrath. Drewcila, he now realized, was no fluke. She hadn't gotten where she was by birth and good breeding, or even by luck. Drewcila had gotten where she was because the little tart was sharp as a box of tacks. She understood people, and she understood business, and worst of all—since he was on the wrong side of her—she understood how best to deal with her enemies.

You killed them.

Dead people couldn't cause any trouble. He had caused her trouble. He had sided with the enemy against her and tried to take over her kingdom. She wasn't likely to believe the same story he had told the reporters that had won them over so entirely.

For one thing, she was painfully—at least for him—aware of the truth that he hadn't treated her poisoning. That he had left her to suffer, and suffer she had. It wasn't something she was likely to forget. Still, if he could somehow prove that he could be useful, even necessary, she might just let him live.

If he had it to do over again, he would have done everything differently. Treated her, done the autopsy on the king, and pointed the finger at Atario. He wasn't stupid enough to think that after this loss the nobles could ever again regain their place in this country. Drewcila had won. She was now in total control without even Zarco to buffer her, and the last time that had happened, she had changed the whole world, and his life.

Still, now that he reflected on it in this new light, he'd had a good life. It just wasn't up to par with what he had before, true. But he wanted to live, and in order to do that he had to find some way to convince Drewcila that he was not only truly sorry for what he had done, and would never do it again, but that it was also in her best interest to keep him alive.

Therein was the real problem. Repentance wasn't going to be enough to buy him a stay of execution. He had to somehow prove that she would be better off with him alive than she was with him dead.

He heard the guards addressing someone just outside the cell block, and then the Valtarian lizard woman strolled in the jail. He could see the blood lust in her eyes. He moved quickly to a corner of the cell and tried to make himself invisible.

She moved around the cell block looking into the cells, and the whole time he was very careful to keep his head down.

She laughed in a maniacal way, and said in that hissing voice of hers that made his flesh crawl, "I feel like a kid in a candy store. There is just so much to choose from, and..." She stopped suddenly in front of his cell, and said, "You!"

Sortas swallowed hard and looked up slowly, wondering what horrible death she had in store for him.

"Not you! You!" she hollered, pointing at another man in the cell.

"Me?" the man asked as the front of his pants darkened.

"Yeah, you, Come here."

The man walked over to the bars where she seemed to check him out the way a client in a restaurant might check out a piece of meat before having the cook sling it on the grill. After a few seconds she either smiled or snarled, Sortas couldn't be sure which, and then she grabbed the guy by his collar and jerked him into the bars. She let him drop to the floor, then opened the door. No one thought it was a good idea to rush her, which seemed to disappoint her. She dragged the still dazed man out of the cell, stood him up and shut the cell door. She looked him up and down, then plunged a claw into the flesh of the man's shoulder. The man cried out and started to fall, but she held him up with that one claw caught up in his flesh.

That's nice of her, Sortas thought.

"You know what you did, don't you?"

"No," the man gulped.

"Yes, you do. You're the shit that pulled the trigger that fired the blast that killed my little blue friend..."

"I...I was just following orders," he cried, then screamed as she twisted the claw in his shoulder again.

"Wrong answer. So...I'm going to let you go and give you a head start. If you get away...Well, you get away, if not..." she shrugged.

"Oh, gods, no! Please," he begged. She pulled the claw out of his shoulder, and he took off running. She gave him a three stride head start, then jumped over his head, landed in front of him, spun quickly and flipped her tail out so that a spike split the guy's head. He fell to the floor with a scream, and she put a foot on the man's head and pulled her tail free.

Sortas cringed. The lizard woman turned to look at them, and him in particular. She put the bloody claw to her mouth and slowly sucked the blood off. "Now you...I know who you are, too, and what you did. Or rather what you didn't do." She just smiled—or snarled—he still couldn't be sure which. "Just a little food for thought. Chew on it awhile. See how treason tastes. I won't make you wait long." She started to go, but stopped in the doorway and turned to look at them all. "And if I ever find out which one of you bastards pissed on my clothes...Well, let's just say I'm thinking of interesting ways to kill you."

She left. They heard her talking to the guard again, and since no one showed up to remove the body, Sortas guessed that she had asked him to leave it there.

Sortas refused to look towards the body. He had to think. He had to think fast, and he couldn't afford to waste time thinking about all the horrible ways she might kill him.

Of course, it was almost impossible to think about anything else.

Arcadia didn't feel like going back to her decimated room alone to brood, and since Drewcila had put a bar in the castle, there was no need to. She made a beeline for the bar, hoping against hope that it hadn't been trashed as badly as her own quarters had been.

Arcadia didn't know what the room had been before Drewcila had it turned into a bar, but it was big enough to harbor a full sized, fully stocked long bar, a small stage, a jukebox, and a dance floor besides a dozen tables.

She didn't know how it had happened. Maybe Drewcila's god, the deity of Party Hearty, had laid a protective hand over it. Whatever the cause, the bar had been untouched. The regular bartender was on duty, and there was at least one customer hugging the bar. Arcadia breathed in a deep breath of normalcy, walked up to the bar and sat down on her usual stool.

Abear walked over to her. "How..." she started.

"Drewcila had a force field installed over the door. When the shit hit the fan I closed the door, flipped on the force field, and hunkered down. It was rough. I had nothing to eat but pretzels and olives for two days."

"Oh…how horrible for you," Arcadia said sarcastically, thinking of how she'd spent the last few days.

Abear laughed. "I wondered why you guys didn't run in here during all the hubbub. I mean…I would have let you guys in."

"And then we would have all been stuck in here with no outside link, and how long do you think those olives and pretzels would have lasted?"

"With Drewcila in here, I would have been more worried about running out of liquor."

Arcadia cleared her throat. "Speaking of which, I'm sitting here, and I don't have my drink yet."

Abear laughed. "Sorry…Hurling Monkey?"

"Yeah…and add a twist." Arcadia plopped her elbow on the bar and then resting her chin in her claw, she sighed.

"Bad day?" he asked.

"What do you think?" Arcadia answered with a laugh.

"I was sorry to hear about Pris."

"Yeah, I just mutilated the guy that shot him, and yet I still don't feel any better."

"Go figure," he set her drink in front of her and lowered his voice still more. "I heard Van Gar's here."

"Yeah."

"I'm guessing that's cutting into your time with the boss."

"Yeah." Arcadia shrugged. "You know…I had her first!"

Of course he knew that, he heard Arcadia's bitches on a regular basis. She told him things she had probably never told another living soul, but then he was the bartender. It was a sacred trust and one he took seriously. People told him their problems, he pretended to listen, pretended to half care. They felt better, they drank a lot, and he had job security.

"Some people have everybody, while other people have no one," a slightly slurred voice said. The creature who had been at the other end of the bar had moved, and she now sat down next to Arcadia without asking. "Hardly seems fair," she added.

Arcadia looked up at the female Chitzsky and cringed. The poor thing had a face not even a mother would love on payday.

"Hello," Arcadia said in a voice dripping with implied 'go away and leave me alone.'

The interloper obviously didn't understand her, because she didn't move, and she just kept talking.

"My name's Shreta. I rode in with Van Gar." Shreta had obviously had more than a couple of drinks, and was well on her way to the worship of the porcelain god if she didn't slow down. Arcadia just wanted the ugly female to leave her the hell alone, and was about to say so when Shreta announced, "I...Van Gar...he was everything I ever dreamed of, and he wouldn't even look at me because he is so completely and totally in love with her."

Arcadia was thinking that he probably wasn't looking because he had a low puke level. However, now it was impossible for her to be rude to the woman. After all, here was someone who understood Arcadia's pain.

"When I was a baby, my parents took me to the supermarket and left me," Shreta slurred out. She was talking with her hands, apparently oblivious to the fact that the drink she was holding was spilling everywhere as she did so.

"They forgot you?" Arcadia asked.

"No, they left me there on purpose. But someone saw them and made them take me back."

Arcadia started laughing. "That's either the saddest fucking story I ever heard, or the funniest."

Abear sighed. He wished they'd leave so he could close up, go home. and get some sleep. It had been two hours since Arcadia had walked through the door, and she was now every bit as drunk as the Chitzsky woman had been when Arcadia walked in. Arcadia's tail was flopping all over the place. She'd already punched a hole in one of the bar stools, and he was literally taking his life into his hands every time he served her a drink. He was well aware that being that close to her put him well within range of her ever-flipping tail, and the dried blood caked onto one of the spikes did nothing at all to put him at ease.

The Chitzsky woman was now completely blitzed. The fact that she hadn't hurled yet was a small miracle and a testament to the Chitzsky race's strong constitution. Still, he wished they would leave before she started making the technicolor yawn.

"I had to take myself to my coming of age dance," Shreta announced in a slur.

"Did you get fresh with yourself?" Arcadia asked with a laugh much better than her joke was.

"Well, hell, yes."

They both laughed hysterically. Arcadia fell off her bar stool, and one of her tail spikes got stuck in the floor. She couldn't pull it out, which only made them laugh harder. Shreta climbed off her barstool and almost fell as she went to help Arcadia. When the two of them succeeded in pulling her tail from the floor, they both went sprawling on their asses—which was apparently the funniest thing that had happened yet.

"All right!" Abear screamed. They were quiet as they turned to look at him. And then for no apparent reason at all started laughing again. "Damn it, girls! It's two in the morning. You fought a dog fight today. Aren't either one of you tired? I would like to go home sometime this year."

"So go! No one's stopping you," Arcadia said with a flip of a claw.

Abear looked around the bar. Could he do that? He supposed he could; it wasn't like there was a till full of money that he was responsible for. The bar was complimentary to the castle staff and visitors.

"Great. I'm going home then," he said and started for the door. "You two try not to get into too much trouble."

They watched him go, than Arcadia levered herself up out of the floor and walked around the bar. She started mixing herself a drink. "What about you?"

"Nah. I drink one more I'm gonna spew."

Arcadia nodded. She sipped experimentally at the drink she'd just made herself. It tasted like shit. She decided to drink it anyway.

"You know," Shreta said, "I never thought about doing it with another female before. It might be fun. You, ah, want to..."

Arcadia made a face. "Geez, girl! I'm drunk, not blind. I mean...nah, that's more or less what I meant. You're a lot of fun, but damn, girl, you're just butt-ass ugly."

"You know, ugly people have feelings, too. Don't you think that's a little shallow of you? I mean, after all I don't actually find you to be physically attractive, but I'd fuck you."

"You've got a point there, but...no." Arcadia smiled then. "Of course that doesn't mean we have to tell them that we didn't."

Shreta looked as if she was about to say something of astute importance, and then she fell into the bar face first and slid to the floor.

Arcadia leaned over the bar to look at the prone body of her new friend. "All you had to say was no!"

Drewcila walked in the door to her office and thought, *And it started out as such a lovely day, birds singing and the whole trip.*

Her office had been purposefully and maliciously destroyed, and it didn't really make her feel any better that the people who did it were more than probably dead.

She had work to do. The whole country was going to hell in a hand basket, and so you would think that a little thing like a destroyed office would be the least of her problems. Of course, what some dumb fucks would fail to realize was that she couldn't actually *do* any of the things she needed to do without a computer, a vid screen, and several thousand iggys worth of high tech communications equipment which was now just so much techno trash.

"Facto!"

"I'm right here. You don't have to scream," he said rubbing at his ear.

"What's the king's office look like?"

"Four walls, two windows, a floor, a ceiling..."

"Your attempt at humor is almost as dull as you are," Drewcila said with a sigh. "Are his computer and communications equipment intact?"

"No. Well, I mean to say I don't know. See, your office was trashed by the nobles, but his was trashed by the locals, and..."

"They stole everything of value to resell it. It's a proud moment for me, and yet I'm still pissed."

"I hate to point out the obvious, Drewcila, but...It is just like you to put a force field on the bar, yet leave the royal offices completely unprotected," Facto said.

Drewcila mumbled a bunch of incoherent curses before explaining herself. "I wasn't expecting all this crazy shit to happen. It's a castle, for godssakes, with a full staff of well trained, armed guards. You wouldn't expect to need force fields and such. On the other hand, I had to put a force field on the bar to keep Zarco from ruining my parties."

Facto cleared his throat. "Speaking of Zarco, you're going to have to deal with his body, the services."

"I thought I made myself pretty clear. Cremate the body, flush it down the toilet. I don't fucking give a good rat's ass. Get rid of it, move on..." She had walked into the middle of her office. She turned slowly and sighed. "You know what? I'm not his widow. My sister is his widow. She loved him, I didn't. She's played me before, let her do it again. Let her decide what to do with Zarco, and you help her. I'll take care of getting the equipment I need myself."

Facto looked shocked past the point of speech.

"Hey...Got to keep up appearances. The kingdom wants a grieving queen, we'll give them a grieving queen."

Facto nodded silently.

"Go find Stasha and tell her."

Facto turned to go, then turned back around, the glimmer of tears in his eyes. "My queen...that's very kind of you."

Drew smiled wryly, "Just good politics."

He nodded and walked away.

She watched him leave, then walked farther into the office. She had to step over a broken bottle of Arcadian gin lying close to the wall under a hole the bottle had made when it hit. "Now that was uncalled for. A victim of senseless violence, cut down in his prime..."

"Are you writing a speech for Zarco's funeral?" Margot asked from the door.

"No." Drew bent over and picked up a piece of the broken bottle, "A fitting send-off for a good vintage. Margot, I need a communicator. Anything stronger than my wrist com, and I need it yesterday."

"I'll see what we can find."

"Since the king's office is apparently empty, I'll be moving in there. Have the staff find me suitable furnishing, I'll work on getting all the technical equipment. And have Arcadia's and Dylan's rooms cleaned. I ran into Arcadia briefly in the hall a minute ago, obviously nursing the father, mother, and illegitimate brother of all hangovers, and all she could talk about was that they had pissed on her clothes."

"Drew... the staff. Well, they still aren't all back. Many of them fled before the fighting started. Others were hurt. I don't know how much they can realistically handle."

"Then we'll ask for workers from the city...no." she smiled wickedly. "Have the guards pull the prisoners out of the dungeon, and have the prisoners muck out the mess. Two guards watching six prisoners. If they try anything, the guards' orders are to kill them immediately. And the guards are to make sure the nobles know this. The guards will work in their normal eight hour shifts, but the prisoners will work in twelve hour shifts until the castle has been completely repaired and cleaned.

Oh...and I love this. Put a member of the household staff over each group as a foreman, and if any prisoner talks back to the foreman, it's an instant death sentence. The nobles did all this because they didn't want to live like the "common" man. Let's see how they like it when they really are living like the "common" man. Read it back."

Margot had written it all down on her power pad, and as she read it back to Drewcila, her smile seemed to grow.

"What's so damn funny?" Drewcila asked when Margot had finished reading.

"Nothing funny, really it's just...well, you're so smart, you always seem to know how to fix everything. How to turn a liability into an asset."

"Yes, yes so true, and I'm so fucking good looking and humble, too. Go now, and do my bidding."

She didn't feel so smart when she was sitting in her newly recycled, refurnished office, trying desperately to find the equipment she needed without having to wait for a week or gut her ship, when Dartan appeared at her door with his crew.

"Ah, fuck!" she said

"Is it a bad time, my Queen?"

"No. Get your luscious ass in here. Listen, I need a transmitter and transceiver with intergalactic capabilities. I need a computer with intergalactic links, and I need it yesterday. Can you get that for me?"

"My Queen, for you..."

"A simple yes or no, Dartan."

"Within the hour."

"You're a good man, I don't care what the others say."

"Can we talk to you?"

"Get me the stuff I need, and I'll do a fucking tap dance for you. Get it here in thirty minutes, and I'll do a strip tease."

He nodded and left at a run with his staff right behind him. She needed to know what the Lockhedes were planning. In order to figure that out, she needed to know how badly they'd been hurt in the battle at Hepron Station. It had looked like the whole of their fleet, but that was probably just wishful thinking.

She had to figure out how to win this war, and do it quickly before it completely bankrupted her. Or at the very least she needed to put out an all-out effort till this crap wore off her tongue and she could open her damn safe.

"So...do you have time to talk to me now?"

Drew sighed. She'd gotten up that morning, showered and dressed, and was almost out the bedroom door when Van Gar had announced that he had an idea she needed to hear. She'd known at the time that *I don't have time to listen to your stupid assed idea right now I'm busy* had probably been a little harsh, and that he'd force her to at least pretend to apologize later.

"I'm sorry I blew you off," Drew said half-heartedly.

Van Gar just nodded, indicating that he knew damn good and well she wasn't really sorry. Then he finished walking in and flopped in the chair across the desk from her. "Half-assed, completely insincere apology accepted. Before you blow me off again, I have a proposition for you."

"Does it include lots of flavored body oil?" Drew asked with a wicked smile.

"Wrong lover. You know that stuff mats my fur up. This is a business matter."

"All right," Drew said her curiosity aroused, "I'll bite, what's your proposition?"

"I have roughly fifteen thousand displaced Chitzskies waiting for a new homeland which they are expecting me to buy them. Here's the thing. If I buy them something, I won't have as much money."

"Well, duh."

"Not only are these my people, but they are also probably the meanest mother fuckers in the galaxy, so I don't want to screw them over. Or at the very least, I don't want them to *know* that I have screwed them over..."

"I'm still busy, Van Gar, a point sometime, please."

"You're fighting a war. I have a small army of some of the most fearsome beings in the universe. They want land. You're queen of half a planet. You need fighters..."

"You fight for me, I give you land," Drewcila nodded appreciatively. It was a good plan. But she couldn't give them shit land, because if she did they'd be pissed off at her. And like Van Gar said, they were some scary mother fuckers. However, all the decent land in the country was owned by private parties or was a damn national monument. If she gave them a national treasure or started kicking the locals off their land to give it to aliens, there was bound to be shit. She told Van Gar as much.

"...the real problem is, Van Gar, that I have a serious battle constantly raging inside me that I have only recently become aware of. You see the forces of *I want everyone to like me* are constantly kicking the living crap out of *I really don't give a damn what people think of me*. I'm in constant conflict."

A noise in the hall drew her attention. She looked out the open doorway and saw the "noble" work detail being prodded along by a pair of exuberant guards who were obviously enjoying their new assignment immensely. It brought a smile to her face, and slapped an idea into her head so fast it made her lightheaded.

"The nobles had vast holdings, huge houses, surely your Chitzsky brothers and sisters couldn't balk about that."

"What about the nobles' families?"

"What about them? They are traitors by proxy. We sling them into the street and let them fend with the common man...offer them the choice of serving in the army or civil service, and redeeming themselves through service to country."

"How do you explain that you're giving the nobles' estates to a bunch of Chitzskies?"

"They pay us for the land. We use the money to help with our war effort. When they fight with pride for our country, they will prove to the common man that they deserve to be citizens."

"Wait a minute, Drewcila. The idea was for me not to have to pay for land..."

"You said you'd give me forty percent if I helped you..."

"...to keep my money."

"You pay the kingdom the forty percent you were going to give me."

"You'd give up your part of the take to help my people and your country?" he said in disbelief.

"Dumb ass! Who is the Queen of this kingdom?"

"You are."

"So if you pay the kingdom, who ultimately gets the money?"

"Oh."

"Yeah, oh." She laughed and reached into her desk drawer to get a cigar. She flipped it up, caught it between her teeth and lit it with her side arm. She threw one to Van Gar, who caught it easily. He put it in his mouth and was about to light it when it sparked to flame.

"Damn it, Drewcila!" Van Gar yelped. "You might at least warn me."

Drewcila smiled back, shrugged and put her blaster back in its holster. "You just can't be nice to some people. You know, Van..." she took a long drag of her cigar and blew out a stream of smoke rings before she started talking again. "I think being around all that religious bullshit has dulled your senses."

Van smiled back at her in spite of himself. "You know you went to sleep in the middle of my story last night. I was really quite magnificent."

"Sorry, that was so insensitive of me, but I was a little tired, oh, you know, what with saving the planet, and screwing you senseless, and all." Drew smiled at him. "Magnificent, huh?"

Van Gar started telling the story again. He was about to get to the part where he was oh so incredibly magnificent, when the reporter dude showed up with all the communications equipment Drewcila had ordered. She completely blew Van Gar off as she started shouting out orders concerning where she wanted this and where she wanted that and what she was going to do with it if they made the screeching noise sliding it across the floor even one more time.

Feeling rejected, Van Gar left in a huff—which was wasted because Drew didn't even notice he was gone. He wandered off in the direction of the bar, thinking a good stiff drink might help clear his mind.

He saw Arcadia sitting at the bar and almost turned around and left. Deciding he wasn't about to let her stop him going anywhere he wanted to go, he walked up to the bar, stepping over Shreta's prone body before picking a bar stool and sitting down. Arcadia looked up at him and pulled a face.

"Van Gar," she hissed out.

"Arcadia," he hissed right back, making the same face. "What happened to her?" Van Gar asked indicating Shreta with a flip of his head.

"I made her come so hard she passed out hours ago, and she still hasn't come to," Arcadia answered.

Van Gar laughed loudly, then stopped, shaking his head. "Come on, Arcadia, who are you trying to kid? You wouldn't fuck her with my dick."

"True. We were hoping it might make you and Drew jealous. I told her it wouldn't work."

"Hair of the dog?" Van Gar asked, pointing at the glass of Hurling Monkey Arcadia held in her claw.

"Is it that obvious that I'm hung over?" she asked.

"Sugar, you're either hung over or you took one of Shreta's ugly pills." Van laughed. "So...how long do you plan to stay pissed off at me?"

"Me?" Arcadia laughed then. "What about you? You have her most of the time, yet you resent the little bit of time I have her, and I had her first."

"Prior ownership seems to be a big deal with her," Abear said standing up from behind the bar. "What's your poison?"

"Bend Me Over and Fuck Me, with a cherry," Van Gar answered. He thought about what Arcadia had said and answered decisively. "You most certainly did not have her first. She said she'd only had six lovers before me, and I know who all of them were. You weren't on that list."

Arcadia laughed. "You believed her? Hell, she probably had six lovers before noon on that day. I've been sleeping with the bitch off and on for six years. I figure that beats you by about three, four years."

After three drinks apiece, and an hour of arguing, pulling up dates and places and times, Van Gar had to admit that indeed, Arcadia had had Drew first.

"I don't really see what difference it makes," Van Gar said.

"How can you say that? You treat me like I'm the interloper, when it's obvious that you, and not I, are the interloper," Arcadia hissed back. "Besides, I love her."

"I love her more than you do."

"Oh, you most certainly do not."

A whole new argument ensued. It was about to come to blows when Shreta came to and pulled herself off the floor. She stumbled over to the bar, and let it hold up her weight as she said, "Why don't you just agree to share her?"

"That's sick!" they exclaimed in unison.

Shreta shrugged. "Like it or not, it's what you've been doing. Sharing her with each other, and every other man, woman, midget, and goat which catches her fancy."

"She said the goat belonged to the midget," Van Gar objected.

"My point is that she obviously has feelings for both of you, since she's kept you both around longer than anyone else. You're both hopelessly in love with her, so neither of you are going to just walk away. Maybe you should agree to share her, and then work together to keep everyone else away," Shreta said, taking the glass of water Abear handed her and downing it in one gulp.

"You know what? That's so crazy it just might work," Van Gar said.

"I'd rather share her with you than share her with you and half the galaxy."

"And between the two of us, surely we can satisfy all her many kinky urges."

"I'm not fucking you," Arcadia said.

"Certainly not," Van Gar said pulling a face.

Arcadia looked over at Shreta and then at Van Gar. "This girl's a genius. We've got to do something about getting her laid."

Van Gar nodded in agreement. They spent the next hour making out a schedule.

When the equipment was in place and functional, Drewcila watched the reports from Lockhede concerning the raid on Hepron Station with a mixture of anger and appreciation. Their reporters were calling Hepron Station an all out victory, no doubt the military had doctored tapes of the raid so that it looked like Barion ships were falling from the sky instead of their own. And they had enhanced the damage on the station. They had even doctored a tape of herself so that it looked as if she were crying for mercy.

She had called in her best communications expert from one of the stations, and he had easily linked her to the Lockhede capital, although they had obviously gone to great lengths to keep her out. Apparently someone wanted nothing to do with any chance of negotiations between the two countries' leaders. Drewcila was pretty certain she knew who.

She was soon staring at the Lockhede President, and he was glaring back at her.

"I need to talk to the lot of you. I suggest you call your colleagues, all of them, and be prepared to talk to me in ten minutes." She closed the transmission and watched the clock.

Reluctantly, President Ralling called the heads of the military and his vice-president to his office. General Tryte had assured him that Drewcila Qwah wouldn't be able to contact them again, and yet she had done so in less time than it took him to

get comfortable with the fact that she couldn't. He was beginning to have less and less faith in Tryte.

Roughly one-fourth of their Air Force had been totally
annihilated by a few small planes and a fistful of salvaging
barges. It was an embarrassment of mass proportions. They
hadn't known Qwah had been there. If they had, it would
have just made them more determined to target Hepron Station. Yet the truth was that if the whore hadn't been there,
their attack most probably would have succeeded.

Drewcila Qwah was an unbelievable problem, and one
he had no idea how to deal with. Without her, Barious would
crumble. But getting to Qwah was impossible, and with her
leadership there was a good chance that Barious, militarily
inferior or not, was going to plow a row right through his
country.

He hated taking orders from anyone, much less that salvaging whore, yet he found himself calling Trailings and his
three generals back to his chambers for yet another telecon-
ference with the ever-growing thorn in his side, the Barion
Queen. They of course arrived just in time, and then she had
the nerve to make them wait for a full ten minutes before
making an appearance again. When she did she was abrupt
and to the point.

"All right, first things first. Someone is trying to make sure
that there can be no chance for negotiations by keeping me
out of your system. I suggest you all find out who the hell that
is and kick their ass to the curb, because negotiations are your
country's only chance of survival."

"No one has set up any such block in the communications
system here," Ralling assured her.

"Yeah, and you kicked the shit out of us at Hepron Station, too. You know what, Ralling? You might get away with
feeding lines of crap to your obviously stupid people, but don't
insult my intelligence by trying to feed the same line of bullshit
to me. I was telling more convincing lies when I was still shitting
my drawers. I'm going to give you cringing, stupid mother

fuckers one more chance to surrender, and then you'd better put on your diapers because we're going to stomp over there and kick the crap out of you."

"We aren't afraid of your threats, Qwah!" Tryte said angrily at Ralling's shoulder. "We have suffered a minor setback at best..."

"You got your fucking lame asses kicked by a fist full of anti-aircraft guns, some small planes, and a couple of salvaging barges. You should see what we can do when we haul out the big guns. You'd better back the fuck off and surrender. My offer still stands, but if you so much as blow a fart in our general direction, I'm going to crawl up your ass and pull your nose hairs out your dick one at a time."

"Your threats mean about as much to us as your salvager slang," Tryte shouted at her.

She laughed as she looked at Ralling. "Gee, Ralling you're just like a spaceport porn theater, everyone's comin' in you."

"You might at least try speaking our language," Ralling sneered back.

"That was my polite way of saying that everyone seems to have their penis up your rectum." She turned her attention to Trailings, who had been silent until then. "Perhaps someone with a brain should explain the complexities of the situation to your president. He obviously isn't the brightest chalk in the box. But then it's been my experience that the very privileged tend to breed ambitious, corrupt, and stupid people with every sperm they spit out of their dicks, while those who must work for their place in the world become increasingly intelligent, because they're constantly having to fight for every crumb they get. Of course, there is nothing quite as sad as seeing a man work his way to the top only to be dethroned by some rich fucker's moronic brat, is there?"

Ralling still had no idea what she was talking about, but it was clear from the look on Trailings' face that he did. Trailings turned to look at him, and this time did not even bother to whisper what was on his mind. "The people want trade, not war. Make peace with the Barions. Stop this foolishness, and bring our country and our people from poverty to an age of prosperity. You can go down in history as the man who brought our country to ruin, or you can be remembered as the man who put an end to their suffering."

"You treasonous bastard!" Ralling turned to glare at the Barion Queen. "His is the voice of a discontented loser. One who would love nothing better than to see me fail. It is for that reason that I know that whatever he says is what I shouldn't do."

She laughed at him as if he had said something of unbelievable humor. "You truly are every bit the idiot I thought you were. Such logic shall surely march your people to their deaths. I will give you forty-eight hours to think about it. If in that time you do not surrender, or you dare to attack even the smallest of our cities, I will unleash the wrath of my army upon you." She closed the transmission.

"We must surrender," Trailings insisted. "It is the only way. That woman and her people are like gods in the sky, and we don't yet know how good their ground troops might be."

"Shut up, you whining traitor!" Tryte screamed. "I tell you that was a fluke..."

"The way her bringing down the Artvail was a fluke? Or their successful attack on our capital was a fluke? You, sir, are a sorry excuse for a general, and if our idiot president continues to take counsel from you, then we shall all perish while accomplishing nothing but the demise of our own country."

"How dare you call me an idiot or question my choice of who I take counsel from?" Ralling screamed.

"I was elected to lead these people. They voted for me. You are only in office through yet another fluke. The people voted for me because they thought I could save them from you and him," Trailings said pointing at Tryte. "In my demoted role as vice-president, I must at least try to stop you as you work at nothing else so diligently as sliding this country into economic ruin and turning it into a smoldering remnant as we fight a war we can not win."

"We can win...we most assuredly will win, and then we will make this country truly rich," Tryte promised.

Ralling looked at Trailings and smiled smugly. "The people will soon be thanking the gods that a *fluke* put me into office instead of you."

Chapter 12

"Well?" Facto asked, looking with displeasure at the bottoms of Drewcila's boots where they rested on her desk.

"They won't surrender. The vice-president, he would in a heartbeat, but he's not in charge. I need to see what I can do about that. In the meantime..." She seemed thoughtful for a moment. "They will attack sometime before the forty-eight hour deadline I gave them. So we need to be on the highest possible alert, Dirty-Dog-Dick-Red-7 or what ever," she said with the flip of her hand. "The minute they attack us we will not only meet them with force, but we will then attack them with everything we have, and we will do it where it hurts, hitting one of their biggest military bases. You want to stop them attacking you, don't lob bombs at their civilian population, you take out their military strongholds."

"Are you forgetting that they are militarily superior to us?"

"To the country maybe, and even that is in serious doubt." Drewcila looked at him and smiled. "But they can't stand against the country and Qwah-Co Industries. I have literally hundreds of ships, all fully loaded with weapons they aren't supposed to have. And I have something else the Lockhedes aren't counting on. An army of the fiercest foot soldiers the universe has ever known. The problem is it's going to take time for me to get them here, and every time they make a strike against us, successful or not, it costs us lives and, more importantly, it costs us money." She took a drink from the bottle in her hand, then looked at him. "Go get Van Gar and send him in here."

"Drewcila...you could call him on his com-link," Facto protested.

"I...I know that. Don't you think that I know that? I need to think, and I can't do that with you standing peering in my brain," Drewcila said.

Facto bowed, then ruined the effect by stomping out of the office.

Drewcila re-ran the fabricated tapes the Lockhede television stations were running. The more she watched them, the madder she got, and then she had a sudden brain storm. "Oh, I am truly brilliant!" She got on her comlink. "Dartan! Get your ass in my office on the double."

He was there before she had time to lower her arm, bowing and scraping, with his full news crew in tow.

"Not them, just you, Dartan." The others quickly left the office as Dartan moved closer to her desk. "Take a load off."

"What, my Queen?"

"Sit down. I want you to see something." She ran the footage again.

"I have seen, my Queen, blatant lies..."

"Brilliant propaganda. They are losing battle after battle, and morale, which was already low, goes right into the toilet. How do you raise morale? Tell the people you won something, even if you have to lie. Problem is they don't know who they are dealing with. When it comes to dishing out bullshit, no one can stand shovel to shovel with me. You get what I'm saying, Dartan?"

Dartan swallowed hard. "Not really, my Queen; if you'd allow me to bring in just the interpreter."

Drew sighed, thought for a moment, and then spoke slowly. "I'm going to make my own propaganda, and you're going to help me."

Dartan chewed on that for a minute, and then his eyes widened. "You mean...We're going to make up the news? Give the people false reports?"

"Yes. And we're going to boost the signal so that it goes not only on every television in Barious, but on the whole stinking planet."

"Oh, my Queen, I don't think that I could..."

"No thinking will be necessary on your part. I will be hiring someone else to do that. All you have to do is follow his guidance. Meet me back here in an hour. I just have a few more things to set up before we go."

He nodded and left the office, head hanging low. He stopped in the doorway and turned to face her. "My Queen?"

"You still here, Dartan?"

"My queen, if I do this...It goes against everything I believe in. When the people learn what I have done, they will never take me seriously again, my career will be over."

"Who says anyone's ever going to find out? Besides, do you want to be a reporter, or a war hero? The fate of the entire country may very well rest on your shoulders. And here's the shit...if you won't do it, I'll find someone else that will, and that mother fucker will be the most famous broadcast journalist in Barious instead of you."

Dartan understood just enough of what she'd said to know that he really didn't have a choice. "Always happy to serve my Queen," he said, bowed, turned, and left.

Van Gar walked in, followed by Facto. "Well?" he asked flopping in the chair across from her.

"I want you to coordinate half our salvaging fleet. Send them to pick up every single one of your people and have them come directly here as quickly as possible. I need as many as possible of both here in the next thirty-two hours."

"Using this equipment?"

"Yes, can you do it?"

Van Gar looked hurt. "Well, of course I can. Shreta can help me. She's homely, but very capable."

"Great. I have to go on a little field trip. Foxtrot! Go and fetch Arcadia."

"Wrist-com, Drewcila," Facto said in a pleading tone.

"Trying to get rid of you again, Factoid," Drew said waving her hand dismissively. Facto sighed and stomped out of the room again. "I only have one little thing left to do, and I didn't want stiff pants to know." She got on the intergalactic communicator, found a closed channel, and after several missed tries finally reached the party she intended. A large speckled alien with three chins and one eye filled the screen in front of her. "Ah, Viny! Good to see you again."

"Drewcila, always a pleasure. What can we do for you?" the creature drawled, his voice coming out strangely as the translator he spoke into interpreted his language into something she could understand.

"I need a top notch assassin, best you got. Money's no object, and I need him here as quickly as possible."

"Money's no object? A sentence I never thought I'd hear from the lips of Drewcila Qwah. It must be very important. Who is the target?" Viny asked.

"Don't want to say that over the air in case this channel's not as closed as I think. My country's at war."

The alien laughed. "It's Barious. Of course you're at war. It's your planet's favorite pastime."

"Yeah, well it's wreaking havoc with my profit margins. I want the war over, and I want it over yesterday, and that's where your people come in."

"You just want one?"

"That ought to do it, yeah. How soon can you get one here?"

"Twelve to fourteen hours..."

"That's too long."

"I have one who can get there sooner, but he's sort of a screw up. Missed his last target, and shot himself in the leg."

"Twelve hours is the earliest you can get someone here?"

"Yes, I'm sorry, they're all on this side of the galaxy. It's the busy season here."

"Do the best you can."

"Don't I always?"

"Yes. Give my love to the wife and kids."

He laughed. "Caught the wife cheating, and I had the bitch killed."

"Just the kids then." The transmission closed.

"Who are you having whacked, dear?" Van Gar asked coyly.

"Now, now, don't spoil the surprise."

Arcadia and Facto walked in the room.

"What's up?" Arcadia asked. She looked better than she had earlier, so she must be getting over her hang over.

"You and I have to take a little trip."

"Did you talk to her yet?" Arcadia asked Van Gar.

"Not yet. We said we'd do it together."

Drewcila sighed. "What's this shit?" Both Van Gar and Arcadia turned to look at Facto. "Fraction, be a good man and go fetch Shreta."

Facto made an unhappy noise, turned on his heel and left. "All right, now that we've completely ruined the royal tight ass's day, you want to tell me what the hell's going on?"

Van Gar looked at Arcadia. She nodded, so he started, "We've been talking..."

"I'm not going to choose between you. Why the hell should I?" Drewcila said with a dismissive shrug. "Everything's fine the way it is now."

"We don't want to make you choose between us," Arcadia said.

"We want you to choose us," Van Gar clarified.

Drewcila was silent as they got into the limo and left the castle. Finally she looked at Arcadia. "So let me get this straight. I can be with Van Gar and you, but no one else, and not at the same time?"

"That's right."

Drewcila fell silent again, brooding. When she finally spoke again, it was to ask. "No one else, you mean like—ever?"

"That's right."

"What if you're both gone?"

"That's not going to happen. No matter how hard you work at it."

She looked at Facto. "I just don't know if I could do it. I mean...only the two of them, for like the rest of my life, it just seems so...restrictive."

"I think if we can share you and only be with you, it's not that much of a concession for you to pledge yourself to us."

"See, and now they're using words like pledge. I'm not pledging shit to anyone. You're my advisor, Fuck Toad, what do you think?"

"I think you're the queen of our country, and that as such you have certain responsibilities. You should find a mate of the opposite sex, and of our race, marry him, settle down in a monogamous relationship, and give the country at least one heir. Since that is about as likely as you ever saying my name correctly more than twice in a row, I think this is a less detestable alternative to what you currently do, which causes the country and the crown constant embarrassment, and has made the tabloids rich," Facto said.

Drew seemed to think about what he said, then looked at him. "I've said your name correctly as much as two times in a row?"

"On several occasions, actually."

"Damn! See? I am losing my touch." She looked at Arcadia. "What if I say no?"

"Lose us both forever," Arcadia said with conviction. Drewcila gave her an incredulous look. "All right! *All right!* If you don't agree to our terms, we are going to be pissy and hard to live with—forever."

Drewcila had no problem at all believing that. After all they'd been doing that for years. Choosing between them would have been impossible. Giving up a long parade of mostly forgettable lovers would have seemed like too much to ask just a few days ago. However after the incident with the sex tattoos, and after sleeping with Zarco and the bad taste that had left in her mouth, giving up what could be equally bad lovers to keep the two best lovers she'd ever had hardly seemed like a sacrifice at all. Then there was that other thing, that thing she didn't like to admit even to herself. She actually cared about them. If she could actually have both of their company all the time without them being at each other's throats...well, she couldn't imagine anything closer to perfect.

"You know, until now I have had to keep the two of you in separate parts of the galaxy to keep you from ripping each other apart, and now you're saying you aren't going to fight. That you're going to share me. I just have trouble believing that," Drewcila said skeptically.

"Do you have any real feelings for me?"

And now the bitch was going to make her say it out loud. Drew looked at Facto, who shrugged and said, "Just pretend like I'm not here, just as you normally do."

"You know I do," Drew answered.

"And Van Gar?"

"You know the answer to that as well."

"And we both love you. So neither of us is willing to let go, and I think we all know that you are never going to just choose one of us, because while you'd never admit it, our relationship is much more than just sex, and so is your relationship with Van Gar. After all these years, I think you owe us some sign that you're committed to us."

"Why do you both have to be so stinking possessive? Couldn't we all just get along and let me do whatever the hell I want to do?" Drew asked "Is that too much to ask?"

"Do you really not give a damn about how either he or I feel? What we want?" Arcadia asked. "Because if that truly is the case, then maybe Van and I should walk away before we invest too much more of ourselves."

Suddenly Drew felt a horrible gnawing pain in the pit of her stomach. *Oh, my gods! I think that's guilt! Well, that just sucks!*

"All right, *all right!*" Drew snapped out. "You win. My life is over, are you happy?"

"Yes!" Arcadia threw her arms around Drew's neck and kissed her. To Facto's dismay, articles of clothing started to be removed. He coughed loudly, and the two women turned to look at him.

"What?" Drew asked. "I'm making out with one of them, so it's all right. I'm not cheating."

"I'd rather not watch," Facto explained.

"Driver! Stop the car," Drew ordered, pulling out of Arcadia's grasp. When the limo stopped she opened the door and kicked Facto out. She threw a fistful of iggys into his lap. "Get a cab. We'll meet you back at the castle."

Facto stood up as the limo took off and brushed himself down. Dartan and his crew, who had been following them, stopped.

"Something wrong?" Dartan asked.

"No...I...I just wanted to stretch my legs."

"By falling on your rear?" Dartan asked with a smile.

"Young man, I assure you..."

"Need a ride, old man?"

"Actually, yes."

The Captain of the Starship Intertwined paced the bridge.

A younger member of his crew turned to look at him for guidance and wisdom, "Captain...couldn't we just go around the planet?"

"No! Damn it, son!" he started in a voice so butch it could change a car's tires, "Don't you understand? It's worse than that. If we continue to travel in these temporal streams, we may very well pop back to a time when we didn't exist at all."

A voice boomed from the darkness that surrounded them. "Cut! Cut! Could you maybe try a little thing we like to call acting?"

The Captain peered into the darkness and screamed back in his true voice, which sounded very much like he belonged in an all-boys' choir. "Don't blame me! I didn't write this Trytee crap. How am I supposed to find any inspiration at all when I'm spitting out such crap as, 'If we continue to travel in these temporal streams we may pop back to a time when we didn't exist at all.' I mean...can that even happen?"

Sabtos sighed. The incompetent little fairy had a point.

Sabtos pulled at his goatee. He was the best producer in the entire nation, and as a director he was a genius. He wondered for the thousandth time since he'd started this project why he was working on such a crap picture. "Someone find out if that's technically possible."

"It's not," a voice said from the darkness.

"Ah...who are you?"

"Does it matter?"

"I...I don't know."

"Well, think about it, and get back to me later."

"Listen, lady, I don't know who you think you are, but I'm trying to film a movie here, and time is money."

"And money is time," a female voice different from the first said.

"I really miss Pris," the first voice said.

"Lights up," the director ordered. As the lights were going up he put on his most angry director voice. "Listen, people, groupies aren't allowed..." he had been standing up out of his chair as he spoke, and when he saw who was standing there he almost fell. But he was able to turn it into a deep bow. "My Queen, a thousand pardons, how may your humble servant aid you?"

"By producing and directing my war."

Stasha was glad she had been in her own quarters and not in the medical unit with Dylan when Facto came to tell her that Drewcila had considered her feelings and was allowing her to make all the decisions concerning Zarco's funeral.

There was a great deal of guilt swimming in her head as she tried to make the arrangements. Mostly because Drew had been right, and after sleeping with Dylan she had all but forgotten about poor Zarco.

She could still feel Dylan's hands where they had touched her, and when she thought about what they had done, her cheeks flushed with excitement.

Drewcila hadn't just been being her usual deceitful self. Zarco *had* been a horrible lover. Oddly enough, she had thought she'd experienced orgasm before, and just didn't think it was the big deal others made it out to be, or worse yet that there was something wrong with her. After her night with Dylan, she knew that *she* hadn't been the problem.

Besides which she now admitted, if only to herself, that what she had felt for Zarco was sick infatuation and not love at all. Because she was sure that she was now completely and totally in love with the human male who made her blood boil.

Then there was that other thing—Zarco had never loved her. She also admitted that Drew had been right about something else—Zarco hadn't loved Drewcila, either. His attachment to Drew, like Stasha's attachment to him, was a sick desire to own someone who didn't want you. He might have once loved Taralin, but Drewcila wasn't Taralin in any way that mattered. Maybe he had truly believed that he could turn Drew back into Taralin, but right now Stasha even doubted that.

So this whole thing was just very hard for her. On the one hand she was pleased that her sister had considered her feelings instead of just flushing Zarco's remains down a toilet, as Drew had suggested at least once. On the other, everything had changed completely for her in the last twenty-four hours, and she was finding it hard to feel anything but relief at Zarco's passing. He had completely disregarded her feelings, slept with her sister, and perhaps most surprising of all, he had been easily replaced in her heart by another.

So it was that she found herself rushing through the arrangements, always doing what was least expensive. The more she worked on trying to feel grief over his passing, the more things she found to be angry about. She would go into the past trying to remember some tender moment they had shared, and would wind up dredging up yet another time when he had completely discounted her and how she felt. By the time she got around to ordering the flowers, she decided he really didn't need them.

She would be expected to give a eulogy, and since she never wrote her own speeches, that meant she really needed to talk to Drewcila. Margot, who had been helping her with the preparations all day, had just announced that Drewcila had recently returned to the castle.

"I've got to go talk to my sister about the eulogy. Keep trying to reach the priest."

"Yes, my lady," Margot said.

Stasha was glad it was a long walk to her sister's office for many reasons, not the least of which that she had to remind herself that she would be expected to still be angry with Drewcila, and that she was supposed to be deeply grieved. The euphoric post-orgasm smile Stasha hadn't been able to wipe off her face all morning wouldn't do. She stopped herself from dropping by Dylan's room on her way. If Stasha had seen him, she would have had to stop at least long enough to have sex with him, and she had many things to accomplish. Besides, then she never would have been able to wipe the smirk from her face.

When she walked in the office, workmen were moving in still more electronic equipment, and maps and charts and graphs were being plastered to the walls—and sur-prisingly—over the windows. Her sister sat in a chair look-ing at where a window should have been, her back to the room. But the strangest sight of all had to be Van Gar and Arcadia working together at a computer console on the far side of the room. Just yesterday evening Stasha had been present when the two had run into each other in the hall. They had addressed each other with such animosity that Stasha had been sure they would come to blows. It had been all Drew could do to keep them separated. Now they were chatting idly as they worked, just as if they were the best of friends.

"My pussy itches. It must be going to rain," Drew announced.

"Drewcila...must you always be so disgustingly crude?" Stasha said, thinking that she should have known that her sister wouldn't make it very hard for her to find something to be upset at her about.

"Stasha, what in hell's name do you have your panties in a knot about this time?" Drewcila spun around in the chair, and there was a cat sitting in her lap. Drew was scratching its head.

"Ah...nothing. Sorry, I'm just a little tense. I thought you were saying...Oh, never mind. Listen, about the eulogy, have you written that yet?" Stasha asked.

"You write it, Stasha. If I write it, it's going to say something I took off a bathroom stall, like...*Here I sit all broken hearted—Tried to shit, but only farted*. I'll pretend like there is some deep hidden meaning to it, people will believe that there is, and soon it will be the prayer recited at every funeral. We don't want that, do we? Royal responsibility and all that good rot. Think of something really nice to say about the stiff. You loved him—I didn't."

Stasha looked from the workmen to her sister. Apparently Drewcila didn't really care who knew how she felt.

Drew seemed to know what she was thinking. "Movie people. If you can't trust them, who can you trust?"

"Just what are they doing?" Stasha asked curiously.

"Making this look like the greatest war room ever. See all that new electronic hooha? None of it's real. It's just painted cardboard boxes with holiday lights stuck through holes and little pieces of plastic glued on to look like buttons. See all the graphs and maps and stuff? None of the information on the graphs means shit, and none of the hundreds of military bases on those maps even exist." She laughed then. "Those rank amateurs will rue the day they decided to screw with me. Right now, even as we speak, a huge battalion of particle board and plastic-coated cardboard tanks are being built in the Taralin Desert. Painted cardboard tubes are being made into hundreds of anti-aircraft guns which will be set up on every building more than fifteen stories tall..."

"Drewcila! You can't fight a war with bad stage props," Stasha said in disbelief.

"A little respect for these people's craft, Stasha. I'll have you know they're very *good* stage props!" Drew protested "I've hired the best studio in the country and some of the brightest stars. We can't lose."

"You are completely insane. However, since I have seen you do crazier things that actually worked, I'm not going to worry about it. But Drew...I don't think I can write a eulogy, not and make it sound like I'm you."

"Would you like to borrow one of our script writers?" Drew asked.

"I'm serious."

"So was I...Listen, Stasha, I don't care what I say about him. Seriously, would you really want to speak the words I'd have to send him off? I'm only good at bullshit when I think it can get me something," Drew said.

Stasha nodded silently and almost asked for the script writer. "I'll think of something that will come from the heart." She was about to leave when Van Gar and Arcadia laughed at something. She turned to look at them, and her face must have shown her disbelief, because Drewcila answered the look on her face.

"They have decided to share me, and in return I have promised not to cheat on them," she said with a shrug.

Stasha smiled back at Drew and said in a flippant tone, "So you've finally decided to settle down."

Drewcila laughed. "Yeah, what can I say? There comes a time in a young salvager's life when you realize it's time to stop screwing around, settle down with a huge Chitzsky male and a Valtarian lizard woman, get a nice ship, maybe buy a couple of small satellites...So, are you still mad at me?"

Stasha sighed and told the truth. "I want to be. I ought to be. It's just hard to stay mad at you. I don't know why, really. You certainly seem to work hard enough at keeping me mad."

A man swept into the room holding up a sketch of a uniform. "Too fluffy, Kraling. I must look tough, ready for battle and smug as hell. And so must all my generals."

The man grumbled as he rolled up the sketch and left the room.

"Wardrobe!" Drew exclaimed, throwing up her hands.

Stasha smiled and left.

Drew threw the cat out of her lap and stood up. Then she scratched her crotch and addressed Van Gar and Arcadia, "I don't know if this crap is ever going to wear off."

"Let's see your tongue," Arcadia said.

Drew stuck it out.

"It doesn't seem as dark today. I'm pretty sure it's fading."

"My crotch itches like a mother fucker," Drew said.

"Drew, I swear, if you give me the space crabs again..." Van Gar hissed.

"Keep your pants on, ass bite, I don't have crabs."

"How do you know?"

"I'd know if I had crabs," Drew said.

"You didn't last time," Van said. He turned to glare at Arcadia, who was chuckling, "You wouldn't think it was so damn funny if you could get them."

"Especially not if you got them on your whole body," Drew said with a laugh.

"That's right, assholes, laugh it up. But I swear..."

"Calm down." Drew rubbed at his shoulders, knowing they were tired from working at the computer all day. "I swear I don't have crabs, and with this new arrangement, if I ever have them again it will be your fault, since as you said Arcadia can't get them."

He turned to look at her, a tentative smile on his face. "Then you've decided to accept our proposal?"

"Yeah, but only if you don't call it a proposal." She shrugged. "What the hell. Crabs wasn't all that pleasant for me, either. In fact, the only thing worse is this stupid tattoo shit, which neither of you are ever to talk me into doing when I'm drunk and feel like experimenting."

"Agreed," they both said.

"Oh, and stop doing that. It's just too creepy."

"Ok," they said. Drew sighed deeply and wondered just what she'd gotten herself into.

Dr. Sortas, who had once held the lofty position of palace surgeon, now found himself mucking pissy clothes from a shower stall. Early that morning when they had first started this work detail, Kentoric, a man Sortas had known since his childhood, had decided he wasn't taking orders from a commoner. The guards had marched him out into the courtyard and shot him. Then they ordered the rest of them to haul his body to the dumpster. Since then, no one had thought it was a good idea to buck the system.

Greed. Greed for money and position had led him to this. He'd had more than any one man should rightfully have, and he'd wanted to keep all of it and get still more. Then Drewcila came in with her maximum wage and her demotion of the nobility and shook his world to its foundations. But he hadn't actually lost anything but prestige, and how tangible an asset was that really?

He wondered about his family and how they were faring at this time. Whether they knew he was a prisoner. If they even knew if he was alive. He'd heard talk that the families of the nobles involved in the failed coup attempt were being evicted from their homes and land. They were being offered a choice of taking up residence in one of the work houses or going into military service. He and his wife had never had a particularly good relationship before, and he was assuming she probably hated his guts right now. Thank the gods both the kids were grown. Of course that meant it was probably military service for them, and probably on the front lines.

What a mess.

"You there! Back to work," the foreman ordered.

Sortas nodded, pulled yet another urine covered piece of alien clothing from the shower and stuck it in the sack. They wouldn't even give them rubber gloves.

"Sortas," the man working beside him said in a whisper. Sortas looked at him. "A few of us are thinking about trying to make a run on the guards."

"Then only a few of you will die," Sortas whispered back. "We're not soldiers, we're professional men. These are Qwah's men. You saw what they did to Kentoric, and that was just for refusing to work. I'll have no part of it. I'm going to get out of here alive if that's possible."

"Do you really think Qwah will let any of us out alive?"

No, he really didn't, but their only real chance was to hope the queen might show a little mercy. Escape was just the quickest way to die. "It's a better chance than escape."

"You two shut up!" one of the guards bellowed.

Zarco had helped the nobles to displace these men from their cushy, well paid jobs as castle security. Now that they were back, it wasn't likely they were going to let him forget it.

They were doomed. Men with a death sentence waiting to be hung. Maybe it was better to at least try to make a break for it. Maybe a quick death was the best they could ask for.

"I'll look ridiculous!" Van Gar protested, pulling on the way-too-small uniform he and five of his Chitzsky brothers and sisters had been dressed in.

"Honey, shut up and do what the director tells you," Drew said as wardrobe went about putting the final touches on the new "general's" uniform she was wearing.

"Tell me again why the uniforms are three sizes too small," Shreta asked, struggling with the collar of her "costume."

"Because it makes you look bigger," the director said. He addressed them. "Now, when I cue you, you will stick these pills into your mouth." He handed them out. "They will then start to foam. Let the foam erupt naturally from your mouth, and snarl and look like ravenous beasts. This is your motivation. You have come here to make your home, but no sooner have you bought your property and started to set down roots than these bastard Lockhedes start bombing your new homeland. You're a warrior race, and you're not going to stand for that. So you will don the uniform of a Barion soldier and do your part at the front lines to protect your new homeland. Do you have that?"

They all nodded.

"Let's see it then! A little maniacal but righteous anger...without the pills." The Chitzskies all started growling. "Very good, I'm living it." He turned to Drewcila. "You, my queen, need no direction." He turned away from her and shouted. "Lex! Lex, get over here!"

The actor who had been playing the Captain of the starship Intertwined ran over, a wardrobe woman still fussing over his general's uniform.

"No offense, but aren't people going to recognize him and realize that your top military advisor is a two-bit TV actor?" Van Gar asked in a whisper at Drew's shoulder.

"No, they'll think, *Gods! Why that general is so good looking he looks just like that actor Lex Icon.* People like to follow and take orders from attractive people, everybody knows that," Drew explained.

Van Gar threw up his hands and walked over to join his Chitzsky brothers and sisters in front of the blue screen, practicing looking mad.

"Dartan, are you ready?" the director asked.

"I suppose so," he said, adjusting the glasses the director had made him wear because he said they made him look smarter.

"Everyone! Take your places and remember you have to get it right the first time. This is live television people, there will be no second take. Are we ready?" He looked around quickly. "Then start shooting in three, two, gods! I hate shooting live television, one!"

Ralling was watching their doctored report of the events at Hepron Station for the fortieth time, thinking what a stroke of genius it had been, when suddenly his monitor fazed out, and then there was a Barion reporter in glasses looking at him. The man was standing in what appeared to be some huge underground chamber carved from solid rock.

"The queen has called a press conference, and we are waiting now for her to enter the war room from where she plans to make her monumental speech concerning the Lockhedes' most recent attack and the state of our military readiness, which has been under fire from the Lockhedes. We are currently in a secret underground bunker, miles below the surface of the planet. This war reaction base was set up three years ago to harbor the king and queen and top aides in case of attack. A facility from which they could conduct a war safely. Special communications equipment has been set up to boost the signal so that the people of Barious can be kept abreast of all that is going on even though we are many miles below the surface of the planet...It appears the queen is now prepared to speak."

Then Qwah's face filled his screen. Ralling wondered if his enemies knew that by boosting their signal to get it above ground they had boosted to every monitor on the planet. Stupid woman. He had but only to watch his TV to learn all of their plans.

"People of Barious. Since these are such urgent times I will try to speak to you in language you understand, so that we won't need an interpreter between us. This is not a time for mirth. I, your Queen, must address you on a matter of grave importance. As you know, the nobles did push us into a war with the people of Lockhede. I have tried to explain our position—that of your king, my dearly departed husband, and my position as well—but most of the leaders of Lockhede want to bring death upon their own heads. Only one of their leaders, who shall remain nameless for his own safety, has spoken out to try and save his people. Unfortunately, the others would not heed."

The camera panned out then, and Ralling could see that Qwah was flanked by a large, good looking Barion man, and a Valtarian lizard woman. All three wore stunning black uniforms with literally dozens of medals hanging from them. All around them were maps and charts and sophisticated electronic devices of all kinds.

Qwah continued, "Still, despite their stubbornness, I have given them forty-eight hours in which to stop this madness. I do not believe that they will. Some idiot has told them that they are militarily superior. Rest assured, my people, and sleep soundly, because this is not the case. They have doctored tapes of the battle of Hepron Station, bringing lies to their people. But you, my people, have seen the reality of what happened and know that while we were out-numbered and out-gunned, we did utterly smite them...That's like queen talk for we killed the shit out of them. I can only guess that they have done this to raise the morale of their demoralized people. These people are hungry, they're poor, and the man who is their president was not even elected by them, but is a man who—unlike the nobles of our country—led a *successful* coup against the people of his country.

"We should not be angry with the people of Lockhede, for this is not their war. Oh no, this is the war of their filthy rich leaders. Leaders who will put their people in harm's way to take that which is rightfully ours. The sad truth, my people, is that they never wanted trade agreements with us. They don't want to enjoy the same wealth as we do—they don't want to share. The leaders of the Lockhede nation want it all, or they want nothing. They want what you have, what we have worked for. They want to take our homes, our factories, our space-ports. *But they will not succeed.*

"I have made an agreement with the Chitzsky people. They have purchased the land the nobles are being evicted from, and the money they have paid for this land will be used to further add to our defensive capabilities. The Chitzskies had just made payment on this land when the first of the bombs rained down on Hepron Station. They rushed to our aide, and this is how we did so utterly smite...I can see why everyone likes that word so much...utterly *smite* the Lockhedes at Hepron

Station. *Our* homeland is now *their* homeland, too, and they consider the attack on us to be an attack against them. They have joined our army, are currently being put into position, and even as I speak to you, my people, they are ready to attack on my command. And now a few words from Four Q General Jurak on the state of our military readiness."

The camera panned up at the big man standing behind her. "Let me first say that our armed forces stand firmly behind the queen. Any confusion caused by the nobles' uprising is firmly behind us. We have never been more willing and more able to serve any monarch in the history of our country. There are rumors flying around that much of our military arsenal has been scrapped. This is simply not true. Yes, military equipment has been scrapped out and sold, but that was defective and/or obsolete equipment, and money from the sale of it has been used to buy state-of-the-art equipment and build underground, covert bases all over the country. It has also been used to place anti-aircraft guns on all of our larger buildings, and to purchase many tanks. We have never been as militarily strong as we are now, and let us not forget that the last time we fought the Lockhedes, we did..."

"Say *utterly smite*. I just like the way it sounds," the queen prompted.

"We did *utterly smite* them. Let me close by saying..." he seemed to be rattled then, as if not quite sure of what he was going to say next. Then his voice rang out strong and true, and with a strength of purpose the likes of which Ralling had never heard before. "We are determined that if they continue to travel in these temporal streams, we will knock them back to a time *where they didn't even exist!*"

"Very well said. Thank you, General," the queen said. "So, my people, kick back, pop a brew, and wait for the fireworks." An interpreter suddenly appeared in a little box at the bottom of the screen, and was busily explaining the queen's words. "If they will not make peace with us, then we're going to kick their asses up around their shoulders so that they have to wear them for collars, walk with their fingertips, and eat with their toes. The decision rests on the shoulders of their country's leaders. They must make peace and start negotiations for trade agreements, or we will turn their country into a smoldering hole. Which, by the way, I understand would be an improvement."

She nodded her head, and the reporter was back on camera fidgeting with his glasses and his earpiece.

"I'm told we have footage of some of the Chitzsky troops and the new tanks which are on the move heading towards a destination unknown. Apparently these are shock troops, and will be deployed at a moment's notice if any attack is made on Barion soil. This is live via satellite and...There we go."

The monitor showed acre upon acre of huge Chitzskies foaming at the mouth and pounding on their chests while uttering alien battle cries. There were thousands of them. The scene changed swiftly to long, straight lines of high-tech tanks rumbling along to a destination unknown. *Thousands* of them, extending as far as the eye could see.

The reporter was back on the screen. "We will try to keep you updated on all the recent events as we have the details."

The screen went black, and then returned to the fake video Ralling had been watching.

He punched a button on his communicator. "Tryte! Get down here now!"

Chapter 13

"That's a wrap!" Sabtos screamed. "Dartan, you were beautiful," he said. Dartan nodded back from where he stood in the fake cavern that had been built in the hallway by hanging a black sheet behind him and spraying foam on the walls, rounding the corners off with it and then cutting, shaping, and painting it so that it looked like rock.

Sabtos walked back into the "war room" and gushed.

"My Queen! What can I say? You were exquisite! Chitzskies, I was totally believing your anger and ability to tear Lockhedes limb from limb." He turned his attention to Lex and clicked his tongue. "Lex...what the hell were you thinking?"

"That...that bumble-fingered grip dropped the cue cards, and I couldn't remember my lines," he said throwing up his hands.

"I thought it was brilliant improvisation," Drewcila said, patting him on the shoulder. Lex made a face at the director and stuck out his tongue.

"How soon will the tanks be done?" Drew asked the director.

"The boys in special effects are wizards. I'd say twelve more hours. Tops," he assured her.

"Good. And the real general tells me the area is well guarded with anti-aircraft guns," Drew said almost to herself.

Van Gar walked over to her, taking off his too tight shirt as he did so, and making her smile appreciatively. "I don't get it, Drew. Why are you pulling protection away from real targets to protect fake tanks?"

"All shall soon be revealed." She looked from Arcadia to Van Gar. "Whose turn?"

"Mine," Arcadia said with a smile.

"All right. Come on, I need a recharge." She looked back at Van Gar. "Meet you in about..." she looked back at Arcadia.

"Hour and a half."

"...in the dining room. We'll all have dinner." She kissed Van Gar on the cheek, took Arcadia's claw and started dragging her out of the room. "You know, this is just twisted enough that it might work."

As Tryte walked into Ralling's office, he was already explaining himself. "The computer has located the area in which the tanks supposedly are. Mr. President, I think I can say without fear of contradiction that the Barion's report is no less a fabrication than our own. I have already ordered reconnaissance to fly out and see if they can send us back proof that these so-called tanks even exist."

"And if they do, what then? You assured me that we had a military advantage. Now the Queen of Barious has a Chitzsky army and thousands of tanks heading towards our borders."

Trailings walked in then without knocking, further adding to Ralling's irritation. "My gods, man! Will you now make peace with this woman before she kills us all?"

Tryte glared at Trailings. "Surely even you know that this was nothing but bold faced lies..."

"What I know is it was no accident that the broadcast we just saw was sent out on such a strong signal that it knocked out every other station on the planet. I know it was no accident that she pretended to feel the plight of our people, or that she purposely reminded them that you were not elected by them. She is trying to tear us apart from the inside out. Even if there is no Chitzsky army lying in wait. Even if there aren't acres of tanks. You couldn't match wits with this woman if she was in a coma—and she's not."

"So what do you suggest I do, Trailings?" Ralling hissed back.

"What I've been saying all along. Make peace with Barious, accept trade agreements on their terms."

"You are a traitor, Trailings. You want us to give our country over to that Salvaging Whore because you know if we try to work with her, if we make deals with her, it won't be long 'til she's taken over here the way she's taken over Barious. Then she'll be running our country as well."

"And that would be so terrible? Why? Oh, I know...because everyone would have proper food, and housing, and health care. The lives of our people are in peril as you stand here and worry about such unimportant things as who's going to be in charge. Wouldn't you rather be a simple citizen in a thriving country than President of a dead one?"

Ralling seemed to think about that a minute before he answered with a simple and truthful, "No."

Sortas now found himself working in the kitchen doing dishes. There seemed to be a never-ending pile of them. He had never thought about how many dishes a staff large enough to serve the palace must make. For the first time, he thought about the people who must normally do these dishes. He had worked days in the palace, going home at night unless some emergency kept him here. His primary duty was to care for the queen and king, as well as the chancellors, but his duties occasionally extended to tending the injuries and illnesses of the household staff and guards—particularly if the injury occurred at work.

He'd never actually bothered to talk to any of them, just treated them and sent them on their way. After all, they were beneath him. Now one of them was barking orders at his back, enjoying the task immensely, and Sortas could hardly blame him. After all, when Sortas had been above this man, he had treated him in the same manner—like a slave.

How many dishes had he dirtied in the years he'd worked here? He'd never once thought about the man or woman who had to wash them. Whether they'd had dreams, aspirations, things they wanted to do with their lives that didn't include cleaning up after other people.

This queen was more than just cunning and resourceful. The woman was wise. And he only now realized that she was also fair. It didn't really match the reputation she had built for herself with the nobles and most of the galaxy. She could blow all she wanted, but when it came right down to it, she cared deeply about what happened to the people—all of the people. The common people of Barious had embraced her as ruler because they had known this all along.

In the end, it turned out that the commoners were smarter than those of noble birth, and that was perhaps the hardest pill for him to swallow.

"You, soap boy!" His foreman popped him on the rear with a wet towel. "The queen is calling for more beer in the formal dining room. Run it out there."

"But, sir…"

"You aren't going to talk back to me, are you, boy?"

"No…no, sir."

"Bring out a six pack. It's in the refrigerator. Get the bottles, she doesn't like the cans."

He got the beer, his hands shaking the whole time. If the queen saw him, she'd recognize him. And if she didn't, it was a sure bet the lizard woman would. Then the queen would no doubt have him executed on the spot. One of the guards opened the door for him, which was good, because in his state if he'd had to do it himself he probably would have dropped his precious cargo. One of the guards had told him that even before all of the recent occurrences, dropping and breaking a full bottle of beer had been reason for dismissal. He could only wonder at the punishment that would be heaped upon the head of he who broke an entire six pack! Of course, he was most likely walking to his death anyway. But why add insult to injury? There was always some hope that mercy might bring about a swift departure from this world.

The guard followed him out, totally washing all thoughts of a possible escape from his mind.

"Put that puppy right here," Drewcila said, pounding her fist on the table beside her. He assumed she meant the beer, since when he looked around he seemed to be the only one bearing any cargo. He tried to keep his face down as he did so, and was careful to make eye contact with no one, but it didn't help.

"You!" Drewcila thundered in an accusing voice.

Sortas quickly set the beer down on the table where indicated. Then he dropped to his knees on the floor, bowing till his forehead touched the ground. "My queen, please! A thousand pardons! When I had realized the error of my ways, I did try to set things right."

To his dismay she laughed. "When you saw you'd chosen the losing side, and that the castle was about to be overrun by the very people you so despised, you did the only thing you could do to save your own ass. Why, if I hadn't continually poisoned myself by drinking large, most probably lethal, amounts of alcohol over the course of my life, and if I hadn't gotten to a hospital where they administered the antidote to the poison, I would have been very ill for many more days."

He raised his head and looked into her eyes, searching for even a slight glimmer of mercy there. "The words you speak are true, my queen, but I swear to you, had I to do it over again, I would throw all my support behind you and serve you. If you but give me a chance, I shall live out my life in service to you, even if it means washing dishes the rest of my days."

"Who is this butt-kissing scum bucket?" the Chitzsky male called Van Gar asked.

"He's the doctor who withheld treatment from our woman," the lizard woman answered.

"You know what, guys? That was only funny like the first fifty times you did it."

"*We* still think it's funny," the Chitzsky and the lizard woman said at the same time.

"And I asked you to quit doing that," Drewcila hissed, apparently at least momentarily forgetting him. She looked down the table to where her sister was picking at her dinner. "What do you think, Stasha?"

"They seem to be getting along very well, and you all seem happy with the arrangement, so maybe you shouldn't worry about something as trivial as the fact that they suddenly seem to be sharing a brain as well."

"As interesting as it is, I wasn't talking about my love life. I was talking about Dr. I'm-not-going-to-give-you-the-antidote-so-that-you-puke-up-small-organs-you're-most-probably-still-using."

He looked appealingly at Stasha. He had treated Stasha for many years, and felt he had a rapport with her. Besides, she was no doubt still angry over Drew shooting Zarco in the leg.

Stasha shrugged. "I don't know. I can't think about anything but the funeral."

"How's that coming?"

"All right I guess. Mother and father are coming in tomorrow. They aren't terribly happy about having a Chitzsky for a neighbor, but said they were happy that at least you weren't slinging them into the streets with the rest of their friends."

"Yeah, well, you tell them I want a birthday present this year, or that could change real quick."

"I think we should kill him," Arcadia said, fixing him with a stare that made his blood run cold. She got up and started moving towards him. Sortas steeled himself for the coming attack, but the Chitzsky grabbed the lizard woman's shoulder and stopped her forward progress.

"I have a better idea," Van Gar said, and fixed his eyes on the ugliest creature Sortas had ever seen, who was sitting halfway down the table.

The lizard woman let out a laugh, then yelled, "Hey, Shreta! Come here!"

The creature got up and lumbered over to them. "What do you think of this one?" Van Gar asked.

"He doesn't have much hair."

"So?" Van Gar asked.

"He's kind of dirty and old."

"Shit! He'll clean, girl," Van Gar said. "Haven't you ever heard the saying, 'Beggars can't be choosers'?"

"Yeah, you got a point there," Shreta said. She looked him up and down. "Could I maybe see his down-below?"

"Yes, that's reasonable. Sortas, rise and show us all your down-below," Drewcila said with a broad hand gesture and a smile.

Sortas got to his feet, "My Queen, I'm afraid I don't understand..."

For answer, the queen poked her finger at his crotch.

"Your package, Sortas. You said you'd serve me the rest of your life if I would pardon you. Well, it seems we've found you a suitable position, and the lady wants to see your package."

Sortas looked the ugly woman up and down as he realized what they had in store for him. "But, my queen..."

Drewcila's blaster seemed to all but fly from its holster, and then she was pointing it at his head. "Drop your pants, show us your goodies, or die."

Sortas wouldn't have thought he could have exposed himself any faster. The creature looked at his privates, licked her lips, and smiled. The queen nodded, and he pulled his pants up and fastened them, feeling as humiliated as he was sure he could feel...until the huge hair-covered creature grabbed him by the collar and started dragging him out of the room screaming, "Come on, baby! Mamma's gonna ride you like a bull!"

"*Noooooo!*"

"Well?" Ralling asked as Tryte walked in flanked by the generals of the Army and Navy.

"There are tanks, lots of tanks. We can't really say how many, though. We saw aerial photos, but...well, they also have anti-aircraft guns, and..." He cleared his throat and continued, "We've sent out three piloted planes and six drones, and none of them have been able to do more than get a couple of pictures back before they were blown out of the sky."

"So...why am I getting the feeling that you somehow think all of this is good news?" Ralling asked.

"Well, sir, because we know right where they are, and they couldn't possibly have many more tanks. It shows that while she may be a good public speaker, she is a lousy general. I'd say she's put all her tanks and those Chitzsky ground troops all in the same place, and we know where that is. So, we send a full aerial assault, and in three or four passes we've wiped them out completely. We cripple their ground capabilities, and without that they can't fight a successful campaign. They're expecting us to hit one of their bases, and then they're going to hit Yeoul base in retaliation with these weapons and troops. But they can't do that if the target we hit are the troops they plan to retaliate with. Her military ignorance will be her undoing. That General of hers is far too pretty to be any good. He gives great speeches, but he's no strategist."

"Tryte...if we go to bomb these tanks and the alien ground troops, and we fail, I'll see you court-martialed and hung before I sign a treaty with Drewcila Qwah. Do I make myself perfectly clear?"

"Yes, sir, Mr. President. I won't let you down this time."

Sortas had never taken such a long shower in his life, but it hadn't stopped the inevitable. He walked out of the bathroom with a towel wrapped around his waist into a room so dark he couldn't really see where he was going.

"I figured it would be easier for you this way," she said.

"Thanks," he answered back. He steeled himself, threw off the towel, stumbled through the dark, and crawled in bed with the huge female, who was easily six inches taller than he was. It was really dark, and it was true that that made it easier, but she was still covered with hair. Of course, when he let himself get over the initial shock of it, he had to admit that it actually felt pretty good against his skin.

"You don't really have to do this if you don't want to," she said in a quiet voice. "I understand, and I'll tell them that you did."

"No! I mean, I told the queen I'd serve her if she would spare my life, and if this is what I must do to please her..."

"Ride me, stud boy, ride!" she ordered, and because he felt like he was being forced to do this, he tossed all his inhibitions aside. He did things with the Chitzsky female that he'd never done with any Barion woman and she did things to him that he'd never imagined possible.

It turned out this wasn't nearly the punishment they had all intended, so that part he'd have to fake.

The door to Drewcila's office—also known as the "war room" in the underground bunker—was open as it normally was. What wasn't normal, even for Drew, was that she seemed to be having an intense conversation with...well, with no one. When Van Gar stopped in the doorway, she looked startled, but much to his astonishment she just kept talking to herself.

"Yes, well, you just do a good, quick, clean job of it, and I'll give you twice that on your return. Do it at the exact moment I want it done, and I'll triple the amount." She stood up then and seemed to shake hands with the air. She sat back down. "Be careful." She waved, and then her eyes returned to the desk in front of her. Van Gar walked on in, and looked around to see if the director or some of the camera crew were there. Seeing nothing, he laughed and sat down in the chair across from Drewcila. "Drew...what the hell were you just doing?"

"It's not important. Hey, listen...When are the first of our ships getting here with your people as crew?"

"Half of them will be here in another couple of hours, tops. Why?"

Instead of answering him, Drewcila got up and started pacing, making symbols in the air and occasionally erasing them with her fist as she did so. At least this was normal behavior. Drewcila was like a walking calculator, and she could figure out even the most complex problems—especially when it concerned money—in just this way. More amazing, Drew could do things a computer really couldn't do as accurately. Drew knew beings, and she knew what they were capable of. More importantly, she seemed to know what they were likely to do, how they would or would not react to a given situation. She stopped suddenly in mid-calculation and looked at him.

"All right, get on the horn. Tell them to gather here," she pointed to a spot on the map, "in the space just out of the atmosphere, and hopefully out of Lockhede detector range. They shouldn't be expecting an attack from deep space, so we should be OK. When we give them the signal, they are to go here," she pointed to a spot on the planet map, "without delay, and open fire. I don't want *anything* to fly away."

Van Gar nodded and moved to the console, where he'd no doubt be the rest of the day, grumbling, "Good morning, it's good to see you, too."

Drew just laughed and mostly ignored him. She didn't have time to mollycoddle anyone this morning. She was at war. She called the admiral of the imperial fleet, who, when his face appeared on her screen, looked as if she might have gotten him out of bed. She just clicked her tongue and shook her head to show her disapproval. In this outfit she looked so damn intimidating she didn't really have to do anything else.

"My queen...I'm sorry."

"Don't be sorry, be ready," she said, working at keeping the smile from her face with an effort. This really was just a hell of a lot of fun. "Do we know the position of the last two Lockhede battle cruisers?"

"We believe so, yes."

"Don't believe so, know. Find them, and then at precisely twenty-hundred hours I want you to take every available ship in our fleet and pound them till they fall from the sky."

"But, my queen..."

"But me no buts, man. This is war. We don't have time for buts. By twenty-two hundred hours I want those ships to be nothing but burning husks littering the planet. Do I make myself clear?"

"Yes, my queen, but surely..."

"What did I tell you about the buts?"

"My queen, if we attack them with every ship in the fleet, that will leave the rest of the country without defense from an aerial strike," the admiral objected.

"Are there no ground to air missiles? Are there no anti-aircraft guns?" Drewcila thundered. "Did it sound like I was asking? Because I wasn't. That was an order, and you have to do what I say because...well, because I'm queen and all."

The admiral bowed low, and answered, "Yes of course, my queen, your every wish is my command. Please pardon my ignorance, for I know that your great wisdom shall lead us to victory."

The transmission ended. As Arcadia walked into the room and took her place behind her own computer console she looked at Van Gar, "Did you hear that drivel? Is it any wonder that her head is so incredibly swollen?"

Van Gar just mumbled something incoherent and nodded.

"A little respect, peasant," Drewcila said with a laugh.

Arcadia laughed and started keyboarding. "Woo hoo! Take a look at this baby." She transferred the data from her screen to Drew's.

Drew read the numbers and started laughing.

"Well?" Van Gar asked.

"Qwah-Co stock is on the rise again," Arcadia announced.

Drew got up and started pacing. "Yes, Qwah-Co stock is on the rise, even though the entire operation has come to a near halt because of this war. Do you know what that means?"

"That you're no longer losing money?" Van Gar answered.

Drewcila stopped pacing and turned to glare at him. "Besides that?"

"I can't guess, but I'm sure you're dying to tell me."

"It means I'm going to win the war. My plan is going to work, and the war will be over by tomorrow afternoon."

"You've garnered all that information from the fact that your stocks are on the rise again?" Van Gar asked skeptically.

"Hey! Stockholders are never wrong." She sat down and made another call, this time to the "real" general of the Barion army. Unlike his naval counterpart, this man was fully dressed, alert, and ready for action.

"General, good news! My stock is up. That means we shall be triumphant in battle."

"Uh...all right."

"That's right, everything is all right. Now, here's the plan." She lined it all out for him in great detail, ending with, "...after they have pounded the area for several minutes, they will fly out, and that's when you will move in. You will sweep the area, taking prisoners and killing any who resist until that area is clean. Then you will hold that ground until the Lockhedes either surrender or we are forced to move further inward."

"I understand, and will carry out all your plans, my Queen."

The transmission closed, and Drewcila started laughing. When her laughter failed to get the attention of either of her mates, she laughed more maniacally until they both turned to give her their undivided attention.

"That's better." She stopped laughing. "Those Lockhede bastards. They failed to understand who they were up against. They looked at our country and saw that we were militarily inferior to them, but they failed to understand the strength of my company. By combining the strength of the country with the strength of my corporation we will slam those bastards back into the stone age."

"Was that really necessary, or did you just need to gloat?" Van Gar asked, returning to his work.

"Hey! Gloating's necessary."

Dartan walked in, minus the film crew. The queen appeared to be in deep thought. "My Queen, I'm sorry to interrupt you, but I was wondering if you'd like me to make any sort of report for you this morning, or if you'd perhaps like to make a statement before you go to the funeral."

She seemed to think about this for a moment, then looked at him and said, "I don't think people should actually say anything during orgasm. What do you think, Dartan?"

Dartan was more than a little taken aback, and he didn't appreciate at all the giggling from the two aliens, who were no doubt laughing at his expense. "Excuse me, my Queen?"

"When you're having orgasm, you just sort of open your mouth and words come out. You know, things like, 'Give it to me, give it to me!' Well, obviously they already are. Then there's the ever-popular begging, as in, 'Please, baby! Please!' As if they're going to stop doing something that's obviously working. And what about the, 'Oh gods! Oh my gods!' It just seems to me like that's a strange time to become religious. And what's with the whole saying everything twice thing? Do you just assume that they didn't hear you the first time? The problem is, of course, that you aren't thinking anything, because there is no blood in your brain. So, what have we learned?"

"I...I'm not really sure?" Dartan said in confusion.

"That you shouldn't speak during orgasm," Arcadia and Van Gar said in unison, which made the queen cringe.

She recovered quickly, "Yes, that's exactly right."

Dartan still didn't understand. "Is that to be a royal decree then?"

"Most certainly not! We are at war. We can't be wasting our time with such trivial pursuits. It was just an observation. What was it you wanted again?"

"My Queen, the funeral. It's in a few hours, and..."

"I just said I can't be bothered with such trivial things."

"Do you maybe want to say a few words about your dear, departed husband?"

"I would, but I'm afraid none of them would help my popularity with the people of Barious. Between you and me, Dartan, he was sort of a prick. My sister will be playing me today..."

"Your sister? I...I don't understand."

"My sister, Stasha. She will be playing the role of myself in today's production of *The Funeral Of A Well-Loved King*, while I will be dealing with more important matters."

"Like whether or not people should talk while they're screwing," Van Gar mumbled. He and Arcadia both laughed, and Drew glared at their backs across the room before turning back to Dartan.

"Like the war and such. The director has gone all out, a large cast has been hired, and I'm told it will be the most beautiful of funerals."

Chapter 14

Lex, posing as the general and high commander of the army, was the first to speak of the deceased. The speech he read off the cue cards was excellent. The audience was beautiful and doing a very believable job of grieving. The flowers, the chorus—all beautiful.

And the tears Stasha cried were very real. Last night after Dylan had made love to her, she'd confessed to her love for him. Then he'd very gently but firmly informed her that he wasn't interested in any sort of permanent relationship. In his delicate words, *Honey, you're great, and I wouldn't mind giving you a tumble now and again, but there is just too much free pussy out there, and I am way too young and far too good looking to get stuck with one woman till the end of time.*

So her tears were real even if they weren't actually for Zarco, the lying cheating, and sexually incompetent bastard!

To make matters worse, her parents disapproved of the funeral being in fact a media production, and they were glaring at her, no doubt expecting her to do the "right" thing and expose the whole farce when her time came to speak.

Suddenly, the cue card man fumbled the cards, and she heard Lex saying, "In closing, let me just say," he turned on the tears, "don't any of you understand? It's so much worse than that. If we continue to travel in these...these temperate times, we may very well go back to a time when our good king didn't exist at all."

There wasn't a dry eye in the house, and no one seemed at all concerned that what he said made no sense. Stasha decided that if the guy with the cards dropped them during her eulogy and made her ad lib, she was going to have her sister kill him. She gave him a look which said as much, as she thought to herself, *All this high-tech shit, and we can't have a simple teleprompter!*

She blew her nose harder than was really lady-like, and walked up to the podium. She dried her eyes with the same handkerchief, trying hard to avoid the blobs of snot, and wishing she'd brought one for the big job and one for the small one. The make up people had done a job on her, and this stuff wasn't likely to come off till they used a ton of chemicals—and maybe some blasting compound. While in the past she'd only really looked like her sister if people were squinting real hard, today she could have probably gone to bed with one of her sister's mates, and they wouldn't have known the difference—except of course when they started having sex, because apparently her sister was really good at it, and she was just as inept as poor, dead Zarco. The tears started to flow again, and Dartan walked up and kindly handed her a new handkerchief, which she promptly forgot to save for tears and blew her nose on. She was glad that after several failed attempts she had given in and let the script writers take care of the eulogy. Stasha dried her eyes on her sleeve, and could just make out the cue cards.

Well, at least I'm giving the country what it wants—a queen in deep grief.

She cleared her throat. "My dear friends and country men. We come here today not to grieve over the passing of a monarch, but to celebrate his life." She sobbed, sniffled, and continued. "My dear husband was a man of the people, and for the people, and it is a crime that the hateful acts of the nobility that killed him made it look as if he had turned his back on the needs of his people in his final days. This was not the way of things. Zarco lived his final hours in terror. In terror for his country, terror for myself, and terror for the legacy he wished to leave behind. Finally, he died in terror for his own life, being forced to accept a war he wanted no part of..."

She paused as realization struck her. *Great! Drewcila may not have written this, but she told the script writer what to say. I'm making a political statement that will forever condemn the nobility, and which will further implicate the Lockhedes as the aggressors in this war...So be it. Zarco should have listened to Drewcila. The nobility had no right to attempt a coup, and why should I give one good damn about the Lockhedes or their fate?*

"Let us not dwell, on this day of all days, on how my poor husband died, but on how he lived. Let us move forward, ever forward, to achieve that which he most wanted—an end to war, and a lasting peace with the Lockhedes. A peace that shall only come about with open trade agreements and the over-throwing of their current puppet leaders. Zarco was a man of vision, and I loved him..." Her voice broke in sobs again. "As he loved me. We had plans for the future of the country, and plans for our future together. We shall no longer be together, but I can make sure that the plans he had for our great nation do not die with him."

Stasha was glad her speech had ended, because she started really crying then, and had to be helped away from the pulpit by Dartan. Her parents would not be allowed to speak, but a long line of fake ministers and dignitaries would be giving hours more of eulogies, and Stasha couldn't stand it.

"Please, Dartan, take me away from this."

He nodded and obliged. He wasn't really needed there any way. The director had everything under control. He led her away from the funeral, which was actually being held in the castle courtyard, although they had broadcast that it was being held on the grounds of the Royal Summer Home in Vardalian. There was a cemetery there in which all of the royals for the last three hundred years had been buried. They easily authenticated the location, which was actually half the kingdom away, with a well painted back drop of the Vardalian skyline. Everything was fake except Stasha's tears.

Dartan led her into the castle. "My lady," he put a strong arm around her shoulders. "Why are you so grieved? Did you love your brother-in-law so much?"

"Oh, Dartan, I'm afraid my reasons for being so grieved are less than pure, and my pain too deep to tell to a stranger as we stand here in the hall. Did you know the castle has its own bar?"

* * *

"Dartan!" Drewcila paced her office. She stopped to look at Van Gar. "That little bastard runs around with his nose up my ass all the time, but when I really need him, I can't find him. Dartan!"

He came running into the office, his hair a mess, and his clothing rumpled. He smelled of liquor and had lipstick smeared all over his face.

Drew smiled.

"My Queen?"

"Do you realize the funeral is over? You were supposed to run around and bug the piss out of the mourners. The director had to grab some half rate actor to take your place."

"I'm sorry, my Queen."

"He smells like your sister," Arcadia said without turning around.

She looked at his rumpled appearance and sudden blush, and she smiled even more broadly. "Well, at least you had a good excuse. Clean yourself up and meet the director in his quarters. You're about to go into the field to talk to our troops."

Dartan sighed. "And where would that be, my Queen?"

"Out in the guards' barracks. Just wait 'til you see what they've done out there, it's great!"

"Yes, my Queen."

Dartan passed Stasha in the hall on his way to his quarters to get changed, and he smiled. She smiled back. A few extra minutes had been all she needed to pull herself back together and look presentable. Unlike Dartan, she didn't seem to mind at all making her sister wait.

"Well?" Stasha asked as she sat down across from Drew.

"I just wanted to say," Drewcila sniffled. "I was so moved by me." She bit her knuckle.

"You aren't funny, Drew," Stasha said with a frown.

"I've had it on good authority that I'm actually *quite* funny. Mommy and Daddy came by after the funeral and called me a bunch of names, most of which weren't in my vocabulary, but

I'm sure weren't nice. Among other things, they seem to think that I have completely corrupted you."

Stasha thought about that for a minute, then smiled. "You know. I think they might actually be right."

"I'm so proud...So, I'm wondering...can we have the folks deported?"

"Don't ask me today. I'd be inclined to agree with you."

"Then what better time to ask?"

"What are they doing?" Stasha asked of Van Gar and Arcadia, successfully changing the subject.

"Van Gar is getting the Qwah-Co armada in position for attack. Arcadia is busy keeping Qwah-Co Industries alive by re-routing freight and keeping us as operational as possible."

"What are *you* doing?" Stasha asked her sister, who appeared, at least for the moment, to be doing nothing more important than sitting with her feet planted in the middle of her desk smoking a cigar and drinking a beer.

"I'm launching a major air offensive against the Lockhedes, which will be followed closely by a deployment of ground troops. I'm writing up trade agreements for the new Lockhede government to sign, and I'm assassinating a high-ranking Lockhede government official."

"Oh, is that all?"

"No, I'm also cleaning my toilet bowl."

President Ralling looked at the screen in front of him. The bitch had once again hacked her way into his private system.

"So...piss head. In a gesture of fair play I'm about to give you one more chance to call off your idiotic war and make peace," the Barion queen said.

Ralling laughed. At that moment he was feeling pretty cocky, and he remembered what general Tryte had said. "You're no doubt a fine public speaker, but you are no military strategist."

She laughed at him. "You underestimate your opponent, butt itch. I'm a business woman, the head of a major corporation. Do you truly believe that a corporation works any differently than the military? There are financial maneuvers, and there are hostile takeovers, and all are governed by *timing*. Do you understand the importance of timing in all matters?" She didn't give him a chance to answer. "No, I didn't think you did. Now, one more time, dunder head. Will you surrender?"

"We most certainly will not. We are one jump ahead of you, Qwah. You will rue the day you decided to tangle with me," Ralling said. He knew his ships and troops were in place, ready to attack within the hour, and there was nothing she could do to stop them now. Now they would be victorious, and he would see that smug grin wiped clean from her face before he danced through the streets of the capital with her head on a stick.

"Let it never be said that I didn't give you a chance."

She was gone, and almost immediately computers started humming in distress all around him.

"Oh, my gods!" one of his aides cried out.

"What is it, man?" General Tryte asked, rushing to stand at the man's shoulder.

"The Crilaten and the Limphondic are both under attack..."

Tryte took over from the man. "My gods! It looks like they've sent out their entire fleet!"

"But...that's not fair! It hasn't been forty-eight hours yet," Ralling said, losing it.

"We must move our ships from the planned attack to save them," Trailings said.

"No!" Tryte said. "That's no doubt just what she wants us to do. She must have figured out that we know just where they are, and that we are about to attack them."

"If we don't help the Crilaten and the Limphondic, they will go down," Trailings protested. "Thousands of lives will be lost, and we will lose our best—our *only* defense in space." He looked at Ralling. "You must now realize that this moron has led us all to our deaths."

Ralling looked from the vice-president to the general. Tryte seemed to have been wrong about everything so far.

"If we pull our ships from where they are and send them to save the Crilaten and the Limphondic, there is no guarantee that they will win. We might suffer heavy losses among the rest of our fleet, and then how will we stop those tanks?" Tryte said. "We must go on as planned. Don't let her pull us away from our target now. With all her ships engaged with our battle cruisers, they can't protect the tanks. This is our chance to blast her. To bring her to her knees. We must trust our troops on board the battle cruisers to be able to handle the Barion armada, and we must move on as planned."

Trailings threw up his hands and stomped around the room. "This man is quite mad. If you won't send aid to the battle cruisers, then do what you should have done all along and surrender now! Stop all this death and madness."

Ralling looked at Tryte. "You had better be right..."

"Gods, man!" Trailings screamed. "He hasn't been right yet. About anything! Not even about toying with Taralin Zarco's brain." Trailings laughed at the look on Ralling's face. "You trust this man totally, and yet you didn't know even that about him? Tryte is the one who ordered Taralin Zarco kidnapped, and he's the one who had part of her brain removed, and he's the one who gave her to Eric Rider to re-program. Your good man Tryte here *made* Drewcila Qwah."

"Is that true?" Ralling demanded.

"No, of course not, this man is a raving lunatic," Tryte said.

"It's all a matter of record. If you aren't too stupid to figure out how to get into the top secret government files—which both you and I have access to—you can look the information up for yourself," Trailings said. "I did."

Ralling glared at him because he didn't have any idea at all how to access the web and find out top secret information—access or no access. Hell, half the time he couldn't figure out how to get into his own web site. Not wanting to show his ignorance, he did the only thing he could do. "We will go ahead as planned." He glared at Tryte with meaning. "You had better be right, Tryte."

Thirty minutes later the Limphondic started its descent, followed shortly by the Crilaten. It became painfully apparent that while they might have had more weapons, the Barions hadn't been lying about at least one thing—the Barion weapons were superior.

Their attack on the Barion tanks and troops started even as they were still living through the shock of losing the last of their inter-stellar fleet. They could hear the voices of the commanders of the raid.

"My gods! They run on for miles!"

"Blue ranger squadron, make your pass."

They could hear the bombs, and then the fleet leader came back.

"What the hell! They aren't real! None of the tanks are real! It's a trap, it's a trap! Get out...Gods! Where did those come from? Oh my gods! We're surrounded! They're everywhere."

"What's everywhere, man! What is it?" Tryte demanded.

"Salvaging barges—fully armed..."

He screamed, there was an explosion, and then nothing more from him. The remaining commanders ended in similar fashion until their was nothing but static to be heard from the transceiver.

Tryte removed his blaster from its holster, put it in his mouth, and fired. No one even tried to stop him.

Minutes later there was a distress call from Yeoul Base. They were being bombarded by the same salvaging ships that had wiped out their fleet.

Ralling laughed, and the others all turned to stare at him. "Well, at least he was right about what they would be attacking." Suddenly he pitched forward in his seat and seemed to have a seizure. Then he was still, his eyes wide open, and drool coming from his mouth. One of the generals ran up to him and tried to get his pulse. The general looked up at Trailings.

"I believe that...he's dead, sir. Mr. President."

"Good. Then someone patch me through to the Queen of Barious, and let's stop this all right now."

Drewcila was throwing a huge party in the "War Room."

"So how did you do it?" Dartan asked, now that they were off camera. "I don't for a minute believe the crap that we told the public, and as for the President of Lockhede having a very opportunistic heart attack, I'm just not buying that, either."

"Elementary, my dear, Dartan. We attacked the battle cruisers with everything we had for two reasons. First, to keep them from seeing the Chitzskies that were piloting the in-coming salvager barges, and second to make them think that there was no way we could protect our 'tanks.' They attacked the fake tanks at the same time that our ships got into position, and we took them out. As they were getting the information that Yeoul Base was being bombarded, the assassin I hired moved into position and killed the president, leaving the vice-president—who wanted to deal with us all along—in charge. And now, because we so totally trounced them, it isn't very likely that they will be able to pull together an even slightly successful resistance from among even their most blatant Barion-hating extremists."

"But why did no one see the assassin?" Dartan asked.

"Now he wouldn't be a very good assassin if he could be seen and caught, would he? They have a device—very expensive and very tricky—but when used by someone who knows how to use it properly, it bends and reflects light so well that the wearer is almost invisible..."

"So you weren't talking to yourself that day in the office," Van Gar said.

"Of course not. Now that would just be crazy."

"Drewcila!" Arcadia called out, weaving with her drink as she walked through the crowd. "Your tongue! It's finally back to normal."

Drewcila held up the champagne glass till she could see herself, and then stuck out her tongue. "Well I'll be damned. It is! Now doesn't that just figure!"

"So what now?" Facto asked.

"What?"

"You can't leave, Drewcila. Not now."

She put a friendly arm around his shoulders. "Now, Sucknoid, I think you're forgetting your place. You don't tell me what to do."

Chapter 15

Van Gar was anxious to hit the road, board the Garbage Scow and get the hell off this planet. He didn't know why he had ever for a second embraced the notion that he could be happy living planet side.

It was more than two months since the war, and that was more than enough time to spend in one place.

Drewcila was walking down the hall towards him, carrying a small bag. Arcadia, who had apparently spent the entire two months they'd been stuck here buying new clothes and accessories, was pulling along a trunk as big as she was. Facto was chasing along behind them. Stasha, Dartan and Dylan were following Facto.

"You can not go!" Facto insisted, shaking his head frantically.

"You keep saying that, and yet here I am, me, still going," Drewcila said with a shrug of her shoulders.

"There are matters of concern which you need to address..."

"Look, I married a nice Barion boy just like you asked," she said pointing a finger at Dartan.

"Your sister married him..."

"The people don't know that. I bought a studio, so now it should be easier than ever to make people believe that she's me. All the press meetings, royal this and royal that, will look better than ever. Anything big comes up, you just ask me and I'll tell you what to do. Dylan, Shreta and Sortas are going to run the recycling business planet side. Hepron Station's almost back on line. The Lockhedes are completely under control, and well on the way to becoming a productive part of our little salvaging empire. There is nothing more for me to do here but lay around drinking and screwing and getting fat, and you don't want me getting fat, do you Fractoady?"

"Drewcila, please reconsider," Facto pleaded. "What about the nobles who picket the castle daily demanding that their family members which you have enslaved here be freed, and that they be treated fairly?"

"I've just this morning dealt with that, and they will all be gone by the end of the day. Don't ya get it, man? I trust you to handle the little shit, and I know you'll contact me if anything big enough to warrant my attention should occur in my absence," Drew said, patting him on the back. "I have places to go and people to do."

Van Gar and Arcadia turned on her, growling. She smiled her most winning smile. "I was, of course, talking about you, dears."

She moved to nudge Dartan. "You know how it is, man? The old balls and chains. He has the balls, she's into the chains."

They all exchanged goodbyes, and then watched as the three walked to their ship.

"Where do you suppose they'll go?" Stasha asked Dylan, no doubt because he was like them—a salvager.

"I have no idea," Dylan said, drying a tear from his eye. He'd really miss Arcadia, but didn't begrudge her happiness. Everyone had to do that which made them happy, and at least for the time being, what made him most happy was servicing as many of the Barion women as he could. It still seemed like a calling to him.

Dylan was glad that Stasha had decided not to hold a grudge. It would have made it hard for him to continue working here if she had. She seemed very happy with Dartan, and he with her, and the whole kingdom was rejoicing over their coupling, even if they didn't exactly know the truth, which was that Dartan wasn't really their Queen's Consort, and that their queen had taken off for parts unknown with her two very different alien "companions."

Everything was happily back to normal, and to celebrate the normalcy, he walked off to the bar. On the way, he passed the guards who were hustling the nobles out of the castle, and from what they were saying, they were gathering up the picketers out by the front gates as well. He didn't know what plans Drewcila had for them, and he really didn't care. The bastards had killed Pristin and upset his normal routine. They deserved whatever they got, as long as it was bad.

He walked in the bar, and found Shreta and Sortas already there.

He laughed as he sat down at the bar next to them. "So, you two decided to start the day early, too."

"Yeah, dude, thought we'd grab a couple ah brews and get in the mood for work," Sortas said. Dylan bit his lip to keep from laughing at him. Sortas' effort to sound just like a salvager would have been really funny if he wasn't so damn sincere. This guy had done the fox hole conversion from hell. He walked, talked, dressed, and acted like a salvager. Hell, he even smelled like one of them, and in a couple of months he had learned almost as much about the business end of it as Pris had known.

Dylan looked from himself to his two new friends and realized the bitch had done it again. Drewcila had put together the perfect crew.

Drewcila sat at the helm. It was good to be in space again. and even better to be in space with her two favorite people. She was very happy with the arrangement. Not that she was ever likely to tell them that. In her experience, other people were only truly happy with an arrangement if they thought you were at least a little unhappy with it.

She was also pleased with her decision to leave Barious, and the direction she now wanted to take with her life. Being queen was only really fun when she got to do it in short bursts. Doing it all the time could turn into a real drag.

"So, where to, Captain?" Arcadia asked.

"In search of Salvagers Gold," Drewcila said.

"You mean..." Van Gar started excitedly.

"That's right. We're going to search the galaxies for the biggest salvaging scores. The rich stuff that's been lost in space so long that no one knows where it's at, or where it came from, or if it's even real."

Pard Jar looked up at the incoming ship. It would carry away the rock they had gathered, and as payment it would leave them food and clothing and farming implements—all by the grace of Qwah-Co Industries. He snarled. He supposed he was reaping what he had sown. But he'd had all kinds of really cool shit, and now he had nothing, and that hardly seemed fair to him.

Twenty of his "followers" had refused to leave his side, which of course proved that they were the very stupidest of a pretty damn dense race. So he spent his days hauling rock with the imbeciles, and his nights sleeping in a dome he shared with "his" female. She smelled so bad, and was so stupid, he'd almost have rather lived alone if it wasn't for the fact that the nights got cold.

Like children, they all eagerly ran towards the landing pad, hopeful that their "parents" had brought them gifts. Something to eat other than that green glop would be nice. The glop was worse for him than it was for the others because he actually knew what was in it.

The engines died, the dust settled, and then the hatch opened. To his amazement, several hundred Barions, wearing the robes of the brotherhood were forced off the ship onto the surface of the planet. A Chitzsky walked out of the ship, unrolled a scroll, and began to read. Pard Jar wondered why they couldn't have just used a palm pilot.

"By order of Her Royal Majesty, Queen of Barious, we do claim this planet, and announce its use as a prison colony." He rolled his scroll up and put it away, then addressed the group as a whole. "Bring rock, and we shall supply you with all you need. No rock? No food."

A Barion man who had obviously been bounced around upon entry limped up to Pard Jar with pleading in his eyes. "Please, sir. This is all a dreadful mistake. I am of noble birth."

Pard Jar looked with total disdain at the man in front of him, then turned to the Chitzsky who stood beside him.

"Well, there goes the neighborhood."

Selina Rosen lives in rural Arkansas with her partner of 11 years, assorted barnyard animals—which she doesn't use for kinky sexual practices despite what you may have heard—and an Amazon parrot with a piss-poor attitude.

She and her partner own and operate Yard Dog Press, a micro press that deals with the oddball children of many Sci-fi, Fantasy and Horror writers. About running a small press Ms. Rosen remarks, "Hey! It's cheaper than paying for a full time dominatrix, and it hurts just as much."

Her hobbies include sword fighting, gardening, building things from trash, drinking large amounts of beer, and seeing if she can belch loud enough to call in wild geese.

Her short fiction has appeared in *Sword and Sorceress 16*, *Distant Journeys*, three of the MZB Fantasy Mags, *Such a Pretty Face*, *Tooth and Claw* and *Personal Demons* to name a few. Her story entitled "Ritual Evolution" appeared in the new *Thieves World* anthology, *Turning Points*. She edited YDP's *Stories That Won't Make Your Parents Hurl*, *More Stories That Won't Make Your Parents Hurl*, and the shared universe anthology *Bubbas of the Apocalypse*.

A collection of her short fiction, *The Bubba Chronicles* (YDP), can be had—as she can—rather cheaply.

Her novels include...*Queen of Denial* (Meisha Merlin Publishing), *Chains of Freedom* (MMP), *Chains of Destruction* (MMP), *Recycled*, the sequel to *Queen of Denial*, (MMP), *The Host* trilogy (YDP), *Fire and Ice* (YDP), *Hammer Town* (YDP), and a novella entitled *The Boat Man* (YDP).

She just finished the third *Chains* book, *Chains of Redemption*, which is slated for May of 2004, and is working on a murder mystery collaboration with fantasy author Laura J. Underwood, tentatively titled *Bad Lands*.

You can contact Selina through her company website **www.yarddogpress.com.** She's the one you get on the "contact us."

Queen of Denial by Selina Rosen
ISBN 1-892065-06-1
$12.00

From the introduction to *Queen of Denial*
by Lynn Abby

And it's funny. Painfully, delightfully, barking seals and whooping cranes funny.

Funny is worse than natural dialog. In "real life" spoken humor relies on timing and nuance while physical humor happens at a speed that cannot be captured with an alphabet. And a lot of what seems funny when written down, dies a lingering death when read aloud. (This I know for a fact.) To write a story that is as funny when read aloud as it is when read silently, and poignant, too, is an act of genius—or dementia, possibly both.

I can't begin to describe the many creative processes that have to be going on to create this sort of synergy. I don't think they can be described. A writer either can do it, or she can't; Selina Rosen can, and she did it with her first novel. If I didn't know her, like her, and respect her, I'd probably have to kill her.

The easy, natural humor of the space merchant-marine, the poignancy of a man searching for something that can never be found, and a plot that brings these two elements together in a thoroughly believable, yet unexpected way. In hockey, they call this a hat trick. In science fiction, it's a book that won't ever be lost in my memory.

Chains of Freedom
ISBN 1-892065-42-8
$16.00

From the inrtoduction by C. J. Cherryh

This crazy book business...readers want the books, but the writers and the publishers have to swim upstream against a marketing system designed chiefly to sell tomato soup.

Rosen has a very good, very funny book with Meisha Merlin. *Queen of Denial* is available for order and should be on the shelves at bookstores.

Let me tell you the short details about Selina Rosen. She's a creative soul, a builder in wood and stone and words...knows farm life, knows how to build a room, or a plot...can cope with goats and chickens, or neophyte writers. Out of this absolute wealth of diverse experience come truly outrageous ideas and a way of looking at the universe with [in some books] humor and [in other books] attitude with a capital A.

Does this honesty and the fact she writes really good, wise, funny and serious books mean immediate, widely reputed success in the writing business? No. It's easier to sell something "just like" the last thing, and Rosen's just-like nothing else. So here we are. *I'm* putting out the word, because I believe in her.
Buy this woman's books!

Chains of Destruction
ISBN 1-892065-69-X
$16.00

From the introduction by Claudia Christian

Selina is an amazing spirit, a woman who literally can suck the air, energy and life out of the best of us. She has left me aching from laughter and cursing her in the morning for keeping me up past my bed time.

So read and enjoy *Chains of Destruction*, and remember as you are lost in the brilliant action scenes and caught up in the trials and tribulations of the memorable characters, that this was written by a woman who I out drank in a cheesy hotel in Houston Texas.

Coming in May 2004:
The dynamic conclusion to
Selina Rosen's Chains trilogy,
Chains of Redemption

Come check out our web site for details on these Meisha Merlin authors!

Kevin J. Anderson

Robert Asprin

Robin Wayne Bailey

Edo van Belkom

Janet Berliner

Storm Constantine

John F. Conn

Diane Duane

Sylvia Engdahl

Phyllis Eisenstein

Rain Graves

Jim Grimsley

George Guthridge

Keith Hartman

Beth Hilgartner

P. C. Hodgell

Tanya Huff

Janet Kagan

Caitlin R. Kiernan

Lee Killough

Jacqueline Lichtenberg

Jean Lorrah

George R. R. Martin

Lee Martindale

Jack McDevitt

Mark McLaughlin

Sharon Lee & Steve Miller

James A. Moore

John Morressy

Adam Niswander

Andre Norton

Jody Lynn Nye

Selina Rosen

Kristine Kathryn Rusch

Pamela Sargent

Michael Scott

William Mark Simmons

S. P. Somtow

Allen Steele

Mark Tiedeman

Freda Warrington

David Niall Wilson

www.MeishaMerlin.com